DANCING IN THE DAINTREE

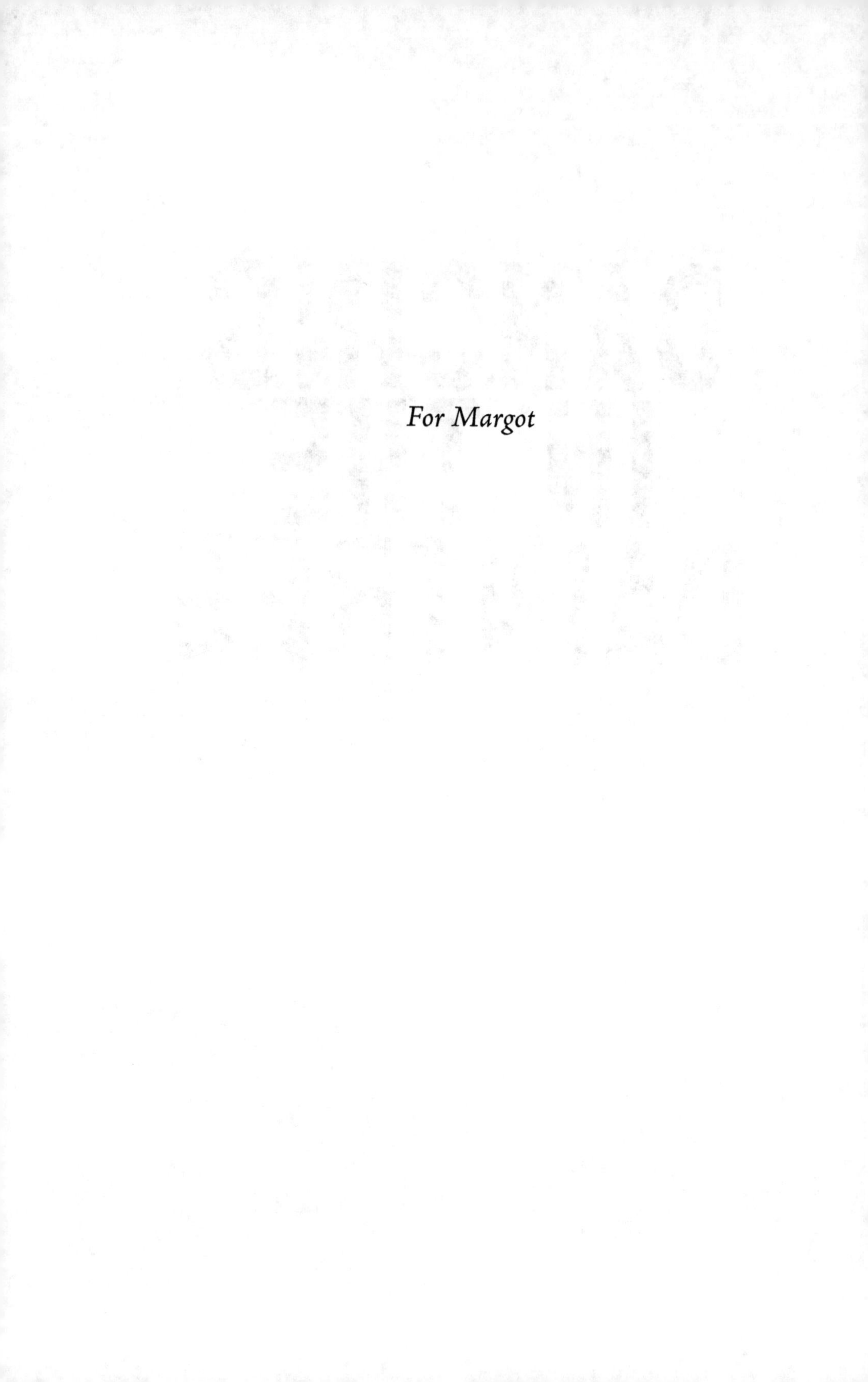

For Margot

DANCING IN THE DAINTREE

Drugs, deceit and danger in the underworld of northern Australia

GARY McKAY

Published in Australia by Sid Harta Publishers Pty Ltd,
ABN: 34 632 585 203
17 Coleman Parade, GLEN WAVERLEY VIC 3150 Australia
Telephone: +61 3 9560 9920, Facsimile: +61 3 9545 1742
E-mail: author@sidharta.com.au

First published in Australia 2020
This edition published 2020

McKay , Gary
Dancing in the Daintree
ISBN: 978-1-925707-37-3
pp330

ABOUT THE AUTHOR

Gary McKay was conscripted into the Army when he was 20 years old. He served as a rifle platoon commander in South Viet Nam and was awarded the Military Cross for gallantry. He decided to remain in the military and rose to the rank of lieutenant colonel before he retired after 30 years service. He  served in the USA, Canada, Papua New Guinea, Malaysia, New Zealand and Fiji.

He is an accomplished non-fiction author with over 20 titles to his credit. He is Australia's most prolific author on the subject of the Viet Nam war. He works as a freelance historian and author. He is a battlefield tour guide in Viet Nam, Gallipoli, Singapore and Guadalcanal. Gary is married and lives in Kiama, NSW. *Dancing in the Daintree* is his first novel and the first in a trilogy. *Dancing* is based on an actual operation that he was involved in during his Army service.

CONTENTS

Six months previously.

At least it was a great night for it. I would be able to get in and get out, and hopefully get away clear without any bastard knowing I had been there.

I pulled the four-wheel drive into a small patch of bush that I had recced a couple of days previously while casing the place. There was bugger all moon so at least that was on my side. The briefing said that these clowns would be switched off because they thought that their bush camp for growing dope was as safe as houses. They probably never thought that some of the local chopper pilots actually did take notice of what flicked past underneath their aircraft on their way to collect tourists to take them out to the Reef.

I shrugged into my backpack after quietly exiting the vehicle and slid on my night vision goggles. At least now I had some vision because it was as black as the inside of a dog's guts. I always remembered Spike Milligan saying "Outside of a dog, a book is a man's best friend. Inside a dog, it's too hard to read". *Why did I always think of that when it was pitch black? God knows.* I checked my wrist compass and headed off quietly through the fairly dense tropical scrub. Within 100 metres I would come across the track that I had spotted from the aerial photo that the Feds had managed to acquire. That footpad would take me very close to where I needed to go. I just had to make sure there were no nasty surprises along the way.

Slow and sure was the way to move. Stealth would give me my security. Stay balanced, and watch for signs of trip wires, booby traps or early warning devices. Move 20 paces, stop, kneel down and listen. My black coveralls and lightweight black balaclava all but made me disappear. My black flying gloves were fine but liked to catch on the "wait-a-while" bushes that fringed the footpad.

Then I heard it. The unmistakable sound of a bloke snoring. *Christ, he sounded like a chainsaw!* Then I saw it. A single wire across the track. I lowered myself slowly to the ground and saw it was connected to a trip flare, and what looked like a small charge of plastic as well. Probably set to provide early warning for the camp inhabitants was my guess. It had been in place a while because there were signs that it was armed and disarmed regularly. *Now that's slack.* They should have been moving their trip wires around.

It took me a good five minutes to disconnect the trip wire so if I needed to, I could beetle out this way and not worry about being illuminated … or blown to smithereens.

I closed in on the snoring. I could make out the silhouette of a rough bush shack. It looked like there were three warm bodies in hammocks: two in one shack and another in a lean-to of sorts. A small kitchen and workshop was under a tarpaulin. And there they were: mounds of marijuana tops ready for baling. I pulled my Minolta out and took some happy snaps with the high-sensitive fast film the Feds had provided.

I heard movement to my flank. *Fuck, it was coming towards me.* I pressed up against a tree to remove my shape from sight. Whoever it was had a torch and was moving towards the kitchen area. A small camp fridge door was opened, and a can of drink taken out. I heard the hiss of a ring tab being pulled. Then I heard a female voice close behind me just dripping with menace say very quietly, 'Move one hair on your head and you are dead.'

Shit. Where had she come from? I felt a gun barrel, probably a pistol, prod me in the back. 'Move, arsehole!' she hissed. I did as I was asked. She held my left arm and started guiding me towards the tent. I needed to get out of here, and real quick. Nobody told me that they had small arms. I thought there was a slim chance but usually these buggers use shotguns to scare people off. Bad guys carrying handguns indicate that they occasionally get serious. I quietly flicked the Minolta onto flash with my right hand and turned slightly to face my unseen captor. I saw she was of Asian appearance and had long black hair. She smelled of lavender or something similar.

Boomph! A brilliant flash of light erupted as I fired the camera flash. Off it went and so did I. As fast as my legs would carry me, I bolted back down my ingress track. Simultaneously, I had ripped the NVGs off as they had been well and truly screwed when the camera flash went off. I had to stop and kneel down in the scrub off the side of the track for a few seconds to recover my night vision. I now had to use the Mark I eyeball to get out of this mess.

The sharp crack of pistol shots and the heavier chatter of a long-barrelled automatic rifle — that sounded very much like an AK-47 — buzzed around me. It was enough motivation to get me moving again. These buggers had plenty of firepower. Thank God they were lousy shots and, like most people tend to do at night, they were firing high. I passed their trip wire and dropped a scare charge with a 10-second delay to give me some time and space. Bullets still kept whizzing around sounding all the world like angry bees. I heard the crack of a round passing close to my ear and knew I needed to change direction and soon.

Into the scrub I went and stopped dead. I waited. Even though this was nothing new to me I could still hear my heart pounding. I would have given anything for a silenced Sterling right now, but 'nah, you won't need a gun, Bob. These crooks are small time,' they said. And I believed them. *Note to myself. Don't do that again.*

The sound of two blokes pushing noisily up the track got closer and then the scare charge went off. Screaming and yells and shouts rent the air as they were instantly blinded by the flash and disoriented by the explosion. At least now I could put some distance between me and my pursuers who would be wary of charging hard after me, now that I had struck back with some of my own persuasion.

It was time to bugger off quick smart. I put the night vision goggles back on and took a circuitous route and after 20 minutes found my way back to the Toyota. A quick scan showed nobody had been around or had tampered with my vehicle. It was time to make tracks and head back to Cairns.

Not my best covert reconnaissance, not by a long shot. And who was that sheila with the long black hair? And how come they had more weapons than our local bikie gang?

Back in my hotel room I finished a shower and took a quick look at the shots I had taken before being sprung. The last image was interesting. It showed half of the face of the woman with the long black hair. Definitely Asian; and as I suspected most probably Vietnamese. The weapon was a 9mm Glock and probably borrowed from our local coppers who had their armoury knocked off about a year ago.

A knock on the door signalled the arrival of my de-brief team. *This was going to be fun. Not.*

CHAPTER 1

Turmoil

I had just returned from my third tour of Afghanistan with the Special Air Service Regiment and had been reassigned to Holsworthy Barracks in Sydney. After attending a training session with our signallers, I was about to leave the headquarters of the 4th Battalion, a Commando unit of the Royal Australian Regiment, and head back to my rifle company to complete my leave application. Little did I know that within a few years my new unit would be lost to the Royal Australian Regiment and become a fully titled Commando Regiment. It seemed that almost everybody in politics and Defence believed the only people who could achieve success in counter-insurgency operations were Special Forces units. What a load of crap. I had six weeks leave coming and as soon as the paperwork was completed and approved, I was intent on making my way back home to our married quarters in Sydney as fast as I could. No sooner had I started walking towards my company orderly room when I was pulled up by the Adjutant. Behind him were two uniformed coppers from the New South Wales Police and they didn't look too happy. I saw our regimental sergeant major in the background, loitering with intent. *What the hell had I done now? Must be bad for the RSM to be here,* I thought.

'Sir?' I responded to the barked order of 'Sergeant McTaggart!'

'Sergeant McTaggart, this is Senior Constable Fleming and Constable Wiggins from the Mosman Police Station. Come into my office please.' The look on his face was awful. The RSM quietly slipped in behind me.

I stepped into the Adjutant's office and removed my rifle green beret.

'Bob,' the Adjutant started, 'We've got some pretty bad news.'

The next ten minutes folded into a blur as Captain McGregor told me how my wife Jenny and our only child had been killed in a car accident that morning as they were driving to Annie's school. A truck had rolled onto our car and they didn't have a chance. The police began telling me what procedures had been taken, how they had arrested the truckie who was as high as a kite on uppers, and what I needed to do next. Identifying the body of Jenny and Annie was my most immediate task.

I had been standing at ease in front of the Adjutant, but I now sat down to try and take this all in. What had I done to have this happen? Who the fuck had I pissed off upstairs to bring this much grief into my life, just when I thought I had everything in front of me? Our family was happy and we were planning on having another child. I was nominated for the next warrant officer's course. I had picked up a few gongs along the way in Iraq and the Ghan for gallantry, and now the sky falls in on me.

'Bob,' the RSM was now in my face. 'Bob, I'll take you down to the morgue.'

'Thanks, sir,' was all I could muster.

* * *

I tried settling down after I took my annual leave following the funeral, but I was just too fucked in the head. I had experienced intense grief when my mum died and thought that was pretty bad, but now I was totally gutted. I felt really bloody empty. My whole purpose in life seemed to have been removed, not even that, more like dug out of me or ripped out like a weed in a garden. I had found real love with Jenny and now it was gone. I actually contemplated taking out the truckie when he appeared in court for his committal, but his world was already screwed. Besides, if I did take him out you wouldn't have to be Sherlock Holmes to figure out who would be a prime suspect. I was listening to his sentence being handed down when he turned and looked at me. Our eyes had locked, and I felt I could see into his soul. I could sense his genuine remorse. His face reflected his own deep anguish and desire to turn back the clock. I couldn't forgive him, but I had realised over the last few months that anger and hatred was just going to eat away at my being.

I had spoken with our chaplain a few times because he asked me to drop in and see him, and although I am not a religious sort of guy, I liked our unit 'Soul Patrol' and I found talking to the padre was a good thing. I had my blinkers taken off and saw a new way ahead. But it didn't bring my girls back.

I had emptied our Army married quarters at Holsworthy and sold almost everything we had owned. It all had too many memories and I had enough of those in my head already. A clean slate was going to be my springboard for getting out of the mental mire that was threatening to drag me down. I was living in a furnished apartment just around the corner from the battalion but realised I was simply going through the motions. For the first time in my life I was not enjoying going to work. My 15-year Army career was now at a crossroad. My time in the battalion, and then six years in the SAS Regiment in Perth had been great. Serving in East Timor in 1999 had been a buzz, especially going in covertly off a Yank submarine to see what mischief the Indons were up to before Peter Cosgrove and the rest of cavalry arrived to help the East Timorese.

I loved the adrenaline flow that came from sitting in West Timor behind the 'front line' of the Indonesians and watching them go about their daily business. After we had come ashore and given the intel on what the bad guys were up to along the East Timor border with Indonesian West Timor, things went a bit quiet. The recently arrived Australian infantry battalion posted into the border area had been given recon tasks beyond their capability, and they asked the SAS Regiment for help. Their recon platoon that acted as the eyes and ears for the battalion was normally only 20 or so strong, but now it was double that number. They needed more patrol commanders and I was asked to be a patrol leader and attached to their unit. We would operate as a five-man patrol, just like we did on close country SAS ops. After a few weeks, we were going really well and the guys in my patrol were as good as any I had served with. They had all the skills, good field craft, great battle craft and tremendous self-discipline. I never once had to tell a man to re-camouflage himself or his equipment. They were switched-on soldiers.

It was a bit like playing cowboys and Indians when I was a kid, sneaking around trying to get the drop on the opposition. Not much had changed in 20 years. We always moved out after dark, using the folds in the ground to quietly wade across the river and insert into West Timor. Finding the Indonesian camps was pretty easy as their cooking led us straight to their base areas. From there we would establish a lying up position, and my scout and I would move forward and sit directly behind the Indonesian forward observation posts that stuck out like a pimple on a pumpkin. Their security was slack; they made a lot of noise and rarely carried their weapons from one point to another even in the forward positions. We could tell who was who in the front line, and once we even took a photograph with a telephoto lens of a section leader perusing his picket list for the night that showed the names of all of his soldiers.

Every week the battalion commanding officer would have a liaison meeting with his Indonesian counterpart. Initially these were held in East Timor but the locals around Balibo got so upset and threatening, the meetings were moved across into "enemy" territory.

Most Indonesian people do not sweat freely, but on the day the CO of the Australian infantry battalion started reeling off the names of Indonesian soldiers on border duties in West Timor, the opposing commanding officer looked like he had stepped out of a sauna. His face almost went white and his eyes visibly widened. Dropping those names and asking if Private Ibrahim was feeling better had the same effect as someone being told that their car was on fire in the car park.

The Indons were good at beating up and terrorising the normally placid and friendly Timorese civvies, but showed themselves to be pretty gutless when it came to taking on well-trained soldiers. They had developed a habit of coming across the border on Friday nights before the big Saturday markets in Balibo and terrorising the local merchants and villagers bringing in produce to sell or barter. The locals had complained about this nasty business and so we asked them to show us where the Indons crossed the river, which was about knee to waist deep and not flowing too quickly. We found their harbour area on our side of the border that they must have used to lay up waiting for dark. We set an area ambush and waited for the nasties to arrive. Sure enough, just before last light one Friday evening, an armed militia patrol started out across the river heading straight for us. We had planted a few plastic explosives around to stun and disorient the group and waited behind dense cover. The way they carried their weapons indicated they were probably not West Timorese militia but Indonesian Kostrad or Special Forces soldiers wearing militia gear. It had the potential to go ugly early.

Once the Indon patrol had reached our side of the river and sat down, we waited for darkness to envelop them. We initiated the explosives and trip flares with a command detonated device and they sat there like stunned mullets as we jumped them and quickly took them captive. After interrogation and getting as much intel out of them as we could, we waited in the bush until first light. We then stripped the Indonesian patrol naked and marched them out of the bush and across the river and sent them back home. Nobody got hurt, except they lost a serious amount of face and suffered enormous humiliation as the locals booed and jeered the naked soldiers as they crossed back into West Timor. The West Timorese militiamen were just thugs doing their country's bidding and making life miserable for the East Timorese people who just wanted to get on with their own lives and feed their families.

* * *

My deployments to Iraq and Afghanistan were memorable. Serving in the land of sand had its moments, but as far as I was concerned, as long as our arses pointed towards the ground it was a waste of time, men and material. As soon as the allies were out of there it would all revert to the tribal and gang warfare it had been before, and just like it had for more than two centuries previously. The whole rationale behind our presence in the Middle East was just to keep our American mates happy and keep them handy as an insurance policy in our region. Our flexibility as Special Forces was sorely tested as we grappled with operating in an environment where long range weaponry is the norm and where all movement is easily detected. Our night insertions became very detailed and we soon got on top of the Taliban in our area of operations. It called for good planning and detailed route and target reconnaissance. Knowing who you could trust as we started training up the locals also provided us with intense moments of betrayal and grief.

But why were we here half a world away from Australia? I was sitting in a classroom doing my international studies course at Deakin Uni trying to make myself smarter when I was posted as a weapons and demolitions instructor at Swan Island. An academic who had been brought down from the Australian National University was answering a question as to why the USA wanted to help Kuwait when Saddam Hussein invaded and his response pretty well summed it up. He replied with a rhetorical remark along the lines of 'if Kuwait only grew bananas, do you think there would have been a Gulf war?' It was a no-brainer.

Delfina

Nine months after the accident, I asked for 12 months leave without pay and thought I would just get out of town and drive until I found something worth looking at or doing. So, here I was just after Christmas in 2008 driving through north Queensland and doing the odd bit of fishing and diving and working as a deckie and part-time skipper on charter boats taking rich bastards out to the Great Barrier Reef. I had gained my master mariner's ticket while working on counter-piracy operations in Somalia as part of a global operation to combat piracy in the major shipping lanes off the east coast of Africa. That was tough work. Boarding ships, usually at night, and taking a ship back off a bunch of thugs who were usually poorly trained in the handling of weapons and keeping the ship from running aground made for interesting and sometimes dangerous times.

But now, up in the peaceful waters of the Coral Sea, the work was relaxing. It certainly lacked any pressure or stress except when wealthy mature ladies wanted a piece of Australian manhood that their overweight husbands couldn't provide. Whenever that happened,

I would quickly move on because the tips were worth more than a bit of hanky panky.

I had served in Townsville during the early nineties and the place had changed dramatically. What had been a small garrison town was now a major provincial centre and economic hub for the vast coal export business inland around Blackwater. I wanted to stay in Townsville for a while. I liked the heat, I liked the dead-casual attitude of the people, and there was no shortage of work for crewmen who turned up at their job on the right day, on time, and most importantly, sober.

I was at the marina doing some maintenance work on a charter boat for Phil the owner when for some reason I looked up and saw this big fat bloke fall arse over tit into the water from the deck of the jetty. He didn't come up in a hurry so I dived in after him, and as I looked down into the clear waters, I could see he was doing a pretty good imitation of a sinking brick. I grabbed him, and with every bit of strength I could muster pulled him back up onto the wharf and started some CPR. Some rubber-neckers were just standing there in their Gucci loafers watching this drama unfold when I had to yell at them to call for an ambulance. But Luigi Zappia, as I found out later, started coming around spitting water and spewing a little. I had him in a recovery position by the time the ambos arrived and before long, he was sitting up and wanting to kiss me. Luigi wasn't my type, so I declined, but I did promise to come and see him at his restaurant in town when he got better.

Luigi owned the biggest and probably one of the best food joints in

Townsville and quite a bit of other commercial real estate in town and Far North Queensland as well. He was a big bugger who only stood about five feet seven but was about as wide. A bit like a fridge, one could say. He was about 50-something and obviously ate a lot of the good cooking that came out of the restaurant kitchen. His penchant for loud shirts and loud conversation was legendary around town. Turns out that on that fateful day at the marina Luigi had suffered a heart attack and subsequently collapsed and fallen headlong into the water. It was just as well I was there because he would have been dinner for the abundant sea life that hangs around the jetties.

About a month after the rescue of Luigi, I got a phone call from his daughter saying that her papa wanted me to come to dinner the next Friday night. I obliged, hoping for a free feed as the tourist season was a bit slow after a recent cyclone, and work was minimal and patchy at best.

I walked into the restaurant that was packed and instantly saw Luigi barrelling towards me with his arms outstretched. I started to panic because it looked like he really was going to kiss me this time. Instead he put me in a bear hug that would have done The Rock proud and dragged me down towards the back of the restaurant where there was a private dining room.

'Bob! Maaate,' he said in his best version of Strine. 'Welcome to my restaurant. Tonight, we will eat and drink, and I will pay.'

I was all for that and nodded my agreeance. 'Thanks Luigi, that's very kind of you.'

'It is the least I canna do for somebody who saved me from the sharks and crocs,' he smiled in a big cheesy grin, revealing a mouth full of pearly whites studded with gold crowns and the occasional gold tooth.

We tucked into a seriously big feed that was punctuated with Townsville identities – all obviously movers and shakers — coming up and saying hello and exchanging banter. It was shortly after a well-known solicitor had left and we were contemplating what to have for coffee that Luigi had the private dining room door closed and he leant forward and pushed a large A4 sized envelope towards me.

'For you' was all he said and leant back motioning for me to open the thick envelope. Jesus, if this was full of money I was sitting pretty.

'What is it?' I asked.

'Justa open it Bob,' he said, trying hard to conceal a toothy smile.

I flipped open the back of the crisp white envelope and pulled out a set of papers. They were the ownership documents for his motor cruiser, the *Delfina*.

'What are these for Luigi?' I asked, feeling something big was about to happen.

'She's yours now Bob. My wife, she has told me I am not going out to sea again until I lose-a the weight,' he leaned forward and added quietly, 'and we both-a know that is a not gonna happen anytime soon, eh?' He started chortling as he leaned back and patted his impressive stomach. Luigi's wife Delfina was clearly one not to be trifled with.

'What, are you giving me the *Delfina*?' I asked. I couldn't believe it. She was one of the most sought-after boats in the region. She was a 60-foot Vitech Flybridge cabin cruiser, and a serious boat in anyone's language. She had a beam of around 16 feet and dual 735 horsepower Detroit diesels. She was only about eight years old by my reckoning and probably worth around 350 to 400,000 bucks.

'Jesus, Luigi, I can't take her, she's worth a lot of money.'

Luigi quickly stood up. Hands on hips, legs apart he glared down at me. 'So, you are refusing a gift from me for saving my life? What, my life is a not worth it to you?' He had his ugly face on now. He looked a bit angry and I had heard he could go a bit if he was stirred up.

'No mate, it is just that this is a lot to give … I …'

'Listen Bob. You give me my life back. Now, I wanna give you a better life. I know a bit about you and your poor family. This is my thanks to you. I will be deeply offended if you do not accept the *Delfina*.' He stared at me, intently waiting for my response to this take-it-or-else declaration.

'Okay Luigi,' I replied. I stood and we shook hands and then he gave me another of those crushing bear hugs. The rest of the night disappeared into a blur of after-dinner drinks, I think a Tiramisu made its way in there somewhere, and then more drinks. It was a long crazy but very happy night.

I awoke a bit dusty the next morning and went down to the boat harbour and spoke to the marina manager Jack Slater. Jack was almost a caricature of what you would expect a tropical bum to look like. Tanned, unshaven, with sparkling blue eyes and clothes that looked like they had come out of a Vinnies waste collection bin. You could put a million-dollar suit on Jack and he would still look like a bag of spuds. Grinning, I dropped the papers onto his desk and he nearly went into apoplexy. 'Christ, Bob, the *Delfina*! No shit!' He spent the next five minutes telling me what a lucky bastard I was, and it should have been him that lifted Luigi out of the drink.

'Well you didn't, Jack, because you were probably shagging that sheila who owns that yellow catamaran from Melbourne.'

'Maybe, maybe not. I wasn't … but thanks for the idea,' he leered at me. 'What are you gonna do now mate?'

'I will go over her and then take her out for a run. Luckily, I have some cash on hand to fill up those diesel tanks.' I knew that was going to cost a bit because they held over 2500 litres. 'Then, I think I will start taking out some charters, maybe do a bit of eco-tourism.'

'Good idea, you will be knocking them back with a stick. Everyone loves that boat. I'll get the people who do our ads to come and talk to you about making up some flyers for the motels around town.'

I hadn't even thought through that far ahead, but I would need to start thinking like a businessman from now on and not just a deck hand.

*   *   *

I spent the next couple of months in Seventh Heaven, taking small groups on charters out to the Reef and showing them the incredible beauty of the region. Some groups went diving, others wanted to fish, and others just wanted to learn about what this massive living organism called the Barrier Reef was all about. I had seen man's vandalism of Mother Nature in a few places around the globe and I wanted to make sure my clients left with the message that we need to protect and conserve what we already have. I'm not a hairy-legged greenie by any means but I do appreciate what we have been given. I had the *Delfina* converted to sleep eight and set it up for small charter operations as far as sleeping and eating were concerned. Business was going quite well. The only thing that irked me was the cost of the diesel fuel that always seemed to be going up. My average bill for a 3-day charter out to the outer Reef would sometimes cut my profit margin to less than $200 a day, but I always saw that as not a bad way to earn a quid.

On more than one occasion I found myself sitting on my apartment balcony, gazing out over a shimmering Coral Sea, enjoying a cold beer after a decent day's work, and pondering where the heck my life was going. I wasn't missing the Army so much, but I was missing all the great blokes that I had served with over a decade and a half. I had been shot at, scared to death, enjoyed the immense satisfaction of doing a dangerous job without losing any of my soldiers and more importantly any of the bits that I cherished most on my person. Now, here I was in tropical Far North Queensland and starting what seemed to be a new life. New challenges and new frontiers. I had decided to resign from the military, and if I wanted to re-enlist, I could and would be back at my old rank in no time at all. I had the runs on the board, and experienced senior non-commissioned officers took a while to breed. I had a good fall-back position if I needed it and was intent on giving this new chapter in my life a good crack.

Recruited

Christmas 2009

About seven months after I had taken ownership of the *Delfina*, my life changed dramatically onto a totally altogether different course. I was renting a nice little unit down near the wharves alongside the Ross River. Nothing too flash but well-located for eating out and meeting up with locals. The bonus was that it had a great deck where I could sit and pluck the fluff out of my navel when things were slack, and I could sit and plan different eco-tours into the hinterland.

Around four in the morning, my door suddenly burst open with an almighty bang. The door jamb was shattered and a couple of very large blokes in black gear stormed into the room, ripped me out of bed and pinned me to the floor. I was taken totally by surprise and didn't even have time to defend myself or react against my attackers. My head was held down firmly and sideways onto the floorboards. All I could see was a pair of shiny shoes standing about three metres away.

Whoever was holding me down knew what they were doing because I couldn't get any leverage at all to try and get out from under their hold.

I could just see a couple of pairs of black military-style boots walking quickly around the apartment checking rooms, searching through the wardrobes and then emptying out all of the cupboards. I was absolutely stuffed as to what this invasion was all about. It was too precise and organised to be a bunch of dope heads intent on burglary. Besides, I didn't have that much to knock off in the place, just my PC and sound system and some small artworks. After half an hour or so the pressure on my head, neck and back was released.

'Clear,' came a muffled voice.

'Clear,' came another from further away. There had to be at least five people in the room in the dark.

The lights went on and the gorillas holding me down lifted me to my feet.

'Put some clothes on Mr McTaggart,' said a suit sitting down at the dining table that also doubled as my desk.

I slipped on a pair of shorts, sat on the edge of my bed, and looked around the room. There were four men in black tactical assault suits that most Special Forces and police SWAT teams use these days. They had been wearing night vision goggles, but these were now off. They were armed with Glock 9mm pistols that were all holstered. They blocked all exits from my apartment that was one storey up off the marina. I concentrated on the bloke in the shiny shoes.

'Tell us what you know about Luigi Zappia,' the suit said quietly and crisply. He had the voice of a bloke in control and of someone who wasn't going to take any shit from anyone. I guessed him to be about 40 years old and in pretty good shape.

'Who the hell are you guys?' I asked. 'And what the fuck are you doing bursting into my apartment in the middle of the night and smashing my door?' I was starting to get a fix on who I would have to take out first to get my hands on a weapon and sort this shit out.

'No good thinking of trying to get away, Mr McTaggart' the suit said quietly, 'we have all the exits covered, and if you make a move to leave, we will take you down, and I promise, you will get hurt.'

He sounded very genuine, so I decided to reappraise my predicament.

'I will answer any questions you want, but if this is a stir from the blokes in the regiment, I will knock all your fucking blocks off.'

'No, Mr McTaggart, this is not a prank or a prelude to a Code of Conduct or Conduct After Capture course like you did when you first entered the SAS. We are from the Australian Federal Police and we need to ask you some serious questions because you are in big trouble.'

The Federal Police? Big trouble? Jesus, what is he on about? And how the hell did he know I had done a Conduct After Capture course?

'Show me some ID,' I said, trying to get my head around what was going down. As soon as I said that the suit started to move forward, and as he did, two of the gorillas came forward with him and flanked me on the bed. They were not taking any chances.

'I'm Peter Bryant,' he started opening his ID wallet. 'I am a senior agent with the AFP, and I work in the area of major crime involving narcotics and firearms, but principally narcotics.' His voice was sincere, and the ID looked real enough. I guessed he was about 183 centimetres tall and weighed about 90 kilos. He went on, 'these men are also agents with the Federal Police, and they are part of our tactical response and operations group. Some of the men who work in our unit you know,' he said with a hint of a smile on his face. 'Mr McTaggart, we know all about you, your military history and your family history. You came to our attention several months ago when you suddenly started moving around in our surveillance area and we need some answers concerning your operations and activities.' He looked at me with penetrating brown eyes, anticipating a response.

'I don't know what you mean by "operations and activities" but all I have been doing for the last couple of months is trying to scratch a living out of taking tourists out to the Reef.'

'How did you come to own the *Delfina?*' Bryant asked curtly.

'Luigi Zappia gave it to me for saving his life.' Peter Bryant looked across at one of the men in the corner who gave a slight affirmatory nod.

'And what do you know about Mr Zappia?' he continued.

'Well, he's generous, noisy, determined, successful and Italian. And oh, and he makes a good frittata,' I replied, wondering where all this was going.

'Don't you think giving you a half-million-dollar boat is a bit over-generous, Mr McTaggart?' Bryant asked, leaning forward.

'Of course it was,' I replied, 'but he was insistent that I take the *Delfina* for saving his life, and his wife wouldn't let him back out to sea in it anyway.' It did sound a bit lame, but it was the truth.

'Has Luigi Zappia ever asked you to do any special jobs in the *Delfina* since you have been the new owner?'

'No … well yes, he did ask me to take a group of people from Melbourne out to the Reef for a day trip a couple of months ago. They weren't that flash once on board because we had a decent swell running and they got a bit crook, so I took them to Magnetic Island for the day instead.' Bryant looked at a notebook that had now been drawn out of his jacket pocket. 'What is this all about anyway?' I asked again.

Bryant stepped a little closer to me as I remained sitting on the bed. 'Has Zappia ever asked you to go to the Myrmidon Reef area and pick anything up?'

'Myrmidon Reef? Nah, there's bugger all out there unless you want to dive or snorkel. But you really have to get your tides right because it fairly rips through there on the incoming and outgoing tides. So, you've only got a two-hour window at best. It's not a place I would normally take people unless they were very experienced divers. Besides, it is over 150 clicks offshore.'

Bryant returned to the dining table and sat down. 'Mr McTaggart, I am going to tell you something now that must remain confidential and must never be repeated to anyone outside this room.' Now he had my full and undivided attention.

'Okay,' I said, 'I can keep a secret.'

'I know you can, but people's lives may well depend on the information you are about to hear.'

'That's a bit dramatic isn't it?' I asked looking around at the unsmiling men in black still alert and ready to react.

'No, it isn't too dramatic, Mr McTaggart, and I will tell you why. Luigi Zappia is a drug lord. He operates a multi-million-dollar business out of Townsville in concert with a few well-known Asian and American drug dealers in Southeast Asia.'

'Bullshit! I have ...'

'Let me finish, please.' Bryant looked directly at me. His eyes were unflinching in his earnest stare. 'Zappia provides resources for those foreign importers by collecting drugs that are dropped offshore in 200-litre drums. They are dropped sub-surface with homing beacons, then collected and brought ashore. After sorting and repackaging the drugs, he or his colleagues — then flies the stuff out to provincial centres in light aircraft for re-distribution around Australia.'

I couldn't believe what I was hearing. *Luigi Zappia, a drug lord ... a kingpin?*

'If you know so much about him, why don't you grab him?' I asked.

'We had Zappia under surveillance for a few months and were about to move on him when he stopped using the *Delfina* to pick up the drugs. Then we noticed you putting to sea and going to areas we were not familiar with. We re-appraised and were led to believe Zappia was moving his operation around to avoid our surveillance and using you as a cover to pick up the drugs.'

'Me?' I asked, 'I haven't even been out to that part of the Reef.'

'We know, and that was diverting our attention and our limited resources,' Bryant responded. 'We now think Zappia is having someone else pick up the drugs offshore, but we haven't been able to pin it down yet,' he said, referring to his notebook again.

'Well why tell me all this if you are trying to nail a crook?'

'Because we want your help, Mr McTaggart. We would like you to get closer to Luigi Zappia and find out who he is employing to bring these drugs into the country.'

'You're kidding, aren't you? I am not a spy and I have never been trained to do espionage work. My specialty was water operations and close reconnaissance. I also know how to shoot and scoot, but I am not a good liar, Agent Bryant.'

'You don't have to be, Mr McTaggart, just socialise with Zappia and keep your ears open.'

'Nope, that it is not my cup of tea. Give me your card and if I hear or see anything, I will give you a bell.'

'That's a shame, Mr McTaggart, I thought a man of your reputation and integrity would be hell-bent on bringing criminals to justice,' he said quietly in what I thought was a sneaky attempt to shame me into becoming a spy.

'Mate, I am a retired Special Forces operative who is now trying to start a new life and get my own shit together. I don't need to play cops and robbers to get my kicks; I am happy being a tourism operator … if you don't mind.'

'Think about it, Mr McTaggart. We will go now, but I remind you of the need for total secrecy and confidentiality concerning this conversation.'

'Sure, whatever. See your own way out. Oh, and who is going to pay for the bloody door?' I asked a little angrily.

'It will be fixed before noon, Mr McTaggart.' They left as quickly as they had come and I was left sitting there on the bed in a pair of shorts with a head full of questions. Bryant's business card was left on the table. It just had his name and a mobile number and nothing else.

*   *   *

The door was fixed before lunchtime. I spent the rest of the day going over maps and checking out Myrmidon Reef and then out of curiosity went down to the *Delfina* to pore over the log to see how many trips had been made out that way. None. Not a bloody one. Either Zappia was a lousy record keeper or whoever was skippering the vessel was keeping trips out that way quiet. I looked through the entire cockpit, trying to see if there was a separate set of logs or running sheets, but there was nothing. I wondered if the Feds had it right. Zappia just didn't come across as a bad hat, but then again, anything was possible if the money was big enough. I had seen corruption firsthand in Afghanistan where the aid money and supplies tended to stay in Kabul and not make it out to the provincial areas where it was most needed. My curiosity was well and truly primed. I needed to find out more.

Luigi

I decided to check out Peter Bryant's story for myself. I had always considered myself a good judge of character and the allegations about Luigi just didn't add up. If he was the bad guy he was being made out to be, then I had been well and truly fooled. I guess my own ego drove me to take the next steps that would give me the answers I wanted. If Luigi Zappia was bringing shit back ashore it had to be stored somewhere, and the only place I could think of for that was Luigi's warehouse down next to the grain terminal on the wharf. I had driven past it a hundred times, but nothing ever drew my attention or stood out as being unusual. The big problem was that the warehouse complex was well protected with security guards and dogs, not so much for Zappia's shed but the Customs and freight forwarding businesses along that part of the Townsville wharf precinct. Zappia's name was emblazoned along the side, promoting his restaurants in town and the fresh seafood business one of his cousins operated. I then remembered the *Delfina* being tied up there a few times, but I thought nothing of it at the time.

The best way to have a look inside the warehouse was to come in from underneath. The local maritime authority had plans of the wharf that I asked for on the belief that I was looking for an alternate site for my business and expansion of the tourism operation I was developing. Zappia's warehouse had two doors, one front and one back, but I was going to come in through the floor via an access hole for water and sewerage facilities when the wharf had once been a berth for coastal traders. The original warehouse plans had been developed by Burns Philp who once dominated that part of Australia's coastal shipping business.

I thought it best not to tell the Feds what I intended to do because they would say no anyway, and forgiveness is usually easier to get than permission. The next week was going to be best for my covert recon because of a lack of moon and poor ambient light. My plan was to drop off the side of the *Delfina* and scuba across to the wharf. Once there, I would locate the access ladder and try and get inside. I would have to make sure the place was empty beforehand because I figured knocking floorboards in would be a tad noisy.

I parked across the road from the warehouse in the afternoon and kept a low profile. At 5 p.m., the warehouse staff left for the day, and through my binos I could see that the place was locked up nice and tight for the night.

Luigi Zappia greeted me like a brother when I called in for a feed at his restaurant around 7 p.m. I chatted with him and saw nothing out of the usual. I felt a bit strange knowing what I had been told, but if Luigi ever wanted another career he should become a professional poker player because I detected nothing in his face to indicate that he was up to no good.

Around 10 p.m., I went back down to the marina, boarded the *Delfina* and got into my wetsuit and scuba gear. I checked all of the gear and waited patiently while a bunch of drunks on the large cruiser three berths down decided to take their party inside their boat. I didn't need this delay as the air temperature at night was still a steamy 28 degrees and I was starting to broil in the wetsuit. But I needed to make sure that nobody was watching because not a lot of scuba diving is done at night. In this age of terrorism and Joe Citizen being alert, I didn't need to be hauled out of the water and asked what the hell I was doing with break and enter gear tied to my weight belt.

I slipped into the warm waters and followed my compass bearing until I could make out the shape of the piers of the wharf below the warehouse. It took me another five minutes to find the access ladder and then another couple of minutes to get out of my scuba tank that I secured to the ladder. I then hauled myself up the barnacle-encrusted steel rungs to the floor of the warehouse. I had my waterproof torch with a red lens and it soon revealed the hatch just above my head. I inserted the jemmy quietly into the gap near where I figured I could get some purchase and nearly fell back in the water when it popped open with almost no pressure on my part. *So much for security.* I slowly eased myself up into the warehouse and looked around. The place was in total darkness. I could hear a compressor running which I figured had to be the very large refrigeration unit for the seafood and a cold room for other perishables. Other than that, the warehouse was packed full of boxes and crates. I slowly circumnavigated the shed that was about 30 metres long and 20 metres wide. It took some time to adjust to the red torch beam, but I was soon moving quickly around the rows of boxes and cartons.

I was beginning to think I was on a wild goose chase when I spotted a pile of 200-litre blue plastic drums in the corner of the warehouse partly obscured by a canvas tarpaulin. My heart skipped a beat as I began to realise that just maybe the Feds were onto something. I carefully peeled back the tarp and saw that the drums had all been opened and their screw-down lids were just sitting on top. I looked inside and saw that the drums were empty. In the last drum I saw a piece of brown greasy-looking plastic and picked it and smelled it. I couldn't tell if it was cannabis or what, maybe it was just fish oil or something. I stuffed the plastic down inside my wetsuit front, replaced the tarp and kept searching. I moved over to where an office was located and carefully opened the door. Then I saw it, a set of scales that I knew were the type that drug dealers use for measuring out the hard stuff like heroin and ice. They definitely weren't the type of scales you throw a fish on. *Fuck you Luigi.* I was happy on one hand and sad on the other. The first thought that raced through my mind was, *they are gonna take my bloody boat!*

I looked around and found a cloth to wipe off the water I had spilled onto the floorboards and began my exit. The floor would be dry by morning in the Townsville heat and hopefully, nobody would know of my intrusion. I pulled the hatch down after me and got back into my scuba gear and swam sub-surface back to the *Delfina*. Once on board, I took out the plastic bag that I had found in the drum at Zappia's warehouse and placed it in a large envelope in the safe in the forward cabin of the boat. I then made a cup of coffee and thought about what I had seen in the warehouse and where I now stood in relation to my Italian benefactor. Things were taking a decidedly interesting turn.

*   *   *

'Bryant' came through the handset of my mobile phone. The words were short and sharp as if the respondent wanted to spend as little time on the phone as necessary.

'G'day Agent Bryant, it's Bob McTaggart here.'

'Mr McTaggart, nice to hear from you. What can I do for you?' Bryant responded sharply.

'I need to talk to you,' I said, playing my cards pretty close to my chest.

'Sure, when and where?'

'How about my apartment, this afternoon at 3?'

'I'll see you then.'

*   *   *

At 3 p.m. on the dot, there was a knock on the new door of my apartment. I opened the door to see Agent Bryant, two of the men I suspected of being callers previously, and another slightly older and heavier man who sure looked like a Fed. All were dressed in casual but neat civilian attire. The two men at the rear wore sunglasses that hid the upper half of their faces. They were the same sunglasses I had worn in Afghanistan and were for protecting one's eyes from minor shrapnel and blast just as much as sun glare.

'Mr McTaggart, this is Superintendent Ballantyne. He is the senior field agent for the AFP in our division.' There was no introduction for the two men behind them.

The Superintendent moved forward and offered me his hand. I shook it and nodded. His handshake was strong without trying to break every bone in my hand. He had a face that reflected experience and I guessed he had been a copper for a couple of decades. His hair was starting to turn grey along the sides. His whole demeanour exuded authority. The door closed quietly behind the group as they entered my apartment. Without saying a word, Agent Bryant moved to the small occasional table in the corner of the room and removed a small listening device that was planted underneath.

'Jesus, how long has that been there?' I asked.

'Oh, about two months, Mr McTaggart,' Bryant replied casually. 'We needed to know whose side you were on.'

Christ, what else did these coppers have in my place? Next thing they will be pulling video cameras out of the bedroom.

'Well, I have never been on anyone's "side", as you put it, but I think I have a good idea who the bad guys are now.'

'Exactly what do you mean, Mr McTaggart?' asked the Superintendent who was looking at me quite intensely.

I explained in detail how I went into Zappia's warehouse and did a recce to see what I could find. The two silent operatives in the background looked down at the floor and I could see one of them smiling slightly as he and his off-sider exchanged quick but knowing glances. Agent Peter Bryant's eyes widened, and he looked like he was about to have a baby.

'And what did you find?' the Superintendent asked with barely a change of expression on his suntanned face.

'This,' I said as I took the plastic bag out of the manila envelope in which I had stashed it. I had seen enough television CSI shows about handling evidence to minimise my own contact with the bag, but before I could extract it, Bryant stepped forward and grabbed the envelope. 'Where was this exactly?' he asked, shaking the bag out onto the dining table.

'In the bottom of one the 200-litre drums.'

'How many drums did you see in the warehouse?'

'I couldn't be sure, but I would say at least half a dozen.'

'What colour were these drums?' he snapped. I could sense he was a just a tiny bit pissed off.

'Blue, yeah mid-blue, and they were plastic with screw lids like they have for farm chemicals' I replied.

'Jesus H Christ!' The Superintendent sat down at the table. He had a look of utter dismay on his face. 'They have got more than double what we thought past our guard.'

Bryant was examining the plastic bag. He looked at the

Superintendent, 'I think this is the same as one of the bags we found out at Myrmidon Reef when that container ship hit a drum a year ago.'

A bloody year ago? How long has this been going on for God's sake?

'I don't want to be nosey, but how long has this shit been coming in through Zappia?' I asked no one in particular.

'Well, Mr McTaggart, it could have been at least two years that we are aware of. It has taken a lot of quiet poking around to get where we are today. Our aim is to catch the major operatives and not just the couriers.' He was about to go on when Bryant stepped in.

'With operations like this we have to have our arses covered all the way. There is a lot at stake here and these men are absolutely ruthless and have no compunction in killing anyone who gets in their way.' His face was stony, and his words chilled me to the bone. 'But first, let's get a couple of things straight, McTaggart. You are NOT an AFP agent, nor do you have any legal authority to break and enter premises of your own accord.' He was staring at me intently.

'What!? You mean just like you probably didn't have authority to kick my fucking door down last week and put a bug in my apartment,' I snapped back feeling smug with my rapid retort.

'Actually, Mr McTaggart, we did have the authority to do both,' the Superintendent said quietly and calmly. That took the wind out of my sails almost immediately. These blokes had some power.

'Now, let's all sit down and see what we can sort out next.'

'<u>We</u> sort out?' I asked. 'We … as in you and me?'

'Yes, Mr McTaggart, we,' the Superintendent replied with authority. He looked like he actually had a slight smile on his face. 'Jim, knock up a brew for everyone will you?' The taller bloke in civvies made for the kitchen. For a visitor I was surprised how well he knew his way around my kitchen. I turned to face Bryant and Superintendent Ballantyne.

'Bob,' Bryant said in a more friendly tone, 'We have a proposition for you. I'm sure this bag is one of the wrappers that they use in the drums when moving very high-grade heroin. We're talking millions of dollars here, and I mean tens upon tens of millions of dollars in street value.'

I let that sink in as Bryant continued. 'Your unauthorised visit to Zappia's warehouse confirms our suspicions, and we now want to move ahead with the next phase of our operation we call *Tropic Lightning*.'

'Jesus, that's original, that's the name of the American division in Hawaii,' I said.

'We know, we are hoping it will draw some of the heat away from the real operation if the name is ever dropped accidentally' Bryant continued. 'We need to confirm some of Zappia's other interests, and we want you to come and work for us.'

'Guys, I don't like drugs and I hate drug pushers even more, but I am not a copper nor have I trained as one,' I said, seeing my idea of earning a living evaporating before my eyes.

'Bob, you have all the skills we want,' Bryant started.

'And the perfect cover for the next part of the operation,' the Superintendent concluded.

'Cover, what cover?' I asked. This was starting to get interesting.

Before they could answer, a mug of coffee was put down in front of me. Black; no milk, and no sugar. Just the way I have my coffee. I looked up at the unnamed agent who just smiled and went back into the background.

'Thanks, Jim,' the Superintendent smiled while sipping at his coffee. 'We need someone who is much like a local, one who works in the area, is seen regularly in the area and has a cover that is plausible to all and sundry. That person is you, Bob. You can blend in with the tourists, your job will take you all over and especially into our area of interest and most of all, we know you can handle yourself if you ever got into strife.' He leaned back in the chair and looked at me over the rim of his mug.

Agent Bryant turned to look at me. He had a plain folder in his hand that I hadn't seen when he walked in. He flicked it open and from my position I could see a photograph of myself in uniform that was taken about three years previously. 'Bob, we know what happened to your family and we know that you have been reassessing what you want to do with your life. Why not permanently separate from the Army and come and work with us to nail these bastards?' For the first time, I noticed some passion in his voice. He had a very calm exterior and showed little emotion, but now he was leaning forward with his jaw jutting slightly forward. He meant business.

'When you say, "work for us" I take it you mean as an agent?' I asked fishing for more detail. 'What exactly would my legal situation be in this regard?' I had seen blokes working for other agencies when I was serving, and they had been left high and dry when it all went pear-shaped.

'You would be covered legally, although your existence would also be denied publicly,' Bryant explained. 'For all intents and purposes, you don't know us and we don't know you. You would be working undercover as an un-badged officer.'

'Okay, so what do I have to do and how much are you going to pay me? This might sound mercenary, but I have to keep paying bills and keep my boat afloat,' I shot back.

'We will cover your operating costs by giving you a special credit card. No one will be able to trace it back to us, and we will also pay you a pretty good retainer for your services. I think a couple of thousand a week should see you looked after.' Bryant smiled thinly as he rattled off the figures.

A couple of thousand a week! There is a God! I sat contemplating my next response.

After a minute or so the Superintendent said, 'Look, Bob, think about it for the next few days and we will get in touch with you again and you can let us know.' He started getting out of his chair.

'I've got one more question,' I said. *Here goes nothing.* 'If Zappia really is a crook, does that mean I will lose the *Delfina?*'

The two senior agents looked at each other and smiled, 'No, the boat is yours as it would be too hard to prove that it was the result of illegal earnings,' Ballantyne said, looking at Bryant as he spoke.

'Well that's our story anyway,' Bryant grinned slightly. 'Don't worry, Bob, we will keep you afloat.'

'Good one,' I said with not inconsiderable relief.

Bryant stood and extended his hand, 'I hope you can join us,' he said, looking me straight in the eyes. 'We need you. And as before, mum's the word about all this. Nobody must know.'

And they were gone. I sat and thought about what had all gone down over the last few days. It was starting to look like I would be changing dance partners in the middle of what could be an interesting dance indeed.

*   *   *

I gave notice of my separation from the Army and got back in reply a wad of bumph about what I could and could not do, and the Superintendent told me to ignore it. I spent about two weeks in Canberra receiving briefings from all sorts of spooks including ASIO who were very interested in my previous security classifications and access to privileged information as part of the Terrorist Assault Group when I spent time in the Counter-Terrorism Squadron in the Regiment. One thing that did impress me was the handle that the AFP had on who was doing what. Their biggest problem was catching the bad guys actually being bad and committing the crimes and retaining the evidence to get a conviction. It must have been frustrating watching crooks go about their business and being unable to grab them because of various legal restrictions. The biggest surprise was discovering just how many clandestine operations were on the go and how heavily involved the Defence Force was in many of the ops. I had worked in Aid to the Civil Power when doing CT stuff, but this side of the equation was a totally different ball game.

I might have pissed them off in Canberra when I told them I didn't have the authority to give them the answers to questions regarding our Special Forces state of readiness and a few other bits that were really a "need to know"' basis. It was nice to screw the guys who usually screwed us.

But for now, I was about to embark on a new chapter in my life. Sitting in the plane on my flight back to Townsville, I wondered what surprises my "handlers" — as I now knew they were called — would have in store.

Bob Bond

February 2010

On my return to Townsville, there was a lot to start putting into play. Greater emphasis would now be placed on me becoming an eco-tourism operator specialising in wilderness and adventurous expeditions. A routine visit to collect mail from my post-office box showed that I even had a registered business name and a registered office and business number. Amazing how fast bureaucracy can work when it wants to. I started being overt in my advertising and preparing flyers to leave at the airport and in motel/hotel reception areas. The price for my tours was exorbitant in the hope no silly bugger would want to go bush with me.

The Feds flew me back down to Canberra and I was escorted into the AFP Ops Room, and after looking around, it was like old home week back in the Regiment, with maps, charts, monitors and stacks of files and folders on desks. I signed various documents that warned me against blabbing off and the likely punishment I would receive for being a traitor to the cause. Just the normal stuff we had in the Army but with slightly more menace. I was going to conduct a preliminary operation up in the Daintree on a "shakedown op" as Peter Bryant put it. 'Get the cobwebs out and flake off the rust' was the way the Superintendent phrased it. Apparently, some people were growing seriously high-grade cannabis on Crown Land up in the Daintree rainforest region. A switched-on chopper pilot had noticed the distinct change in vegetation in an area that he flew over regularly and saw a reflection from what he thought was a vehicle window in an area where there normally wasn't and, more importantly, shouldn't have been anyone. The area was closed to campers and the like and so he let the authorities know.

My job was to go in covertly, check out their operation and gain intelligence for a full-scale Queensland police raid in conjunction with the AFP. Normally the State police would have handled this sort of job, but they were stretched to the limit chasing crooks further south and had run out of warm bodies to put into the field.

'So, how many are there in the area?' I asked during the initial briefing.

'We're not sure, Bob,' Peter Bryant responded. 'But looking at some aerial shots we were able to get from a RAAF recon mission, it looks like a camp that would hold at least four if not six people.' He turned and pointed at an enlargement of the map of the area over which the photograph had been superimposed. 'It looks like this is their main camp. They park several vehicles – four-wheel drives mostly — as the track in is not passable for two wheel drives. It looks like they have a water point here.' I moved closer and saw what looked like irrigation pipes coming out of the river about 50 metres from the camp site.

'Is this their water supply for crop irrigation?'

'Yep, you wouldn't think they would need to draw water for growing marijuana up in this part of the world, but they are pushing this stuff along at a great rate of knots.'

'What's that?' I asked, pointing at a dark object near the river.

'We think that is their generator for running the pump to get the water up to the crops.'

'Are they armed?'

'Not to our knowledge, however you should take every precaution not to be caught in there. We have had run-ins with some of these types before. We even had a group of Calabrians growing dope just outside Canberra back in the 80s, and they all carried shotguns.'

Bryant walked back to his desk and sat down.

Lovely, just what I need. A bunch of crooks who might have shotguns and not give a shit about taking out someone snooping around their campsite.

'Will I be armed?' I asked hopefully.

'Bob, we don't think you should go armed at present,' Bryant said, looking up from a folder.

'Why not?'

'One, we don't expect you to compromise yourself and have a confrontation with these criminals. Secondly, we don't want to escalate what is already a delicate situation on Crown Land with the possibility of civilians in the area,' Bryant stated coldly.

'Hang on a tick. You said I should be ready, what if I am confronted with armed villains up there?' I was getting a bit testy because having a credible response to a threat was important.

'We will be giving you every imaginable support and equipment so you don't get confronted,' Bryant shot back. He looked across at one of the support team who I recognised from a previous meeting. 'Jim, tell Bob what kit we are going to give him.'

The agent walked over to a table that was covered with a sheet of black plastic. He drew it back and motioned for me to come and look at the goodies laid out on the table.

'We have got Series 4 night vision goggles. You will carry a compact UHF and HF transmitter with frequency hopping, rapid encryption and burst transmission capability. We know you have an explosives and demolition ticket so we thought some scare charges and a few other bits of C4 and F1 switches would come in handy if things got dicey.' He smiled and stood back and let me handle the equipment. I had to admit the NVG were the very latest and had greater capability than those we had used on night ops in Afghanistan.

'Who will I be talking to on the radio?' I asked.

'Hopefully nobody,' Bryant said coming across to the table. 'We only expect to hear from you if you need help. Jim will give you a set of code words so you can keep in touch if things get out of hand.'

'Right, so no traffic unless absolutely necessary?' I needed to pin down the type of control they expected to run with this job.

'And we will not be calling you. The last thing we want to do is compromise your position,' Jim said.

'There will be no need for scheds, we expect you to be in and out in one or two days … tops,' Bryant added.

Piece of cake, I'll be dancing in the Daintree.

*   *   *

The plan was to drive up to the Daintree via Port Douglas. The rainforest area is massive at around 1200 square kilometres. The Daintree is unique in that it is the oldest continually surviving tropical rainforest on the planet. In many places, especially north of the Daintree River, the jungle grows right down to the edge of the sea. It can get soggy up there because they get about two metres of rain every Wet season between December and March, and access can be tricky. Most tourists only venture into the region on organised tours or are very experienced campers with seriously good four-wheel drive vehicles and trailers. The area was strictly managed by the Queensland Parks and Wildlife people who were quite zealous when it came to protecting their environment. The rainforest is well over 100 million years old and also contains some unique fauna and flora. It is a special place and one had to tread carefully especially when it came to things that bite, like crocodiles and seriously venomous snakes.

I would set up my cover on the premise that I was heading up into the Daintree and then heading further north and going through to Cooktown to see the lay of the land with a possibility of starting up some eco-tourism. The Queensland Parks and Wildlife blokes in the town office thought I was nuts but gave me some good advice on which roads were best to travel on. I enquired about rivers and water and crocs and they were more than willing to share some crocodile war stories with me. I made a mental note to carry a large handgun next time I came up this way. I recalled running into Les Hiddins, the *Bush Tucker Man* from an old ABC television series, and he carried a massive Magnum .44 revolver that he reckoned was the best thing to change a croc's mind if it was contemplating making you his next dinner.

I had logos on the side of my Toyota Land Cruiser claiming to be a tourist operator and charter boat operator (which was partly true) and drove around town for a while, making sure I wasn't being followed or under any sort of observation. My iPad was kept in a compartment under the driver's seat the spooks had made for me, and I had a series of storage panels built under the vehicle for holding stores and equipment one wouldn't normally associate with a tourist operator. The C4 explosive in a storage bin I could always say was "expanding bait", but some of my other paraphernalia would have been a bit hard to explain.

I arrived in Mossman on the Cape Tribulation Road just after sunset and booked into the Demi View Motel in town. I wandered into town looking for a place to have a feed and found a great little Thai restaurant. Just as I was settling into an entrée of fresh spring rolls, I heard the voice of an old Army mate behind me.

'Jesus, they'll let any riffraff in here.'

I turned and saw the compact and lean shape of Ian Taylor.

Christ, he still looks as good as he did ten years ago.

We had served together in East Timor and before that, he had tried to convince me I should get out of Water Troop and give the HALO section a try. High altitude low opening parachute jumps were not my idea of fun. I didn't mind jumping but leaping out of a Herc at 30,000 feet on oxygen and flying ten clicks through the dark and then opening less than 1,000 feet above the ground was not my idea of a good career move. Ian had set an Australian HALO record up at Exmouth years before and stepped out at something like 35,000 feet. He reckoned when he looked down at Exmouth Gulf, he was sure he was going to miss landing on Australian soil altogether. As it turned out he came to the Water Troop and became very skilled in sub-surface operations including teaching the rest of us how to exit a Collins Class submarine in the middle of Bass Strait at night.

'G'day Squizzie.' I could never figure out why all blokes whose name was Taylor were called Squizzie. It was an Army thing but nobody I knew could ever tell me why. Legend had it that it was because some guy in the Army was a bit like Squizzy Taylor, the notorious criminal from Melbourne from the 1920s. We shook hands and I asked him to join me for dinner. He explained that he was on a job for the Government but would say nothing other than that. Normal rules, don't ask and nobody has to tell any lies. "Need to know" and all that secret squirrel stuff. It was a credo and iron-clad rule drilled into us in the Regiment and seemed to stay with us after that as well.

'What are you up to mate? I heard that you had taken leave without pay,' he asked while looking around the room slowly. He was taking it all in and seemed to be right on his guard.

'I'm trying to expand my business up here. I think I will give it a go in Banana Land for a while.'

Ian was a dyed-in-the-wool New South Welshman and immediately started telling me all the reasons why Queensland was a crappy place to live. I told him about saving Luigi Zappia and the *Delfina*. I didn't expand on anything else about Luigi or the AFP. No lies, just not everything. He gave a low whistle and said that fortune always favours the brave. We enjoyed a few beers over dinner and were having a coffee afterwards when Ian asked me to do him a favour.

'Mate, anything. What is it?' I replied.

'I can't tell you everything Bob, but I pulled the pin after the last tour of Afghanistan. I figured six tours was enough and I am now working for an agency out of Canberra.' He looked around very slowly to make sure nobody was within earshot. In a low voice he then told me that he suspected something was wrong and that there was a bad apple in the mix and that he was anticipating trouble.

An agency in Canberra? Nobody in the AFP had told me about Ian, so he must be working for another group of spooks.

'What sort of trouble?' I asked, keeping my voice low.

'It seems that every time we are closing in on our target, things just fuck up,' he added with a look of resignation. 'It seems like the bad guys we are trying to locate always know when we are coming.'

I prompted Ian to tell me more, but he put his hand up and shook his head.

'Nope, too dangerous mate. It is better you don't know, but if something happens to me will you promise me to check out what happened?'

'Christ, Ian, that's a bit cloak-and-dagger isn't it? You're not having a lend of me, are you?'

'No mate, I am dead serious. For God's sake, keep this to yourself and watch your back.' He had an earnest look on his normally smiling face and I could tell that something was chewing away at him.

'I better go, I have an early start tomorrow, we are going out to one of the cays off the main shipping channel. Give me your mobile number in case I need to call you,' he said while still scanning the emptying restaurant. 'And one other thing mate,' he said as he stepped nearer, 'Do NOT trust anybody you don't know really well.' He smiled faintly and shook my hand.

I handed Ian one of my business cards that had my "real" phone details and not the phone that the AFP were using for my operation.

'I am going up to the Daintree tomorrow, so don't expect me to answer. Even the sat phones have trouble getting through up there,' I said.

We shook hands again and told each to take care and went our separate ways. I watched him walk off down the street keeping in the shadows as much as possible until he turned the corner and was gone.

*   *   *

The next morning, I headed up towards the target area and checked out the road leading past where I would have to leg it in to reach the camp. I didn't want to have to walk too far in case I had to scoot out of the area. I stooged around for a few days, checking all the roads in the area, most of which were not shown on the tourist maps but came up on the iPad that the AFP had so kindly given me. Just love that technology.

*   *   *

I drove down the road I knew would take me to within a few kilometres of my ingress point. I had seen a dense piece of bush off the road where I figured the vehicle would remain unobserved from the main track. I slowly crept the vehicle in to the hiding spot, trying hard not to damage or break the vegetation. Once I had immersed the vehicle in the dense undergrowth, I took my backpack and moved 25 metres away from the vehicle and sat down next to a large ficus tree and waited and listened. The sounds of the bush soon became familiar and I could hear small animals and insects moving around next to me, obviously reacting to my body heat.

I was completely clad in black from head to foot. I set my wrist compass for a point where I knew I would intersect the footpath leading into the camp. I would now start moving about 100 metres every 20 minutes to close with the track leading into the camp site. Every 5 metres I would stop and listen. It was not yet the Dry season but the Wet had been really lean, with very low rainfalls recorded. As a result, there was a lot of dried vegetation and dry leaf matter on the ground. As one of my mates in the Regiment once put it, it was like trying to sneak down a footpath walking on corn flakes. Once darkness fell, I would put on a nylon face mask to reduce the shine on my face.

*   *   *

Slow and sure was the way to move. Stealth would give me my security. Stay balanced, and watch for signs of trip wires, booby traps or early warning devices. Move 20 paces, stop, kneel down, and listen. My black coveralls and lightweight black balaclava all but made me disappear. My black flying gloves were fine but liked to catch on the "wait-a-while" bushes that fringed the footpad.

Then I heard it. The unmistakable sound of a bloke snoring. *Christ, he sounded like a chainsaw!* Then I saw it. A single wire across the track. I lowered myself slowly to the ground and saw it was connected to a trip flare, and what looked like a small charge of plastic as well, probably set to provide early warning for the camp inhabitants. It must have been in place a while because there were signs that it was armed and disarmed regularly. Now that's slack. They should have been moving their trip wires around.

It took me a good five minutes to disconnect the trip wire so if I needed to, I could beetle out this way and not worry about being illuminated ... or blown to smithereens.

I closed in on the snoring. I could make out the silhouette of a rough bush shack. It looked like there were three warm bodies in hammocks; two in one shack and another in a lean-to of sorts. A small kitchen and workshop was under a tarpaulin. And there they were: mounds of marijuana tops ready for baling. I pulled my Minolta out and took some happy snaps with the film the Feds had provided.

I heard movement to my flank. *Fuck, it was coming towards me.* I pressed up against a tree to remove my shape from sight. Whoever it was had a torch and was moving towards the kitchen area. A small camp fridge door was opened, and a can of drink taken out. I heard the hiss of a ring tab being pulled. Then I heard a female voice close behind me just dripping with menace say very quietly, 'Move one hair on your head and you are dead.'

Shit. Where had she come from? I felt a gun barrel, probably a pistol, prod me in the back. 'Move, arsehole!' she hissed. I did as I was asked. She held my left arm and started guiding me towards the tent. I needed to get out of here, and real quick. Nobody told me that they had small arms. I thought there was a slim chance, but usually these buggers use shotguns to scare people off. Bad guys carrying handguns indicate that they occasionally get serious. I quietly flicked the Minolta onto flash with my right hand and turned slightly to face my unseen captor. I saw she was of Asian appearance and had long black hair. She smelled of lavender or something similar.

Boomph! A brilliant flash of light erupted as I fired the camera flash. Off it went and so did I. As fast as my legs would carry me, I bolted back down my ingress track. Simultaneously, I had ripped the NVGs off as they had been well and truly screwed when the camera flash went off. I had to stop and kneel down in the scrub off the side of the track for a few seconds to recover my night vision. I now had to use the Mark I eyeball to get out of this mess.

The sharp crack of pistol shots and the heavier chatter of a long-barrelled automatic rifle — that sounded very much like an AK-47 — buzzed around me. It was enough motivation to get me moving again. These buggers had plenty of firepower. Thank God they were lousy shots and like most people tend to do at night they were firing high. I passed their trip wire and dropped a scare charge with a 10-second delay to give me some time and space. Bullets still kept whizzing around, sounding all the world like angry bees. I heard the crack of a round passing close to my ear and knew I needed to change direction and soon.

Into the scrub I went and stopped dead. I waited. Even though this was nothing new to me I could still hear my heart pounding. I would have given anything for a silenced Sterling right now, but 'nah, you won't need a gun, Bob. These crooks are small time,' they said. And I believed them. *Note to myself. Don't do that again.*

The sound of two blokes pushing noisily up the track got closer and then the scare charge went off. Screaming and yells and shouts rent the air as they were instantly blinded by the flash and disoriented by the explosion. At least now I could put some distance between me and my pursuers who would be wary of charging hard after me, now that I had struck back with some of my own persuasion.

It was time to bugger off quick smart. I put the night vision goggles back on and took a circuitous route and after 20 minutes found my way back to the Toyota. A quick scan showed nobody had been around or had tampered with my vehicle. It was time to make tracks and head back to Cairns.

Not my best covert reconnaissance, not by a long shot. And who was that sheila with the long black hair? And how come they had more weapons than our local bikie gang?

Back in my hotel room I finished a shower and took a quick look at the shots I had taken before being sprung. The last image was interesting. It showed half of the face of the woman with the long black hair. Definitely Asian, probably southern Viet or Thai by the look of it. The weapon was a 9mm Glock and probably borrowed from our local coppers who had their armoury in Sydneyham knocked off about a year ago.

A knock on the door signalled the arrival of my de-brief team.

This was going to be fun. Not.

'Bob,' Bryant said sternly.

'Peter,' I smiled back.

The other two accompanying agents remained in the background. One stood about near the door and another near a window overlooking the marina. The atmosphere was cool if not frigid.

'Well, that didn't go down too successfully as a covert recon, did it?' Peter Bryant said with his opening salvo.

'Not really,' I answered back, keeping calm.

'Jesus, Bob, what the fuck happened up there?' Bryant asked sitting opposite me at the dining table.

I gave a long and detailed brief on my recon, ingress, and extraction. I also told him about the woman with the long black hair.

'A woman?' he asked, looking up at the field agent near the window.

'Yeah, she was tall for an Asian, and from the grip she had on my arm I would say quite strong as well,' I said, looking for some further idea of what was going on.

'How do you know she was Asian?' Bryant asked, opening up his ever-present folder.

'Because I took a photo of her.' I smiled back while passing it across to the table to Peter Bryant.

He grabbed the photograph up and while it didn't show her complete face, we could make out the almond shaped eyes, the jet-black hair, and a collar of a denim jacket.

'Well done,' he said with genuine disbelief that I would have a photograph of one of the crooks. 'However, it doesn't alter what I need to say concerning your mission,' he said in that earnest tone that indicated a rocket was about to follow. 'The bottom line, Bob' — he paused to add gravity to his next remark — 'is that this op was supposed to be covert and it ended up far from being that.' He waited for my response.

'True. But I have to say running into a bunch of criminals that were heavily armed was also not on the agenda.' I watched his face change ever so slightly to one of slight acceptance and agreement. 'These were not a bunch of weekend amateurs growing dope to fund their annual holidays. That sheila was carrying a Glock, and from what I could hear being unleashed in my direction upon my exit, they had heavier stuff in abundance. This was not a good result, granted, but neither was the basic intel in my briefing. I also believe I was at risk because I was not forewarned, nor was I able to respond with reasonable force.' There, I had said it.

I fucked up and they fucked up.

'Okay, okay, let's not get twisted around the axle on this,' Bryant said quickly. 'By the time the local Police were able to respond, they had pulled up stakes and left. No doubt they will re-emerge somewhere else before long. The only good thing was they left a lot of juvenile plants behind.'

Before he could go any further, there was a knock on the door and the Superintendent walked in with a shitty look on his face. Behind him was a bloke I had not seen before, but he looked like someone that belonged in Canberra and flew a desk.

'Superintendent,' I offered.

He held up his hand in a gesture that indicated nobody should speak. He passed a note to Bryant who immediately had the two agents with him start sweeping the apartment for listening devices. I sat and watched as they produced small hand-held monitors that looked like mobile phones but were clearly detectors of some sort.

'Clear,' one said after 10 minutes.

'Gentlemen, I want you to meet Frank Benning. He is from the Office of National Assessment and has been working in concert with our people in Canberra.'

I looked at Benning and thought that I recognised his face. He reminded me of a bloke who used to be the Army's Provost Marshall back in the early 1990s. We had been working with the State Police in Victoria as part of the SAS Regiment's Aid to the Civil Power training and he was the liaison between the Military Police and the State coppers. He was a tough nut and ruled his Corps with an iron fist. He looked at me but showed no recognition at all.

The Superintendent continued. 'Last night, one of the men working undercover for the AONA was killed. We are not sure yet how he died, but at present we will await a coronial investigation before we proceed any further on our current operation.'

'What happened?' asked Peter Bryant.

Benning stepped forward and said in a flat tone, 'We believe that our operative drowned whilst undertaking a sub-surface reconnaissance of a likely target out on the Reef.' Benning paused and added, 'Tides and currents are tricky in the area and my belief is that the agent underestimated the conditions and lost his way and drowned accidentally.' He moved towards the table where the photograph of the Asian woman was laying. I watched his face and saw a flash of recognition cross his dark eyes. But he said nothing.

'Who was the agent?' Bryant then asked.

Benning swung around to face Bryant and replied, 'Taylor, Ian Taylor'.

I sat stunned. I didn't believe my ears. I worked hard to show no emotion on my face.

Squizzie? Dead? It couldn't be. No way. He was too good a bloody diver and swimmer to drown.

I remembered what he said in our conversation in Cairns and sat saying nothing. I also recalled how we used to say he must have been a dolphin in a previous life, so good were his aquatic skills.

Do not trust anybody you don't know really well.

I kept my counsel, but my mind was racing.

'So how exactly did this bloke Taylor drown?' I asked trying not to sound too inquisitive and not letting on that I knew Ian.

'Poor judgement in my opinion,' Benning shot back dismissively. 'He should have done his homework regarding the currents.'

'Meanwhile,' the Superintendent went on, 'Let's talk about last week's little fiasco, shall we?'

Bryant flushed and I looked up at the Superintendent, waiting for the burst that was sure to follow. 'From what I can gather, it seems that the camp was better protected than anyone gave those people credit for?' he asked, enquiringly glancing between Bryant and myself.

'You could say that,' I offered. 'They were packing a fair bit of heat as I found out.'

'Yes, sorry about that, McTaggart,' Ballantyne responded, 'they caught us off guard as well.'

'It would have been nice if I had had a weapon ...'

'Let's get one thing straight, McTaggart,' *Uh oh, here it comes.* 'This was a covert operation and you are not James bloody Bond.'

'I know that,' I said, 'I look like shit in a dinner suit ... and I don't like martinis,' trying but failing to lighten the conversation. *Well, that went over like a lead balloon.*

Peter Bryant stepped in. 'He has a point, sir, he was unable to defend himself ...'

'Forget it, Peter, we will not have our special agents running around with lethal weapons.'

'Superintendent Ballantyne, I have carried handguns for most of my time when I served in the Regiment, especially when doing counter-terrorism work. I think you can trust me not to go firing indiscriminately if I ever get into strife.' I pleaded with as much integrity as I could muster.

'I would support his request, sir,' Bryant added, looking at me trying to recover some trust from his team.

'I'll think about it. Meanwhile, everyone just sit tight until we hear from above what our next move will be. McTaggart, go about your normal business and keep the *Delfina* operating. I want you to be our eyes and ears out towards the Reef.

'Sir,' I responded.

Benning took one last look at the photograph on the table but said nothing as he turned and followed the agents and the Superintendent out of my apartment.

The Enemy Camp

A bloke who could have been president of the Far North Queensland Ugly Man's Club strode into the camp site that was hastily being pulled down and packed into several four-wheel drive vehicles. He was 185 centimetres tall, weighed around 120 kilograms and had a shaved head that was covered in scars. Tattoos ran down both of his heavily muscled arms.

'Carina, what the fuck went down here?' the ugly man asked.

The long-haired Asian woman turned to face him, 'Franz, we had someone snooping around last night and he was probably a copper,' she said in perfect English.

'And why do you say that, Carina?' the man asked with menace dripping off every word.

'Because he was wearing night vision goggles and had explosives,' Carina answered calmly. She hated every fibre of Franz Nesbitt's being. Ever since she had kneed him in the groin when he thought he could take advantage of her when they were in an isolated camp up near Black Mountain near Cooktown, their relationship had been very fragile. He was a cruel and sadistic man who had no compunction using force or violence or both to get his way or win an argument. His volatile temper ran off a very short fuse. She thought he actually enjoyed inflicting pain on others.

'So how come we were sprung?' Franz looked around as two men were hurriedly packing up the portable generator while two others were tying bundles of mature cannabis plants into stooks and loading them into a trailer behind another four-wheel drive.

Thuong Thach Carina responded carefully, trying not to shift blame onto any one person in particular. 'Maybe they saw the crops, maybe they saw the camp, I am not sure,' she replied.

'Bullshit, Carina, somebody here fucked up and I want to know who,' Nesbitt shouted angrily. 'I flew over this camp and everything was sweet a week ago. Tell me who fucked up!' he yelled, his face starting to change to a darker shade of red. His massive frame started to heave as he looked around the remains of the camp site. His fists were clenched, and he started kicking at the ground.

'Franz, I do not know,' she replied honestly, becoming just a little wary of what this man was likely to do in a fit of rage. She felt for her Glock that was hidden underneath her shirt that hung outside her jeans. She was anticipating the worst.

'Well, I just happen to know, Carina,' he sneered and turned looking at the two men who were now lifting black irrigation pipes into the back of a Land Rover, 'One of these fuckwits didn't put his cam net over his fucking vehicle when he came back from town last week.'

The two men stopped what they were doing and looked towards Carina for help.

'Jeez, Franz, the vehicle was only out in the open for a few minutes, it takes time to pull the nets over, doesn't it, Kegs?' the skinnier of the two said, looking towards his bulkier mate.

'Don't look at me, Stretch,' Kegs responded fearfully, 'It was your truck — not mine — that they must have seen. I haven't moved mine until today.' He said doing his best to squirm out from under the accusing and terrifyingly menacing stare of Franz.

'So it was yours, Stretch, was it?' Franz growled walking towards the skinny man who had now paled visibly. 'What have I always said about leaving the cam nets up on poles so you can drive straight in?' He was now right up in front of Stretch. 'It is common dog-fuck, Stretch, and you, my son, have really screwed this lovely little set up here,' he spat, as he looked back at the other two men who were now closing toward the group. 'Every time we have to decamp like this it costs us hundreds of thousands of dollars, and in this tight economic climate, Stretch, we can't afford stupid fuck-ups like this.'

'I'm sorry, Franz. I won't do it again, I promise,' Stretch pleaded.

'I know you won't, Stretch,' Franz said quietly. He quickly pulled a large .44 Magnum pistol out of his waistband, and with an outstretched arm shot Stretch between the eyes at point blank range. The man's knees buckled, and he dropped backwards onto his backside. The back of his head had erupted in a pink mist as the copper jacketed round exited Stretch's skull and embedded into a tree

15 metres behind him. There were blood spatters on Franz Nesbitt's shirt front and lower face.

The group stood in stunned silence as the life blood oozed out of the back of Stretch's shattered skull. Nesbitt looked down at the still corpse, turned and said casually, 'You two, pick up this bag of shit and chuck him in the river.' He moved towards Carina who immediately felt for her Glock but kept it undrawn.

'Get this place packed up and get the fuck out of here before 3 p.m. The cops will all be here by last light. Head towards the Daintree and we will move as much as we can out by plane tonight,' Franz growled. 'I am heading back to Townsville. Don't leave anything behind that can link us to the mob in Townsville. Torch it if you have to.' He picked up the spent cartridge of his handgun, turned and strode towards his vehicle, nonchalantly wiping blood splatters off his face as he went.

The airstrip in the northern Daintree that the group would use was unmonitored. It had been unused and abandoned after a nearby cattle station went broke when live cattle exports were stopped by people who should have known better. Franz Nesbitt had used it many times to fly drugs and illegal immigrants further south.

*   *   *

Just before last light, the Queensland State Police conducted a sweep through the abandoned camp just as Franz Nesbitt had predicted. Unsurprisingly, they found very little apart from rubbish that was collected for forensic examination. One young constable noticed some creamy pink shiny material on the ground and asked for an evidence bag. The young copper knelt on one knee and carefully lifted the spongy material into a bag, not realising that it was part of Stretch's brain matter that had been blown out of the back of his head. As he stood, a glint of metal caught his eye about 10 metres away. He walked over to the tree where he saw the flash of light and after a few seconds realised he was looking at the base of a spent round lodged into the tree. He called his senior constable and team across and he was then told to dig the round out of the tree and bag it.

Meanwhile, further north the convoy of vehicles carrying stores and equipment, driven by Carina and Kegs, was winding their way up the Cape Tribulation Road, heading for Helenvale. They looked like any campers with their four-wheel drive vehicles and trailers apart from the fact that they were heavily armed and had about a hundred thousand dollars' worth of harvested cannabis plants in large plastic bags under the tarpaulins on the trailers. As they drove up the gravel road, Carina was thinking of the last minutes Stretch had spent on Planet Earth and how careful she would have to be around that animal Franz. Kegs was wondering how long it would have taken before the crocs ate Stretch. He shuddered slightly because they had seen crocs in the creek when they were setting up the irrigation pipes. They had heard dogs barking at night until one night when Franz reminded them that the dogs were in fact crocodiles doing the barking. Stretch slept on top of his Land Rover for several nights after being told what the dogs really were.

By midnight, the group had arrived just south of Helenvale and prepared for a 1 a.m. arrival of a Twin Otter that would take their cannabis further south for onward sale. Kegs and another man set out the landing lamps for the pilot, and within an hour they had loaded and despatched their illegal cargo. Carina called the group together and told them to split up and regroup in Townsville in a week's time for their next job. It was likely to involve another camp, but she gave no further details, mainly because Franz had kept her in the dark. Knowledge was power.

*   *   *

'Waddya mean, they lost it?' Luigi asked Franz.

'Luigi, we had to get the hell outa there because the coppers were gonna raid the place.'

'How did the coppers know where it was?' he asked. They had grown marijuana in many places up and down the coast for over a decade and had very rarely been sprung, usually only by accident when some dopey Grey Nomad got lost on his northern adventure.

'One of the guys fucked up,' Franz offered, 'but I fixed it, it won't happen again.'

'It better not, Franz, because this is costing me big money when we have to dump the stuff like that. Where are the crew now?' Luigi asked while poring over a National Parks' map of the Black Mountain district.

'They put the dope on a plane last night and they are returning in separate vehicles back here,' Franz said, hoping his boss wouldn't penalise him for this latest disaster.

'Okay, bring them together in about ten days. I think we will head up to here,' he said, stabbing the map with a pudgy forefinger. 'Lakefield Downs. It has good access to the coast, and we will be able to combine two jobs with one and maybe give ourselves some more security.'

'What about the owners?' Franz asked, peering at the map.

'It's no longer a cattle station,' Luigi snarled. 'The bloody Feds confiscated it from a gooda friend of mine a few years back. He was my best link to the US and had really good contacts in Thailand,' he added ruefully. 'The bloody AFP put people in there disguised as Army paratroopers and monitored the place without him knowing. Poor bastard got 25 years and lost the lot.'

Franz looked closer and noticed how large Lakefield was and that it was now called Lakefield National Park.

'Christ, it must be 100,000 hectares that place,' Franz said, straightening up.

'I tella you, it was so big they never even bothered to ride the boundaries on that station,' Luigi said. 'They said it would take too long, so they used to check the fences by air.'

'What do you want to set up at Lakefield?' Franz asked, breathing a little easier as Luigi had seemed to move on from the screw-up the week before.

'I wanna grow some more dope but we are gonna start dropping some more stuff offshore in a coupla weeks. The Feds will probably be abandoning their idea of putting in monitors along the shipping lanes.' He looked around the room as if someone might be listening and added in a low voice, 'One of their boys drowned last week and they are reconsidering their options,' he said smiling and showing his prominent gold tooth.

'How much more?' Franz asked.

'More than you can imagine,' Luigi said, bringing the conversation to an abrupt close. 'Now start getting the gear ready for a long stay up north.'

'Okay,' Franz said, starting to walk toward the exit.

'Oh, and Franz?'

'Yeah, boss?'

'If this one screws up, someone is a gonna die real ugly. You make sure that nobody fucks up again, okay?' Luigi said, pointing a stubby forefinger at Franz with a look of menace in his eyes.

'Okay, boss, got it,' Franz replied and quickly headed out into the hot bright sunshine.

*   *   *

'What have you got for us, Sergeant Bryant?' the Superintendent asked.

'Well, sir, it would seem that the mob up north of Mossman, which Bob McTaggart ran into, did a bit of their own housekeeping.'

'How so?' the Superintendent asked.

'The Queensland Police found brain matter and a spent .44 round in a tree,' Peter Bryant said, looking down at the manila folder with the after-action report. 'We believe that someone was probably killed and disposed of in that camp site. They probably put the body in the creek and let the crocodiles dispose of the evidence,' he added.

'Nothing surprises me. Anything else?'

'Yes, they took most of the mature crop with them and most of their camp stores, but we have no indication yet in which direction they fled. It was probably north as the Police raiding group came in from the south and saw no suspicious movement, although at this time of year, there is always a lot of traffic during the Dry.'

'Thanks for that. What is McTaggart up to?'

'He is out doing charters and keeping himself busy. He has a reputation of being thorough, and from all accounts is running a very good business as a boutique tourist operator. It is not cheap what he is providing, but they are lining up to go out with him,' Bryant finished.

'Has he reported anything yet?'

'No sir, I have set up a drop system for him and all he has to do is ring my phone and tell me the marlin are on and we will meet,' Bryant said. 'Sir, have we got anything back about that operation the ONA were running?' he asked.

'It has gone quiet, Peter. I do know the Coroner has asked for specialist assistance concerning the diver's equipment. Other than that, they have left town,' the Superintendent added with a look of resignation on his face. 'From what I am hearing, it seems that the agent may have run into foul play, but keep that to yourself,' he said, looking up over the rim of his glasses.

'Roger,' Bryant replied.

'Let's get McTaggart in and see what he might have heard around town,' Superintendent Ballantyne said.

*   *   *

Friday night and I am in the Sportsman's Bar of the Exchange Hotel and my latest clients are bragging about their fishing exploits of the past few days. The atmosphere is friendly and the banter and chatter is non-stop as arms are spread wider as stories of ones that got away get more exaggerated.

'Hey Bob, tell 'em how big that kingie was that I caught just after lunch yesterday,' one of the men from Melbourne yelled.

'I tried to take a photo of it, but I didn't have a wide-angle lens,' was my ready response. It was also my favourite way of avoiding arguments about who had the biggest catch. Laughter erupted, and back-slapping continued. Just as I was about to make a move to head off to my apartment, my mobile phone went off indicating I had a message. I moved away from the noisy bar to check the screen and there was a message from Peter Bryant asking how the fishing was. I texted back that the marlin were on and he responded with an RV point and time out on the beach near Cape Pallarenda some 15 minutes north of town. The meeting was scheduled for 10 a.m. in a small café near a popular fishing jetty.

As I was heading out the door, I bumped into one of the dive operators who had a berth just down from the *Delfina* and we often talked on the radio about weather and surface conditions when we were heading out. We might have been competitors, but we were also colleagues looking out for each other in the Coral Sea.

'G'day Bob, how are you goin'?' he asked with a big smile on his face.

'Not bad, Bazza, how are you?' I said.

'Things are pretty good, plenty of tourists to take out these days, which surprises me given how strong our dollar is.'

'True, but there are always plenty of Asians who want to go out,' I said, enjoying the trade chit chat.

'Wanna beer?' Bazza asked.

Why not?

'Sure mate, maybe only a couple as I have an early start tomorrow,' I said, trying to avoid collateral damage as Bazza really could put the grog away. I wanted to chat because he always had the latest gossip on what was going on around town.

Bazza ordered a couple of beers and after a swig I asked him, 'So what's new mate?'

'It's been an interesting week.' He smiled as if he had just won a trip to Hugh Hefner's mansion for the weekend. 'I got asked to check out some gear down at Police Central for the coroner.'

'Oh yeah?' I answered as my early warning lights started to come in inside my head. 'How so?'

'Some fella drowned out on one of the distant cays last week and they wanted me to give his gear the once over. The Police divers weren't sure, so they asked me to come down and check it out.'

Straight away I thought this had got be Ian Taylor's gear, but I kept my mouth shut.

'What did you find?' I asked, taking a pull on my beer and looking up at the big television screen showing a rugby league game.

'Strangest thing. They said this bloke was an experienced diver, but he drowned owing to a lack of air.'

'What's so strange about that?' I asked.

'Well, if I didn't know better, I would say someone has slipped him a faulty regulator or somehow his air was cut off during his dive.' Bazza responded with a perplexed look on his face. 'I checked everything out, but it wasn't until I pulled the regulator apart I found that the brass actuating clip for his air supply had been worn so badly that it must have given a false reading.'

'So what does that mean?' I asked trying not to make a big deal of it, although I now had a good idea that Ian Taylor had been murdered.

'It will be inconclusive as there is no hard evidence that the item was tampered with unless they send the gear down to the Tonge crime labs in Brisbane. We haven't got that sort of kit up here,' Bazza said, resignedly bringing it to an end.

'He probably just screwed up,' I said. 'Diving is like explosives, I guess. First there is fear, then familiarity, then carelessness and if you survive that, you have respect.'

'Too true, mate. You can never have enough checks and counter checks when going down.'

I bought another round of beers and we chatted on current weather and when we thought the Wet season would kick in. This always affected tourist numbers and made going out to the Reef a bit of a gamble because sometimes the weather 100 kilometres off the coast could be perfect but seriously shitty closer in to the landmass. We said our goodbyes as I headed back home. I wondered what the Feds had up their sleeve for me now.

Melanie

The meeting out at Cape Pallarenda with Peter Bryant was just to see how I was doing and if I had seen anything unusual while out on the Reef. That was easy; nothing to report apart from one yacht that was crewed by topless females and skippered by a bloke who looked like Hugh Hefner but wasn't – he just thought he was. I wanted to find out what the Feds knew about Squizzie's death, so I gently broached the subject.

'That op that the ONA were up to, what was all that about … or is it too hush hush?' I said, pretending to look furtively around the room of the café.

Bryant looked at me for a while, studying my face before he answered, 'Why do you want to know?'

'I just want to know if my career as a spook is over or not,' I said, trying to maintain a poker face but probably failing badly.

'Oh no, it's not over just yet,' Peter Bryant said reassuringly. 'We have a lot to do yet … and the bad guys haven't stopped being criminals,' he added with a slight smile.

'I don't know a lot about ONA but aren't they supposed to be watching out for external threats to Australia and stuff like that?' I asked. *At least that's what Wikipedia said.*

'Exactly,' Bryant countered, 'and that is what they were doing but sometimes our stuff overlaps.'

'And how is that?'

'Well, without giving away too much, and you probably know a bit about it anyway, having done a fair bit of time in Water Troop with the SAS. But, our masters in Canberra are worried about unauthorized and incorrect use of the shipping lanes, and the likelihood of illegal immigrants — or as the politicians prefer to say,' and he raised his fingers in the inverted comma signal, "asylum seekers" — attempting to gain a foothold in Australia,' Bryant stated in his best deadpan voice.

'How the hell are they going to do that?' I asked, 'They are flat out just keeping a watch on the northwest side of the country as it is.'

'Would you believe using underwater sensors and ultra-low frequency radar?' he said somewhat smugly.

'I know we use ULF for submarine transmissions, but I didn't know we could track people smugglers as well,' I said, somewhat astonished at this revelation. 'It would cost a lot of bucks to set up something like the barrier that they had in the North Atlantic during the Cold War.' I had studied this sensor system during my studies at Deakin and was amazed at the ability of the NATO forces to track Soviet submarines as they transited into the North Atlantic Ocean.

'I don't think they are thinking along those lines Bob,' Bryant said, 'I think it will be more of a point-to-point system to try and track vessels passing a certain location and recording the size and speed of the vessels.'

I was finally able to get to my question regarding Ian Taylor. 'So that bloke Taylor was helping to set that up?' I asked with my best innocent expression.

'Not sure, but it was at least the preliminary part of the operation. Anyhow, now that it has gone pear-shaped, there will probably be a hiatus to the whole thing.' He paused momentarily and looked down. 'It will probably be put on hold while things calm down,' he added. 'But to more immediate things, we want you to continue your surveillance on the outer Reef, and if you go quiet with clients we will stump up money to get you out there on a regular basis.'

Thank Christ for that. Filling the tanks on the Delfina usually ran into four grand.

'That will be handy, she takes 2500 litres of diesel,' I added to underline how much I needed financial assistance.

Bryant whistled. 'Wow, that much?'

'Yep, but it gives me great legs and endurance while I am at sea. Enough to escape a big blow if one arises,' I said.

We arranged for a meeting in a fortnight if he didn't contact me sooner and I climbed back into my Land Cruiser and headed back into town. Back in my apartment I had an email from the Outrigger Hotel who wanted to know if I could come up to Cairns for a week and take a group of six American tourists out to Green Island and then onto Arlington Reef. My initial thought was no way because of the travelling time and fuel cost, but then I read down to the bottom of the email and read that the retainer for my services was double what I normally charged, and in addition my redeployment costs would be covered plus a bonus for the charter. I was looking to clear ten grand for the week. I changed my mind and said I would be there in two days. That would give me enough time to get a deckie to handle a group of six and allow me to do my job properly. I sent a text to Peter Bryant saying the marlin were on in Cairns and I would be away for a fortnight.

*　　*　　*

The trip up to Cairns was uneventful. The waters inside the Reef in July are usually like a millpond unless a big trough manages to squeeze its way south. I asked Jack Slater, the manager of the Townsville marina, to ring his mate in Cairns and see if they could rustle me up a deckie for a week. The sea was very calm, winds were light, and the weather was almost perfect. I berthed at around 3 p.m. a day before the charter, allowing me plenty of time to refuel and stock up the *Delfina* with provisions, which for Americans usually meant plenty of Jack Daniels and half a slab of beer per man per day. I was tying up my forward lines when I heard a voice ask, 'Bob McTavish?'

I looked up at the wharf and saw a pair of tanned long legs running all the way up to a tall female's armpits.

There is a God.

'Nope, Bob McTaggart,' I replied and stood up to get a better view of the woman on the jetty. 'What can I do for you?'

'Sorry about that,' the blonde apparition said, 'I can hardly read this bloke's scribble. I heard you were looking for a deckhand for a week's charter.'

There really is a God.

'Um yeah,' I stammered, 'What experience have you got?' hoping she didn't take offence at my question. But so help me, she certainly didn't look like your average deckie. She stood about five foot ten and was well toned in the arms and legs that were brown all over. I reckoned her to be about 28 years old, but I had given up trying to guess a woman's age because I had got it wrong so many times. Her hair was blonde and short, and even though she had a baseball cap stuck on her head I could see her big green eyes. She was wearing denim shorts that had seen plenty of wear, and a large black T-shirt that read "The liver is evil and must be punished". I liked that. On her feet were a pair of sneakers that were probably once blue but now a colour that defied description. "Work wear" best described the colour.

'I've worked on prawn trawlers and cruise charters and I've got my junior mariner's certificate, so I can navigate all the channels around the Reef and navigate at night,' she said, handing me a folder with her credentials. 'How much are you going to pay?' she asked bluntly.

'Straight to the point eh?' I shot back, climbing up onto the deck. I stood next to her and my six-foot-two frame was enough to make her smile. 'I need you to do the cooking and normal boat maintenance. I don't see us doing any work at night, so it won't be a tough one,' I said, leafing through her papers which all seemed to be in order.

'Have you worked the Reef very much?'

'Yep, for the last six months, I have been out every week, even during the Wet with the CSIRO and people from James Cook Uni,' she stated matter-of-factly.

'Sounds good. How does a grand sound?'

Her green eyes widened and with a big grin showing immaculate teeth she said, 'Sounds great. When can I start?'

'Hang on Miss …,' I said, looking for her name in the papers.

'It's Melanie, Melanie Adams,' she said, looking me straight in the eyes and offering her hand. 'Pleased to meet you, Skipper.'

'Call me Bob, Melanie. Let me check your references and we will see what we can do,' I said, watching a flicker of disappointment cross her face. 'Is your mobile number in here?' I asked, watching her face change to one of disappointment if not resignation.

'Yeah, how long will this take?' she asked, giving me the big green-eyes look when women want something. 'I need a job soon.'

'No more than a few phone calls,' I promised. I looked down at her papers and when I looked up, she was gone. I watched her tight backside disappear down the marina jetty towards the manager's office. I hoped she was clear. I rang a few numbers including the university and a number in Townsville and all seemed okay. On a whim I thought I would get Peter Bryant to check her out and when he answered his mobile phone it sounded like he was in an airport.

'Bob?'

'G'day Peter. I am doing a job in Cairns for a week or so. Can you guys check someone out for me?'

'Sure, what's his name?'

'Not a "he", a "she",' I came back quickly.

'Got a hot date have you, mate?' he asked laughing.

'No, I just want to check this sheila out, she wants a job as my deckhand,' I said, trying to keep it quick.

'Okay, give me her details and I will get back to you. It could take a day or two.'

'Mate, I haven't got that much time. I have to go out tomorrow morning,' I pleaded.

'Alright, keep your pants on; I will see what we can do.' He hung up, saying maybe an hour or two for a "quickie" and that should be a good check unless she was a terrorist from Al Qaeda. That boy had a sick sense of humour.

By the time I had refuelled the *Delfina*, Peter Bryant had rung back and given Melanie Adams the all-clear. Her credentials were fine, and it seemed that as of last month, she was still very single. I got on the blower and gave Melanie a ring and offered her the job. She sounded very casual about it, given she had said she was searching for work. Maybe I had pissed her off by checking her out.

'Where's your gear, or have you got digs ashore?' I asked, hoping she wanted to sleep on board.

'I'm staying at the "Y" and I have paid up until the end of the week,' she said. 'What time do you want me at the boat?'

'I have almost got everything ready, so you can start tomorrow. Be here hot to trot at 7 a.m. We will be out for a week.'

'Thanks, Skipper,' she said and hung up.

* * *

I got my bike off the rack on the back of the Land Cruiser and decided to take the treadlie for a push around town. I was going to be stuck on a boat for the next week and there wouldn't be much chance to exercise the legs. I hated running but I could bike for days. Too many scrums as a forward holding up lazy hookers and too many jumps onto hard LZs had not been kind to my knee joints. I preferred the low impact workout from a good hard 30-kilometre bike ride than a 10-kilometre run. As my mate Gazza would say, "you shouldn't run, that's why God invented the combustion engine and motor cars".

Cairns is a nice town and reasonably flat so there are plenty of places to go for a walk or a ride, especially along The Esplanade where one can also check out the people trying to maintain their fitness. While pedalling along, I thought about how good Melanie Adams looked. I hadn't hooked up with a woman since Jenny had been killed. I just hadn't wanted to. The thought of going down that emotional pathway again just seemed to hurt too much, so I shoved those sorts of feelings and actions into the background and got on with rebuilding my life.

And then the world's best looking deckie appears and I have to admit when I was looking up at those gorgeous legs, I actually thought of things that I hadn't thought of for quite a while. It had been hard coming to grips with my loss, but the pain was gradually wearing off. As my dear old dad used to say, "time heals all wounds", which may be true but it doesn't stop the memories. I hadn't even jumped in the sack with anyone since Jenny and Annie had been killed. I just hadn't had the urge, although in the last few months I had been taking notice of all the good-looking female backpackers that were washing through

Queensland on their rite of passage. I could never figure out why Pommie sheilas always tanned up so well when they spent most of their life being white from the weather in England. The sight of young women in bikini tops and short shorts and sandals was beginning to thaw me out. I would have to be on my guard.

*   *   *

Melanie Adams turned up on time, but I couldn't say the same for our American shipmates. They were about an hour late which was going to mean a slight change of plan owing to the tides. But the customer is always right, and there to be plucked, so we were all smiles welcoming them aboard. There were more than a few admiring glances being shot Melanie's way because she was in a tidy pair of shorts and a white top that showed off her tan and toned arms.

The trip out would be fairly uneventful for the next couple of hours, so I gathered the clients together and gave them my usual chatty welcome brief, did the normal housekeeping and concluded with a comprehensive safety brief. I talked about always having a buddy with you, even on what seemed simple activities, and reminded them that Australia has its fair share of wildlife that would like an American as breakfast, lunch, or dinner. To emphasise my point, I anchored off a small cay about 30 clicks from shore and let the tourists walk around. The cay was only about half an acre in size and almost disappears at high tide.

'Hey Barb,' one bloke in a floral shirt yelled, 'what are these marks over here?' he asked pointing at the sand.

'Those?' I said, trying to sound as nonchalant as possible and lifting my sunnies to get a closer look at the feet and tail marks of a large saltie, which was probably a 15-footer. 'Those prints there, Hank, are from a saltwater crocodile.'

'A goddam crocodile!' he exclaimed while turning to look around the cay. 'Jeeesus!' he whistled with his eyes widening, 'But we are at least 10 miles from shore!'

'More like sixteen or seventeen,' I responded as the rest of the group gathered around. 'And see that tail mark there?' I said to no-one in particular, 'Well that tells me is he is probably 15 feet long, which would also make him about ten years old.'

'What in the hell would a crocodile be doing out here?' another of the group asked.

'Looking for American tourists,' I said with a deadpan voice.

There was a round of nervous laughter as they all suddenly seemed keen to get back on the *Delfina*.

Melanie had made a salad lunch while the group had been sightseeing, and once we were underway again, she left them to their meal and brought me a plate up in the wheelhouse.

'You made an impression there, Skipper,' she offered as she handed me a plate of freshly cooked prawns and tropical fruits.

'Yeah, I like to make sure they don't go running around without thinking of the nasties that lurk beneath,' I smiled.

She nodded and sat down on a bunk in the wheelhouse as she started demolishing her lunch.

Silence ensued as I kept the *Delfina* headed towards Green Island where we would stay for the night. It was always a good time to sort out those who would not be able to handle the rougher seas of the outer Reef. I had worked on Green Island when I was about 17 and had taken time off after finishing high school and lugged beer kegs from the wharf up to what was then a very basic pub. Now it was all golf buggies and porters in white shorts and Hawaiian shirts and four-star luxury accommodations. However, the charter group would be sleeping on board the *Delfina,* as would Melanie and I.

We tied up about 4.30 p.m. after some light fishing where we snagged some nice mackerel and coral trout that I would use for meals over the next few days. The pub put on a great seafood barbecue, and I used the opportunity to give a briefing on the Great Barrier Reef and what the group could expect to see over the next few days. The Americans finished their meal and we sat around sharing stories and getting to know each other. The men all came from the American west coast and from what I could gather, they had all gone to UCLA together and played college football. They were an articulate group; mostly professional types, and from the way they were buying drinks, they were not short of a dollar or two.

Several of the men split off from the group to chat up a group of young women from Germany. They ordered drinks for the girls and all seemed to be proceeding swimmingly. The men were all in their mid-40s and playing out of their age group, but it was no deterrence to their mission to work their way through the cocktail list while they entertained the fräuleins. I wanted to get a good night's sleep because the next day would be a slog out to Arlington Reef and we would be heading into a morning sun, which is never a good mix with a hangover or headache. I had a crew cabin at the rear of the passenger section and Melanie was okay with having to share the heads and the bunk room with me. I certainly didn't mind, but from the cool reception I had received when she checked on board and the general body language, my antenna was telling me that Melanie was a "no-go zone". I played it cool and adopted the role of captain and leader and had plenty else to worry about besides a little hanky panky.

Melanie was still ashore when I hit the sack and I was almost in the land of nod when I heard a commotion up on the jetty. I clambered up the stairs to the aft deck and was confronted by Melanie and a drunk member of the charter group whose name was Carter. He was a big man, standing over 190 centimetres tall or six foot three in the old measurement, and would have tipped the scales at a beefy 120 kilograms. He was a big sucker. In rugby terms he would have been a second rower or a bloody big prop. Carter was now trying to grab hold of Melanie's arm as she was trying to board the *Delfina*. They had been wrestling all the way down the wharf for about 100 metres.

'Last warning, Carter. Let go of my arm or there will be trouble,' Melanie said firmly through clenched teeth.

'Aw c'mon, Melnee,' he slurred, 'Just give a guy a chance, will ya?' He continued grabbing at Melanie's arm as she worked her way towards the gangplank to board the boat. As she moved past him, Carter grabbed her around the waist with his big bear-like arms and tried to kiss her on the face.

I could see this was going to get ugly pretty quickly, so I started moving towards the wharf to get Carter off Melanie. *How on earth was I going to stop this gorilla in his tracks?* I would have to wait until I got up to the deck. A rifle would have been real handy.

'Carter!' I yelled at the top of my voice, 'Get your hands off her!'

'It's all right, Skipper, I can handle this,' Melanie said calmly from underneath a bear hug. For a woman being molested she was sure taking it easy. No sooner had I got up onto the jetty decking than I saw Melanie swivel smoothly out of Carter's drunken embrace. She swiftly brought a knee up into Carter's groin and immediately took his mind off groping Melanie. He was now doubled over, clutching at his bruised nether regions and groaning loudly. With a short sharp upward thrust of her palm Melanie then collected Carter under the chin and laid him out flat on his back. He hit the wooden jetty like a sack of spuds.

I was seriously impressed, as were Carter's friends who had been walking back down to the *Delfina* when they saw Melanie unleash her anger on the drunken American. They started running towards the prone hulk of the still prostrate Carter.

'Holy shit,' one said quietly.

'Goddam! Man, are you okay?' another asked of Carter, who was still coming around after being well and truly flattened. He was now sitting on his sorry arse with his friends gathered in a semi-circle.

'Wha … hoppen?' Carter asked as he looked blearily around the group.

'I'll tell you what happened, Carter,' I offered. 'You tried to force yourself on Miss Adams here and you got your arse kicked.' The group of Americans all straightened and looked down at Carter.

'Is that right, Carter? Did you molest young Melanie here?' an American named Dwight asked.

'She came onto me,' Carter offered lamely. 'She wanted a real man,' Carter said to an audience that was quickly swinging against him.

Melanie had moved onto the boat and was starting to pack her kit bag.

'Where are you going?' I asked.

'Ashore,' she said sharply.

'No, you're not,' I said, lightly restraining her arm that was about to shoulder her bag. 'If anyone is going ashore for the night it is our friend here, Carter.' I turned to face the remainder of the group. 'If it's okay with you, gentlemen, I think we will let Carter sleep ashore tonight, and tomorrow morning we will see whether or not he continues the trip.'

The men all looked a little sheepish, some looked at Melanie with what I thought was hostility and one just looked embarrassed. Their unofficial spokesman Hank stepped forward in front of me and said, 'I think that would probably be a good idea, given what has just happened, Captain.' He turned towards Melanie and stated as if in a court room, 'Ma'am, on behalf of the group we offer our sincere apologies for our colleague's behaviour. We can assure you it was out of character.' Then turning to his friends, Hank ordered, 'C'mon guys, let's get his gear and get him into a room on the island.'

For the next ten minutes they packed Carter's kit, and then steered him towards the hotel to find him a room for the night. While the boat was empty, I went into the galley and called to Melanie, 'Would you like a cup of coffee?'

'Thanks, Skipper, that would be nice.'

We sat on the aft deck under a million stars of the Milky Way and enjoyed the brew. I looked across at Melanie who looked as if she didn't have a hair out of place on her head.

'You certainly know how to handle yourself.'

She looked back at me and said over her coffee mug, 'I grew up in a family with three older brothers.'

I nodded and said, 'Did they also teach you unarmed combat and self-defence?'

Melanie smiled slightly, 'Sort of, we didn't play anything other than footy in the backyard and I either mucked in or missed out.' She stood and walked into the galley, heading for her bunk. 'Thanks for the coffee, Skipper. See you in the morning.'

'Sure. Good night.' And she was gone.

I found the episode of Melanie versus Carter interesting, because normally, after a confrontation involving physical violence, there is a period of unsettlement. The adrenaline of fighting is still surging through the body and it is hard to sit still, let alone remain cool, calm, and collected. But Melanie was all of that and more. The efficient manner with which she dispatched the Yank was quite a sight, and I made yet another mental note not to cross Melanie Adams when she was pissed off.

*   *   *

The remainder of the evening passed without incident. I heard the group minus Carter make their way back to their bunks, and when I approached Hank, he told me that they had found a "room" for Carter on the island. With no police on Green Island, the hotel, which was also the main employer, had found a unique way of controlling patrons who were a danger to themselves and others when intoxicated. A shipping container that had washed off a ship that ran aground in the Coral Sea years before, now doubled as a drunk tank.

I woke the group for breakfast and Hank went ashore to collect Carter. He returned alone, saying that Carter sent his apologies but would not continue to Arlington Reef with the *Delfina*. He would make his own way back to the mainland on the daily tourist boat or get a chopper back to Cairns. That was fine with me; it would avoid any awkwardness arising from a big bloke like Carter constantly seeing Miss Adams, who was about half his size, and remembering that she had put him on his backside. There was not a lot of room on a boat even as big as the *Delfina*, so all things considered, it was a good thing the humiliated Carter was not continuing the trip.

We arrived at Darlington Reef just after midday, and I soon had the group fishing for all manner of reef fish with the proviso that we only kept what we wanted to eat unless the guys had a way of getting their catch back home. By late afternoon, the wind had come up, so I headed onto the lee of the reef and found some clear calmer water for a bit of snorkelling. The guys had a ball as they swam amongst shoals of brightly coloured fish and saw "the biggest goddam turtle in the world". Luckily, the weather was favouring us, and we spent the night anchored near Arlington Reef. The following day, I planned to take the group down to Thetford Reef where there were spectacular coral islands, and then move on to Fitzroy Island to get stuck into some really good fishing. I wanted to show the group how to fish with hand lines and not have to worry about expensive rods and reels.

Melanie was proving herself to be a great deckie; she kept the galley in good order, which is never easy with a boat full of men. Unsurprisingly, nobody tried to make a move on Melanie, not even after a day's fishing and diving, and then a big meal washed down with icy cold beers did anyone even look sideways at Melanie. But I did, and I kept finding little things about her that slowly built up a picture of just who this woman really was. Born in Sydney on the upper North Shore. Her dad was a merchant banker, mum was a speech therapist and she had a shed full of older brothers. She went to Hornsby Girls High School and then went on to university to attempt a degree in science but soon tired of that and having a future as a lab rat, so she went to London in a delayed rite of passage, as most kids do in their gap year between high school and university. After a year of working in all manner of jobs, she eventually ran out of money and returned to Australia. I tried to find out more, but our work kept on getting in the way and I figured if she wanted to tell me about herself then she would. I had told her my life story – seriously abridged – but I wanted her to know I was single and available. I wasn't confident because Miss Adams was playing her cards very close to her tidy little chest. If anything was in my favour it was that I came with no baggage and no in-laws as both my mum and dad had passed. Mum from a heart attack while water skiing and Dad from cancer that was probably caused by heavy smoking when he was a young bloke.

*   *   *

The charter was successful, with the group tipping Melanie and myself handsomely. From the look on Melanie's face I had a feeling her tips were going to outweigh her wages. Hank came back to the boat while we were cleaning the *Delfina* for the return trip to Townsville. He was carrying a bunch of flowers that were obviously not for me, and a bottle of Chivas Regal that was. They were from Carter with a note of apology. Hank left, saying that the group wished us well and they would be recommending the boat to friends of theirs stateside.

I was trying to figure out how I could keep Melanie on as a deckie, given she seemed to be based more or less in Cairns and long-distance relationships were not my bag.

What was I thinking? Long term relationships? I haven't even asked her out on a date yet.

We finished squaring the *Delfina* away and I wrote Melanie a cheque for her wages and thanked her for her efforts and hoped she would work for me again. She smiled and nodded at my comments on her crewing skills saying, 'That would be nice Skipper, maybe soon.' And without so much as a backward glance she shouldered her kit bag and was off down the jetty.

Coming towards me was the manager of the marina, holding an envelope. 'Hey, McTaggart,' he yelled. 'Got a message here for you.

The bloke that delivered it said you needed to read it as soon as you got back in.'

Well, that was handy, I had tied up four hours before.

'Thanks, mate,' I shot back, 'When was this dropped off?'

'About 8 this morning,' he said, beetling back up the jetty, knowing I was about to give him a serve for his tardy delivery system.

I opened the plain envelope that was simply addressed to me care of the *Delfina*.

"Ring me ASAP. P.B."

Bryant wanted me to call, so I rang him on my mobile. He was short and sharp.

'I need you to do a ground recon for us, Bob.' His voice sounded urgent.

'Sure mate, when and where?' I asked.

'I will brief you tomorrow. Book into a pub in town and I will call you.'

It all sounded very sneaky. Nothing over the phone, and he also wanted me to get off the *Delfina*. Bloody spooks, running around as pseudo James Bond characters half of the time. But I did as I was told and would wait and see what job Peter Bryant had in store for me.

A Run Ashore

I checked into the local Best Western motel and treated myself to a spa and then a decent shower. It was nice to be able to wash again without worrying about how much water to use and not knock your elbows every time you turned around or wanted to scratch your bum. I sent a text message to Bryant, telling him where I was and he came back with a time for our meeting the next day. I thought about where I would eat out for the night and asked at the reception desk where I could get a serious steak. I walked about a kilometre downtown just as the sun was setting, wandering along the beachside promenade, and eventually found myself outside a Hog's Breath Saloon that proclaimed on a chalk board that they had the world's best steak. The price of their scotch fillet didn't require a second mortgage, and I ventured in. I needed a beer to wash the humid Cairns air down my throat, so I sat at a small bar and ordered a Heineken for no other reason than I felt like a Heineken. Tomorrow I would probably feel like drinking a Corona or Carlton Draught, I am just that sort of beer tart.

I was looking over the wine menu when I heard a familiar voice behind me. 'Hello, Skipper. Looks like they will let anyone in here after dark.'

I spun around on my bar stool and there was Melanie Adams. Her hair seemed blonder than before, her eyes were a brighter green, and her teeth were dazzling. She looked fantastic in white slacks and a silky shirt thing that showed off her tan.

There still is a God.

'Hi Melanie. How goes it?' I asked, looking over her shoulder to see if she had a date with her.

'Not bad, I thought I would spend some of my hard-earned cash on meat joined together instead of fish for a change,' she quipped. A tall good-looking woman in a skirt and blouse sidled up to join us. 'Oh, Skipper, this is Karen, a good friend of mine. Karen — Bob, Bob — Karen,' she smiled.

I shook Karen's hand and asked the women to join me for a drink.

'No thanks Skipper, we have secret women's business to discuss … maybe later,' Melanie said as they headed off with a waiter to a table they had booked overlooking the water.

Bugger, she's a lesbian.

Such is my male-dominated homophobic thinking that if any woman knocks back a free drink, she is either a lesbian or a camel. When I used to drink at the Cottesloe pub that the regiment used to frequent in Perth, I found that after 9 p.m. there were a lot of women around, but they were all lesbians and didn't drink. Or so it seemed in my alcohol-fuelled haze at the time.

Before I could order another beer, the manager of the Cairns harbour marina walked in with a few blokes who looked like they needed a drink. Introductions were made all round and they sat and ordered beer. After a small while, they decided it was time to put on the nose bag and we sat at a table about ten metres from where Melanie and her friend Karen were sitting, looking into each other's eyes in deep conversation.

Her legs weren't that good anyway. Damn it, yes they were. They were great legs.

Sigh.

A couple of bottles of red wine were ordered and we tucked into some steak. Typical of blokes trying to find common ground, the conversation swung around to football, and in this case it was rugby league. I love the way blokes who never got out of sub-district footy can become instant experts on the way National Rugby League teams should approach the game, and how they know the frailties and strengths of every senior football player who ever pulled on a jersey. Every now and then, I would cast an eye over at Melanie but never caught her eye. I dismissed my campaign as a lost cause and re-joined the banter on who was going to win the next premiership. Dinner was over, but now it was time to get stuck about those big-hitting reds. I became heavily immersed in man talk.

A one-man band started playing across the restaurant. A few couples started dancing to some tunes from the seventies. As the wine level dropped in the bottles on our table, so the noise level grew. Another bottle of shiraz was ordered, and Friday night was looking good. I was deep in conversation with a bloke who was an engineer from the Blackwater coal mines, and he looked up over my shoulder. I followed his gaze, and standing above me was Melanie.

'Would you like to dance Skipper?' she smiled.

'I … ah …' For some inexplicable reason I hesitated. Melanie's face changed to one of a frown. The engineer sitting next to me in the booth dug me hard in the ribs with his elbow.

'Of course he would,' he interrupted, sternly giving me one of those get-off-your-arse-now looks.

'Yes, of course I would,' I said, hurriedly catching up as quickly as I could, and standing abruptly, nearly knocking over the wine bottle in front of me. 'I'd love to, Melanie,' I blurted.

I followed her lovely backside onto the small dance floor, and we danced the remainder of the number. I kept trying to sneak a look into her eyes without wanting to be a dork, but every time I did, she looked up at me and smiled.

Okay, so she's a lesbian who loves to dance.

The number ended, and Melanie took my hand and led me over to where she and Karen had been standing at a tall table. In front of them was a bottle of champagne in an ice bucket and several glasses.

'What's the occasion?' I asked. Melanie jumped straight in with 'Well, Karen here has just had word that a house she inherited from her recent divorce has been sold. Not only that, for much more than what she was expecting, so it is a night of celebration,' she said, smiling at me and looking at me differently from what I was used to seeing from her normally reserved and serious countenance.

'Oh, so a place here in Cairns?' I asked, trying to keep the conversation flowing.

'Nope,' Karen said, 'Down in Brisbane where I live, or lived. I think I might take a small holiday overseas to clear out the cobwebs and recharge my batteries,' she added. 'It was not a nice divorce.'

'Oh?' I offered.

'Yes, I came home sick from work one day and found my dear ex-husband doing some horizontal folk dancing with a girl who I thought was one of my best friends.'

Ah, so they are not lesbians. There is a God. Didn't doubt Him for a minute.

'Yep, so Karen came up here on a short break, and the word came through about the house this afternoon, so we are celebrating.' Melanie was still looking at me differently. I couldn't put my finger on it, but her eyes were roving over my face and upper body.

Jesus, was my fly open or what?

'Do you drink bubbles, Skipper?' Karen asked, offering me a flute.

'Yes, sure, I think I will take a break from the red. It was starting to get a little untidy with that mob over there,' I said, taking a long sip from the glass being pushed toward me.

The music started up again and before I could ask Melanie for a dance, a guy from a group over near the bar came over, asked Melanie for a dance and she was gone. I stood there like a stunned mullet. I was going to have to watch my back more carefully. Where was a wing man when I needed one?

I engaged Karen in small talk and discovered that she and Melanie went way back to primary school and even attended high school in Sydney together until they graduated and went their separate ways pursuing their dreams. Karen was a graphic artist and did advertising work but had more recently got into website design. It meant she could work from home or anywhere, as long as she had access to the internet. I kept looking across at the dance floor where this boofhead was trying his best moves on Melanie and working hard at cutting my grass. The number finished and Melanie headed straight back to where we were standing.

'Christ, that bloke had bad breath,' was all she said as she took a swig from her flute.

'Now, Skipper …'

'Melanie, can I be Bob, please?' I asked, looking into her green eyes that were still dancing.

'Oh, so this is the boat captain you have been going on about?' Karen grinned, her eyes twinkling mischievously.

'If you mean the captain of the charter boat that I mentioned in passing, yes, it is,' Melanie said with what looked like a blush passing over her face.

'Mentioned in passing!' Karen almost shouted. 'You wouldn't shut up about him,' she guffawed. Melanie now turned crimson and I could see she was really uncomfortable. I grabbed her hand and led her onto the dance floor.

'Have you been telling lies about me?' I asked watching her squirm.

Let's see her wriggle out of this one.

'Not at all. I mentioned you and the *Delfina*. Karen is a bit materialistic and I think she got confused with what I said about you and the boat,' she added defensively. She avoided my eyes and kept dancing to the up-tempo music. I liked the way her hips moved. I liked the way she did anything … actually.

We spent the next couple of numbers moving and circling around each other. It was reminiscent of a bull fight with constant manoeuvring and positional changing. Occasionally, we caught each other's eyes but the contact was always brief and quickly lost. I was busily trying to plan my next move. It had been a long time since I had done this. I had a flashback to the days in Surfers Paradise when I was a young digger with bugger all money. My mates and I would sit drinking at a table eyeing off the girls who looked like they had potential for exchanging bodily fluids. Drinks were expensive, so we sat on our beers until about half an hour before closing time, and then would make a move on a girl we fancied and if worse came to worse you were only up for one drink. It was all about the law of diminishing returns.

We finished dancing and Melanie stood very close, not making a move. I felt a warm feeling wash over me.

Perhaps she has seen the light and seen me for the stud muffin I really am. Yeah, dream on, Robert.

The champagne was almost finished and as I offered to buy another bottle in the hope of prolonging the interaction, which I was thoroughly enjoying, the two women excused themselves and headed for the powder room.

Why is it sheilas always go to the dunny in pairs? If blokes did that we would be seen as pillow biters.

The restaurant was slowly emptying, and I needed to come up with a plan to separate Melanie from Karen so I could engage her one-on-one, and hopefully some hand-to-hand contact. I thought back to my hotel room and tried to recall if the bar fridge was stocked. I wondered if I had thrown my dirty clothes into the laundry hamper or left them laying all over the floor like I usually did. I wondered where in fact Melanie actually lived. While all this devious pre-planning was rushing through my head, the two women reappeared arm in arm.

Uh oh, this doesn't look good.

'Well, Bob,' Karen started, smiling somewhat lasciviously, 'I am going to leave you two love birds to each other's company. It has been a big day and I am off to bed.' And with that she asked Melanie for the key to the front door of her apartment and was out the door. *Apartment? I thought she said she was staying at the YWCA? Maybe I had it wrong or mis-heard.*

Melanie kissed Karen on the cheek, and they said their goodnights. Things were looking up. She turned to face me and said, 'If you asked me to have a cup of coffee somewhere, I wouldn't say no.' Her eyes were locked on mine and I could feel that warm sensation again.

'Sure,' I said, 'There's a great little place around the corner.'

Why didn't I ask her back to my motel?

'Sounds good. Let's go,' she said, sliding her arm through mine as she picked up her handbag. 'For a minute there, Skipper, I thought you might put the hard word on me and invite me back to the boat for a nightcap,' she said as we walked out onto the footpath.

'It's against regulations, matey,' I said in my best pirate voice. 'No fraternising with the lower decks.'

Melanie thumped me on the arm as she pulled away from me. 'Lower decks! Hah!' But her frown quickly disappeared, and she linked back into my arm as we walked along the promenade. It was a balmy night and just a hint of a breeze. *Yep, things are looking good.*

We sat and talked over coffee for almost an hour and were soon given the hint that the place was closing when the staff started putting the chairs on the tables as a pre-cursor to cleaning. I had enjoyed just sitting and talking. Exploring each other's wants and discovering what helped make this good-looking woman tick. I had almost lost track of time and the desire to grab her and make her mine, but fate played a tricky hand.

'Gee, is that the time?' she said with almost a frightened look on her face. 'God, I've gotta go!'

'What's the hurry?' I asked, hoping not to sound too petulant. 'It's only 1 a.m.'

'Yes, I know,' Melanie said, grabbing her handbag, 'but I have got a really early start tomorrow and I haven't packed my gear yet.'

I was thinking about saying something smarmy like 'I'll help you pack' but could tell that this wasn't the time or place to try and wriggle my way into the remainder of her shrinking time and space.

'Okay, do you need a cab or can I walk you back home?' I asked hopefully.

'It's not far, we can walk,' she said, steering me out of the café and pushing money into the waitress' hand as we slid out the door.

It was only a ten-minute walk back to Melanie's apartment in a modern block of well-maintained units.

'Do you own one of these?' I asked, wondering just how much money she was earning as a deckie on other jobs.

'Hell no,' she laughed, 'Only boat skippers can afford these swish flats. I only got it when I came ashore. I rent a two-bedroom unit in here at mate's rates from an old friend. I would need half a million to buy what I live in.' Melanie turned and looked up at me.

'I really enjoyed tonight, Sk … Bob,' she corrected. 'I hope we can do it again soon.'

'Me too, Melanie,' I said rather lamely, 'Maybe …' and before I could say anymore her soft warm lips were on mine, and then she was onto the security key panel punching in her access code and gone.

Damn, I really wanted to do more of that kissing stuff.

* * *

I meandered back to my motel that was a good 30-minute walk away, passing drunks trying to maintain their balance on their round-bottomed shoes and watching their legs walking toward me but their bodies wanting to veer off at an angle. I was so glad I didn't get that whacked anymore. It had only taken a couple of hundred seriously bad hangovers to wake up to myself.

As I walked, I wondered how I was going to maintain my cover and still do what the AFP wanted and try to develop this growing interest I had in Melanie Adams. It was going to get tricky. I thought about how much I had enjoyed her company. I was delighted that she was an intelligent person who could carry a conversation on almost any topic but still be seriously attractive at the same time.

This was no bimbo, my boy.

I was going to have to play my cards very well indeed.

I arrived back at my motel and quickly checked that nobody had entered in my absence. I opened my wall safe and made sure my Glock handgun was still there, along with two spare magazines. I wasn't going to get caught out without some way of protecting myself if I got into the poop again like I did on that bungled camp recce in the Daintree. Superintendent Ballantyne wouldn't have approved, but then he wasn't the bloke who was being shot at, was he?

I settled in for the night, thinking delicious thoughts about Melanie Adams and what my strategy would be in our next meeting, whenever that was going to be.

The Drop

The large cruiser swept quietly through the dark channels of the outer Reef. The deep throb of the diesel engines was barely discernible above the sound of a light wind washing across the calm sea. This stealthy crew were east of Gordonvale and northeast of what was known by the locals as Sudbury Reef, a particularly treacherous piece of water with highly unpredictable currents. The lookouts on the foredeck and flying bridge were dressed in black coveralls and carried machine pistols. The men methodically scanned the horizon, keeping a vigilant eye out for any other craft. The captain of the boat had slowed the vessel to 15 knots, which was way below her top speed of 48 knots. She was showing no navigation lights, and all interior lights on board were red. A navigator was hunched over a radar and depth sounder, reading off the depths every 30 seconds. The skipper was peering into the inky blackness, hoping he would not find his way onto a shoal or reef. The skipper was not overly concerned about his illegal activity being uncovered. He was aware that his client had very reliable inside information that allowed them to track inside the reef virtually undetected. He felt relatively safe, but at the same time just a little uneasy as his cargo would attract seriously heavy penalties if he and his crew were caught by the authorities. He thought about the lucrative payoff and inwardly smiled as he studied the chart on his desk.

'How long till we reach Sudbury Reef?' a heavy-set man in dark blue jeans and a black long-sleeved shirt asked. His thick eastern European accent was always difficult to fathom, and many had found that asking him to repeat his remarks usually resulted in something bad happening to them.

'About 15 minutes, Mr Kudlov,' the navigator replied, hoping not to upset the burly Russian.

'Dah, ist good,' the Russian said as he stepped out onto the deck. 'Tell your men 15 minutes until we drop. Keep your farking eyes open,' he snarled.

There was no moonlight at all over the ruffled ocean, which was just the way it was wanted. They would be dropping a series of 200 litre barrels into the water. Each barrel was fitted with a homing beacon that would allow Kudlov's people on shore to collect them and bring them back to the mainland for onward distribution. Getting into the area was easy; it was getting out again and not being discovered by Coastwatch or any other Australian agency that there might be a problem. He was confident that the operation was safe. Sure, there were risks navigating the Barrier Reef and the shipping lanes at night without lights. And the risk of being caught and the subsequent jail term was something he didn't want to think about. But the rewards were huge. Actually, they were staggeringly enormous. But having someone on the inside who could warn him when things were unsafe or if surveillance was getting close meant his losses were minimal. Killing the diver, who was too close for comfort last month, was simply collateral damage and no skin off his nose anyway.

His Vietnamese colleagues were now pushing very high-grade heroin through their links in Thailand and southern Viet Nam. It was no problem getting stuff out through the Mekong Delta. All he needed was a boat capable of transiting across the South China Sea, and one that would be able to outrun any likely pursuer. He was more likely to allow an official boarding for inspection anyway as the hull of the boat was cleverly designed with a sub-surface hold much akin to the bomb bay of an aircraft. It had cost plenty to retrofit after purchase, but it was now paying big dividends.

'Five minutes, Mr Kudlov,' the skipper announced.

'Good. Arm the beacons.'

The boat kept a steady course until it was just east of Sudbury Reef.

'In position,' the skipper said quietly as he studied his sonar and depth finder.

'Begin ze run,' Kudlov said, looking at the chart on the table in the wheelhouse.

'Bearing one eight zero,' the captain announced and the helmsman brought the cruiser gently onto a heading of due east and called back, 'One eight zero, sir'.

After ten minutes at five knots, the boat began dropping its cargo of drums at 30-second intervals. The drums settled on the bottom in 30 fathoms of water in a part of the Great Barrier Reef where few tourists ever ventured and which dive companies avoided owing to the savage currents that swept around the Sudbury Reef extremities. Once the last drum was despatched, the skipper closed the bay underneath the vessel. He turned to Kudlov, awaiting instructions.

The normally surly Russian was almost smiling. 'Let us head for Cairns, kapitan. It is time for wodka and wimmen,' he said through uneven and badly stained teeth.

'May I turn on our running lights?' the captain asked.

'Sure' Kudlov replied, slapping the captain on the shoulder, 'Ve haf nothink to hide… do ve?' he laughed as he went onto the aft deck and lit a large cigar.

*   *   *

Carina Thuong sat in the Land Cruiser with headphones from the UHF receiver firmly positioned on her head. Her long jet-black hair was tied back in a ponytail so she could monitor the radio that would soon tell her if the drop off shore had been successful. She hated this part. Kudlov had insisted that Carina be within 20 kilometres of the drop point so that any radio transmissions would be short range, and as brief as possible. She loathed the waiting, the boredom, the inane small talk of the male cretins that Kudlov saddled her with to manage this most important part of the operation.

Why was it that the men recruited for these duties had an IQ that matched their shoe size? Getting into the area around Grey Peaks

National Park undiscovered was always a challenge, but the cloak of darkness provided the opportunity to get within a few kilometres of the coastline. Most tourist traffic stopped about an hour before sunset, so the chance of being seen, let alone identified, was slim indeed.

Kegs appeared at the rear of the vehicle and leered at the slender body of Carina. He had never made it with an Asian woman and wondered what it would be like.

'How's it goin', Kreena?' he asked with a stupid grin on his fat ugly unshaven face. He felt secure up here in the bush with Carina and their new recruit, Bart. Stretch needed replacing and Kegs had found him attempting a break-and-enter on a liquor store in Townsville while on parole. Kegs hauled him out of the alleyway and literally threw him into his ute just as the alarm went off and saved him from being arrested. He was now in the gang. Little did he know why he had been recruited.

Bart Jackson was known to the police as a petty criminal. Their opinion of him was that he was a person who really should have sought honest employment because he was such an incompetent crook. Franz thought that Bart would make good material for their crew, not because he was light-fingered and on the wrong side of the law, but because he was expendable.

'We should hear soon. Keep an eye out on that track leading in here. I don't want anyone wandering into us,' Carina shot back.

'Okay, okay, keep your shirt on.' *Or rather off, you stuck-up bitch.*

'And make sure the new guy is on his toes,' she added as the radio hissed into life.

'Viper, this is Rattlesnake. Over.'

Carina grabbed the handset and responded, 'Rattlesnake, this is Viper, send over.' Her radio voice procedure was immaculate and reflected the signals training she had covered while in the Army Reserve when living in Sydney.

'This is Rattlesnake, all good this end. Your parcel will be at Apple sixty-two, Orange forty-five. You have seven days to collect your goods. Over.'

'This is Viper, I copy Apple six two, Orange four five. Seven days, roger out.' Carina smiled to herself. Good, the drums were in the water and she had the coded coordinates. She entered the grids into her notebook and stepped out of the vehicle. She needed a pee real bad. Kegs and Bart were 25 metres down the dirt track, smoking and talking quietly between themselves. *Some sentries those two make.* She slipped into the bush and quietly pulled her shorts down around her ankles and squatted next to a tree. She took the Glock from the waistband of her shorts and placed it carefully on the ground within easy reach. She revelled in the joy of relief as her urine splattered onto the dead leaves on the ground between her boots. A rustle in the undergrowth made her start. She hated snakes, and the last thing she wanted was a snake bite on her backside. As her urine dribbled to a halt, she slowly took up the handgun and looked carefully around her. She pulled her shorts back up over her dampness and stood motionless. The bushes behind her moved again and she rapidly moved out from behind the tree to confront Kegs who was standing not more than a metre from her toilet. His eyes widened as he looked down at the black metal of the Glock.

'Hey, h-hey steady on there, Kreena, I was just coming to have a slash,' he stammered.

'Like hell you were, you sleazy bastard,' Carina spat at him. 'What, do you get your rocks off watching women pee, do you?' she asked, bringing the barrel of her Glock up under Keg's pudgy nose.

'Well, if you really want to know, I could get my rocks off watching you have a shit,' he said with a throaty voice while looking down at her crotch and shapely legs.

'Make one move in my direction or one more filthy remark like that to my face and I will blow your nuts off, Kegs.' She paused for the dramatic effect to sink into her colleague's thick skull. 'Is that clear?' The menacing look in her black eyes at his groin convinced Kegs that she meant business. The fact that she was packing a pistol quickly changed his opinion of this secretive woman.

'Sure, sure, no problem, Kreena,' he mumbled as he headed back towards the Land Cruiser.

'Now, find Bart and get in the truck. We are heading back to Cairns.' She hated working with men she regarded as morons. But it suited her purpose and her plans for her own future in a business she knew could pay her enormous dividends if she played her cards right.

A Twist

It was a quiet morning in Cairns. It's funny how once you got above the Tropic of Capricorn in Australia, the tempo of life slows considerably and the vowels in Australian speech get longer and lazier. I finished breakfast, grabbed a taxi, and made my way to a coffee shop on the beachfront promenade. I had been busy contacting real estate agents to get me a lease on a flat because it was starting to look like the centre of gravity for ops was creeping north. The house that I owned out near Swanbourne Barracks in Perth was leased to a couple of gay blokes who were looking after the place, paying their rent on time and causing no dramas. I wasn't ready to sell that house just yet, but I knew I would never be able to go back and live in it as it held too many memories of my late wife. So, renting in my newfound occupation was the way to go and Peter Bryant said that if I ran into problems to give him a yell because rental assistance was not out of the question. In the meantime, I had been in luck and had found a reasonably priced unit that I was sure the AFP wouldn't baulk at when I explained the need for a second base to operate from. An advanced tactical HQ was how I intended to put it to Peter Bryant. I would move in at the end of the next month.

I had decided to try and blend in with the local populace, so I wore leather sandals, denim knee-length shorts and a pastel coloured short-sleeved cotton shirt. I had found a panama hat in a local shop with a tag that said it was allegedly made of 100 per cent paper, and I had my aviator Ray Bans protecting me from glare and identification. I looked just like a tourist not wanting to look like a tourist.

It was not even 10 a.m., and the heat was starting to kick in and the relative humidity was on the rise. It was expected to hit 32 degrees by noon. *Just another day in paradise.* Bryant and Ballantyne would meet me and give me my next briefing. It was sounding as if things were heating up. Pretty appropriate for this part of the world, I thought to myself. I saw the duo walking towards the rendezvous point, looking like two businessmen. Their lack of suntan gave them away as people who worked indoors. They both wore a look of concern on their pasty dials.

'G'day, Peter. Mr Ballantyne,' I offered, nodding at the senior man who really had his game face on. He nodded back but didn't offer a sound. *Hmmm. Serious shit.*

'How ya going, Bob?' Peter Bryant said in his neutral voice.

'Ah, not bad,' I responded and waited for their next announcement.

'Good. Good,' replied Bryant, looking around the café and sitting at a small table at the same time. He waved at the waitress who immediately headed our way. We ordered coffees all round. I noticed that the superintendent kept looking over my shoulder and periodically sweeping the area behind us. His surveillance scan paused momentarily on a bloke who was standing about 25 metres away, leaning up against a post of a souvenir shop next door. I stood to get my wallet out of my shorts and as I did so, I checked out who had caught the Super's eye. It was Frank Benning, the spook from Canberra. If this bloke was supposed to be conducting a covert overwatch of our meeting, he must have been a graduate from the Maxwell Smart School for Spies. He stood out like dog's nuts and he had copper written all over him.

Superintendent Ballantyne was about to launch into a spiel on what was likely to happen in the next phase of the operation when the waitress came back with the coffees. A pregnant pause filled the warm tropical air as we waited for her to withdraw out of earshot.

'McTaggart, things are moving pretty fast at present and we need to kick it up a gear.' I could tell he was focused but also unhappy.

'Sure,' I said, keeping it short and sharp. 'What do you want me to do next?'

Ballantyne looked over my shoulder again at the man leaning against the post. A cloud crossed over his face as he said in a lowered voice full of frustration, 'Peter, go and tell Benning to stop standing around looking like a spy.' He leaned forward at Bryant and whispered, 'In fact, tell him to get the fuck out of my sight.'

Whoa, serious shit. I hadn't heard the superintendent use the F-word before in all of our dealings, so this bloke must be pissing him off. I wondered what it could possibly be that was pulling his chain.

'Sir,' Bryant replied and headed in the direction of Benning.

The superintendent looked across at me and smiled weakly. 'Sorry about that. We have been blessed with a visit from our Canberra office, and special agent Frank Benning is now overseeing the escalating situation we have up here.'

'Overseeing?' I asked, trying fit the jigsaw together.

'Probably more like over-watch, would be a better way of putting it,' Ballantyne said in a voice dripping with resignation and frustration.

Ballantyne was clearly unimpressed.

I had met Frank Benning in Townsville when I had been told of Ian Taylor's drowning. 'I thought that was Benning,' I said, looking across at where he was standing. 'Why isn't he in on this brief?' I asked, trying to get a handle on all the secrecy.

'It's not that, Bob,' Peter Bryant said as he sat back down. I turned casually and noticed that Benning was no longer hanging around. 'It is better for everyone if you deal with as few people as possible.'

'What, so I can't give too much away if I am captured and tortured?' I joked, trying to add levity.

'Something like that,' Bryant replied, looking me right in the eye, but not smiling at my attempt at light humour.

'Okay then,' I countered. 'Let's have it.'

'We'll give you a folder when we get into our car,' the superintendent said in a low voice. 'Do not open it until you are back in your hotel. Once you have digested it, secure it so it cannot be found or read by anyone without authority.' I felt like making a crack about eating the paperwork as part of my 'digesting' it, but from the serious faces opposite me I decided light humour was not on the menu.

The superintendent then gave me a five-minute heads-up on the drug drop offshore and the likelihood of a pickup and flyout of the stuff from a remote airstrip. My job would be to conduct covert surveillance on the point where the drugs were expected to come ashore.

'It's pretty sensitive information and intelligence, Bob,' Peter Bryant added, looking down at the floor. 'But,' he paused, and I thought his shoulders slumped just a little, 'we have another problem as well.' He leaned back and rubbed his hands over his face while exhaling a deep sigh.

'What's that?'

'We believe that some bastard is leaking information out of our national headquarters' office and we can't pin it down.'

'Oh, that's nice. Just what we need. A mole who could easily set us up,' I said with just a touch of sarcasm to indicate my concern.

This was not good. I thought back to what Ian Taylor had said, *'It seems like the bad guys always know when we are coming.'*

'No need to tell us how it is, Bob,' the superintendent smiled through thinly pursed lips. 'We have already lost one agent when Taylor drowned.'

'What? Are you saying he was murdered, Superintendent?' I tried to keep myself from speaking too loudly. 'How the hell can you put a guy into a situation where he loses his life without backup?' I thought it was a pretty good question.

'Listen, Bob.' Bryant now leaned forward and spoke very slowly. 'We had no idea that Ian Taylor was in any danger when he was tasked to do surveillance on a likely drop point. We only found out two weeks ago from the forensic lab in Brisbane that his death was most probably not an accident.' The superintendent was visibly upset. After all, he had lost one of his men on his watch. No commander likes to lose people in battle, but murder? A different circumstance altogether.

I knew it. Squizzie was like a fish. He was so meticulous when it came to water safety.

'So, how are we going to deal with this?' I asked.

'For a start, we are all going to have to be extra careful on who we deal with both in and out of the AFP,' he paused with what I suspected was quite deliberate emphasis, 'and any other Federal or State agencies,' the superintendent remarked. 'You must trust no one.' That sounded like an echo to me and confirmed what Ian Taylor had suspected before his murder.

'I assume I can now have a carry gun?' I asked. I knew I would feel a whole lot safer if I had deadly force in my back pocket. I didn't think telling them I had already acquired a pistol through an old mate would be a good thing at this time.

'We are not happy about it, but given what has happened, we have been given approval for you to go armed,' Peter Bryant replied. 'But mate, be sure about one thing, this is not a war zone. There are still Rules of Engagement. I have put a copy to that effect in your briefing folder.'

'Fine by me. Where do I draw the weapon and ammunition?'

'We have arranged for you to get your handgun from the local Army Reserve armoury. We wanted to keep you away from the local coppers and you can use the cover of visiting an old Army mate in the

Far North Queensland Regiment to pick it up.' Bryant smiled at me when he added, 'They know nothing about what is in the box marked for you to collect. They think it is a project for adventure training, so be prepared to ad lib on that one. The details are in your folder.'

'No worries.'

Things are looking up, now I will have a backup weapon. Hope it's a 9 millimetre.

'Okay then,' the superintendent stood to close our meeting. 'Let's get out of here and get you started.'

'Before we do that,' I started on my spiel for a second base to operate out of in Cairns, 'can I set up a forward base here in Cairns so I am not in and out of motels all the time and can establish some security?' I hoped I sounded convincing.

'Sure, but keep it down on costs,' was all Superintendent Ballantyne said over his shoulder. I couldn't believe it. That was easy peasy compared to other bureaucratic organisations I had fought tooth and nail with over housing and accommodation when serving in the Army.

As we made our way across to the vehicle to take me back to my motel, I looked across the promenade and at the shore lined with impressively large Weeping Fig trees. The esplanade along the beach front is popular with tourists and locals alike wanting to take a stroll, go for a jog or a leisurely bike ride. Underneath a very large Ficus I thought I saw Melanie Adams walking slowly and talking intently into her mobile phone. Those tanned legs and that great backside in shorts were not easy to miss. *She should have been on a boat*, I thought.

Maybe the job fell through. I made a note to ring her and see if she was around for a while. Hope springs eternal.

The briefing notes were thorough. Whilst the AFP knew what was going on, they had been unable to catch the bad guys doing it, and more importantly nail the ringleaders. The Mr Bigs were the ones that they were really after. I just found it strange that they had never been able to grab the people bringing the stuff in. They had come close on numerous occasions, but their prey was slippery indeed. The more I read about Zappia and his nasty bunch of cronies, the more I realised that they were not the big fish; someone else was driving the operation. Zappia was just a middleman and making very good money from it as well. The estimates of street value were staggering. I knew there was money in drugs, but this was unbelievable. One estimate was close to 100 million dollars a year … that they knew about! I could see why these blokes ran the risk of jail time. And why they were prepared to kill without compunction to remove obstacles in their way.

The tricky bit was going to be getting hard evidence on the people bringing the stuff ashore without tipping off the mob who were importing the heroin. Somehow, we would need to contain the land party and simultaneously grab the people dropping it offshore. With a bad apple in the AFP barrel, this was going to be bloody difficult and a lot easier said than done. I would rather have set up a sting to catch the mole. *Just like the French copper did in* Day of the Jackal. *Now that was cool.*

Back in my motel room I re-coded some vital information such as drop points, airstrips, and likely crooks that I had to be careful not to run into. I rang the 51st Battalion, Far North Queensland Regiment and asked for the Regimental Sergeant Major and introduced myself. He told me there was a package awaiting collection and invited me to drop in and have a beer. He said he had heard of me through one of his cadre staff senior NCOs. I arranged to call into the Sergeants' Mess at 5 p.m.

The visit to the snake pit at 51 FNQR was pretty uneventful. I met a few young sergeants who were reservists and had just returned from a tour of duty to Afghanistan, and from the way they carried themselves and spoke of their operations, I could tell that a few lessons had been learned. You can teach people just so much about combat and war fighting, but the real classroom is on the battlefield. It was evident that deploying reservists on operational duty was going to benefit the young people who volunteer their time to defend our country. I collected my "adventurous training" package and headed back to the motel.

Peter Bryant was certainly looking after me. I opened up the carton and unwrapped a barely used Glock 23; my favourite 9mm handgun that came complete with a night sight, a tactical aiming sight, two holsters; one for sidearm and one for underarm, and three spare 10-round magazines. I now had spare mags for both Glocks and two holsters. I had about 120 rounds of ammunition that would be plenty, considering I wasn't supposed to get into a shoot-out with the crooks. That would be someone else's job. Things were looking up. I stripped and assembled the pistol to make sure everything was okay and loaded everything into the day safe in my room. It was starting to look like a small armoury in there.

I rang Melanie Adams' apartment and was told by her answering machine that she was out of town on a job and wouldn't be back for several weeks. I was beginning to doubt my powers of observation. I knew Melanie's face and legs very well. I was very familiar with the way she carried herself. Either she had a twin, or somebody was telling porky pies.

*   *   *

I went about half a block downtown and bought the worst looking floral shirt I could find and a large straw hat. I needed to look like a tourist with bad taste, or any Pommie tourist would do. I had my camera with me and my telephoto lens that allowed me to see how many gold fillings a person had if they yawned within half a kilometre of my camera. I walked past Melanie's apartment and saw that her blinds were open. I continued past and wasted a few minutes taking photos of a large clump of Strelitzia or Birds of Paradise. It was one of the few flowers of which I knew the horticultural name as my Mum had grown them and loved to show off her knowledge of the plant.

Across the road from Melanie's flat I made my way down a side alley and stayed in the shadows, watching her window on the first floor of the unit block. It wasn't long before I saw her profile in the window. I grabbed my camera and zoomed in on her. I was busy trying to make out who was in the room with her, but I needed some elevation to get a decent look into the building. A tradie's ute was parked nearby, and I quietly took the ladder off the vehicle and climbed up onto the balcony of an apartment opposite.

Two figures came into view and I brought the camera up to my eyes and wished I hadn't. Inside the apartment were two men who were pointing to what was either a chart or a map on the dining room table. I managed to get a few shots away before I heard an angry voice down in the alleyway.

'Hey you!' The angry voice got considerably louder. 'Hey, fuck knuckle! What the hell are you doing with my bloody ladder?' I looked down onto the face of an unshaven and very pissed-off looking plumber.

'I-I'm so sorry sir,' I pleaded in my best nerdy voice, 'But I just saw a chestnut-breasted cuckoo and I had to get a photograph of it. They are extremely uncommon, you know.' It was my best impersonation of naturalist David Attenborough. *Sorry about that, David.*

'You're the only fuckin' cuckoo around here, mate,' he snarled. 'Well now you can find your own way to get down, you bloody drongo,' the plumber growled and quickly took the ladder, slammed it onto his truck, tied it down and drove off shaking his head.

I hoped the brief but loud altercation hadn't been heard by Melanie Adams and her visitors. I scrambled down the drainpipe and headed back to my motel. Once inside the room I downloaded the digital imagery onto my laptop. I enhanced the photo of Melanie and the two men. One looked familiar. I was beginning to think that somehow Melanie Adams was a baddie. I thought back on every conversation I had managed to have with her in private but couldn't for the life of me think of anything that made me think she was or just might be a crook.

I went back through the file that Peter Bryant had prepared for me, and in the photographs, there was one of the blokes I had been told was probably involved in collecting and distributing the drugs. His name was Alan Williams. He had several aliases and a string of charges for which he had done jail time. Most included crimes had to do with possession and dealing in drugs. He also had a firearms offence and a few assault and battery charges. He was a large unit but more fat than fit. His nickname was Kegs. The other hombre I couldn't identify, but he was skinnier than his mate. He must have been trapped in 1980 because he also had a mullet haircut, and not even a good one.

I wondered about telling Peter Bryant what I had seen but would then have to explain what I was doing taking photos of people inside Melanie's apartment. I couldn't decide whether to sit on what I had discovered or tell Bryant. Stuff was zinging around inside my head. *Why had Melanie told me she was going offshore and clearly wasn't? What were two bad hats doing in her apartment poring over maps or charts? And what was her relationship with this bloke called Kegs?* Too many questions and too few answers for my liking.

I decided to confront Melanie and sort out what the hell was going on. I also decided to tell Bryant about Melanie Adams; after all, it was he who had told me she was clean when she applied for the job as a deckie on the *Delfina*. I rang his mobile phone, but it went to voice mail. I had to be on the road at Zero Dark Hundred in the morning to get to Gordonvale, about 40 clicks south of Cairns, for the surveillance task. I didn't want all these unanswered questions in the back of my thoughts about Melanie so I decided I would just bowl up to the front door and see what her reaction was when I was standing in front of her. Like any good attack, the element of surprise carried a lot of combat power.

I knocked on her apartment door and it opened to reveal Melanie Adams in shorts and a T-shirt. Her eyes widened and without saying a word, she grabbed my arm, dragged me inside her apartment and slammed the door shut. She clamped a hand over my mouth and put her forefinger up to my mouth to indicate I shouldn't utter a word. She moved quickly to draw the curtains to prevent me being seen from outside. I sat down on the lounge chair and watched her quickly but efficiently circulate around the apartment, securing doors and making sure nobody could see into the unit. Once she had done this, she came back to where I was sitting and walked me into the bathroom. I started to speak but she put her hand over my mouth and again indicated I should be quiet. I did as I was told. *What the …?*

Melanie turned on the shower and let the water pelt out noisily onto the shower cubicle floor. She sat me down on the toilet lid cover and leaned over and hissed in my ear.

'What the hell are you doing here, Bob?' Her face was drawn with intent. 'And keep your voice to a whisper.'

'Me?!' I responded and started to stand but she pushed me hard down back onto the toilet seat.

'What am I doing in town?' I repeated, 'More of a question, isn't it, Melanie, of what are *you* doing in town?'

'Christ, Bob, why can't you just do what you are told?' She looked seriously concerned.

'Me? What the hell are you talking about?' I said in my best voice of innocence.

'Bob, I work with Customs and I know what you are doing up here,' she offered, looking intently into my widening eyes.

Fuck, how could she know? Nobody outside of the AFP was supposed to be aware of what we were doing.

'Show me some ID,' I asked.

'Later,' she shot back. 'First things first. You have got to get the hell outta here because this place is probably under surveillance by people who would rather shoot first and ask questions later'.

'Okay, but who were the two clowns who were in your apartment this afternoon?' I asked, waiting to see her reaction.

Her green eyes bored into the back of my skull. 'How did you see who was in here?' she asked. I explained how I had got up onto the balcony across the road. 'Did anyone see you?' she asked with a voice that started to sound tentative.

'Just a tradie whose ladder I borrowed.'

'For both our sakes, you better hope he was a tradesman, or we could both be in really deep shit.'

'What do you mean, "deep shit"?' I asked, watching her eyes and facial expression for signs of a tell or even worse, a lie.

'Bob, I am working on a long-term mission to find out how people are circumventing the normal ports and airfields to import illicit substances – drugs.' She certainly sounded like a copper.

'Go on,' I ventured.

'I know that you have been asked by a federal agency to find out what you can about the illegal importation of drugs into Far North Queensland.'

'Really?' I responded, not wanting to blow my cover, which now for all intents and purposes appeared to be torn to shreds.

'Yes, really.' She had stood back hands on hips. 'And my job was to check you out on the *Delfina* to make sure you were straight.'

'Oh, and am I?' I said, trying hard not to smile.

'You are definitely straight and definitely not a crook, Bob McTaggart.' She now smiled just a little.

She walked across to the shower cubicle, turned off the water and motioned for me to follow her into the lounge room. She wrote on a note pad that I should leave after she turned off the outside lights.

'Why the secrecy in here?' I whispered into her ear.

She took my hand and walked me over to a lampshade on a side table. She wrote "bug" and pointed at the lampshade base.

I nodded and mouthed 'bad guys?' to which she nodded her head in the affirmative. I moved toward her front door and as I stood there while she turned off the outside lighting, she signalled that I should call her mobile phone after midnight. I nodded and exited Melanie's apartment and walked quickly into the shadows and headed back to my motel. My mind was going at hundred miles an hour. She still hadn't explained what Kegs and his mate were doing in her flat. What were the charts they seemed to be looking at? It seemed I now had even more questions than before. This was all starting to get murky.

*   *   *

I decided not to return the way I had arrived and spent a good half an hour backtracking to see if I was being followed. I wasn't.

I rang Melanie on her mobile not long after midnight. She had slipped out of her apartment and could now talk freely. She explained quickly that she couldn't talk for long, but I should call her when I was back in town. She knew I was off on a surveillance mission but didn't say exactly what it was. Maybe the security wasn't leaking as bad as I had speculated.

'Okay, I'll give you a ring when I get back to Cairns. I don't know how long, maybe a week or two,' I said, not giving anything away.

'Good. And Bob?'

'Yes?

'Please be careful,' she said in a low voice.

'I will. See you later,' I responded, trying not to sound concerned, and I hung up.

Things were starting to get more than a tad uncertain. There was a mole in the system, and now a woman who I thought was just a really good-looking sort, was a bloody federal Customs agent! *Jesus, why did life have to be so frigging complicated?* I didn't want to compromise our op so I decided I wouldn't ask any more questions, especially over the phone because I didn't know just how secure even that line of communication was.

I finally got to bed around 1 a.m. after double checking all of my gear before setting off at first light. I wanted to be well and truly out of Cairns and heading south towards Gordonvale by mid-morning. That would get me to an insertion point just on dark to allow ingress under the cover of darkness. It was imperative I got in early and hopefully unnoticed by those going about their daily work. Inserting myself into where I needed to be was going to be a long and slow process. It was imperative that nobody saw or heard me or the whole operation could be blown wide open and we would be back to square one. I reckoned on establishing my lying-up place within two or three kilometres of the suspected pickup point where the drugs would come ashore. I had deliberately not showered or shaved to keep any foreign smells and odours from unveiling my presence when in the bush. Sleep did not come easily.

Gordonvale Surveillance

I started driving south down the Bruce Highway, a drive that can quickly change from being as boring as bat shit to incredibly frightening in the blink of an eye. Stray cattle wandering out of the scrub onto an unfenced major arterial and where semi-trailers and B doubles are sitting on 110 kilometres per hour can very quickly get the heartbeat racing. Even the odd kangaroo suddenly wanting to feed on the other side of the road could grab your attention quick smart. You could not relax. My aim was to do an old ambush occupation deception manoeuvre and cut back on my own track to make sure nobody was up my backside. I remembered what Peter Bryant had said and trusted no one. I went past my target area and after 30 or more minutes pulled into a roadside café and service station on the pretext of breakfast and watched the road for another half hour. Nothing stood out, nothing suspicious caught my attention. So far, so good. Everything looked as it should; kids going to school in bright yellow school buses. Mums dropping their kids off at the bus stop. Tradies calling in for a wake-me-up coffee before pushing on to wherever they needed to be. Farmers calling in and picking up packages and the paper. Locals stopping and chatting to each other before going their own ways.

I hit the road again, heading back north but turned off the Bruce Highway near a small country town called Kamima with a population of seven and a black dog. This place is so small and insignificant it doesn't even get onto the towns' register. I then used my GPS to take the secondary roads into Grey Peaks National Park. There were a few old abandoned homesteads and properties that had been unprofitable as mixed farms dotted around the area, and one on the boundary of the national park and the Yarrabah Aboriginal Community had an airstrip capable of taking a Twin Otter-sized aircraft. This was to be my surveillance target.

My cover was simple; I was looking for places to bring tourists for some eco-trekking and adventurous training. I drove slowly along Pine Creek Road and found the area I was looking for. I got out of the Toyota and noticed a dirt track leading down to the water of Mission Bay. It had been used in the last week by a four-wheel drive with a reasonable load in it. In fact, not much traffic had been in the area at all. I drove another couple of clicks along the road and found a track that had been highlighted in my briefing notes. I turned off the gravel road and headed into the bush. After another 800 metres I ran out of track and almost into a small creek. This was going to be my home for the next week or so.

I disabled the Toyota by flicking a switch hidden under the passenger side door that cut the ignition and would prevent the vehicle being stolen. I then shrugged into my backpack and walked on a compass bearing through the bush, which was primarily tropical rainforest, until I came to a small rise. On top of the hill I was able to look down onto the former homestead of Pine Creek Station and was able to make out the overgrown but still usable airstrip. Looking northeast, I could make out the shoreline and relatively placid waters of the Great Barrier Reef shimmering about two kilometres away. I walked slowly around the area to find myself a good hidey-hole for my lying-up position, and where I could stash my survival gear if I would ever need it. I needed an escape plan and egress route if things went pear-shaped. Been there, done that.

My briefing notes said I might have to wait a few days for anything to happen, but my experience with ambushes and surveillance ops was that if you ambush three tracks leading into a killing zone, the enemy will always take the fourth track, and, if it can fuck up – it will. I started a slow but methodical sweep of the area below the rise and found that there was plenty of wildlife in the area, and down near a swampy bit of ground feral pigs had been rooting through the mud. Their presence put an end to my idea to use trip wires to provide early warning of my lying-up position. Now I wished I had a rifle because even a 9mm handgun against an angry pig can be just a little too close for comfort. An angry 90-kilogram hog can take a bit of stopping, and dropping one at night even harder. Their black fur blends in with the dark rainforest at night and makes them a difficult target.

I found no visible traces of people having been in the area around the boundary of the airstrip. It was now time to call it a day and I headed back to my LUP. I saw one brown snake slithering off into cover when I came across an open piece of grassy ground. As long as I minded my business, he would mind his and I moved past it a little quicker than normal patrol pace. I set up some branches and deadfall on the track I had made entering my camp spot to give me some early warning if someone or something was following my scent. I felt pretty secure that I was alone in my little neck of the woods for the time being and made a hot meal from my ration packs and enjoyed a mug of coffee before resting against the base of a tree. I made a plan in my head for the next day, and eventually crawled into my lightweight sleeping bag and put out some serious zeds. It was going to be a case of sleeping with my ears open.

Around 5.00 a.m., first light started to break so I moved quietly out of my sleeping bag and sat with my back against a tree and listened to the bush coming alive. Once I could see about 50 metres, I stood and cast a wary eye around my camp site. I did a circuit around where I had slept about 50 metres away from the vehicle and found no trace of human movement. After breakfast I packed my backpack, put my shoulder holster under my bush shirt and secured the second Glock inside the vehicle in the storage box under the rear seat. I had a waist belt with three water bottles and carried a civilian cadastral map of the area to explain what I was doing in the area if anyone asked. I set off to finish my circuit of the airstrip, staying in the tree line at least 100 metres in from the verge. It was slow going because the vegetation along the side of the strip was thick and laced with all manner of shitty vines and lantana bush. By mid-afternoon, I was back on my rise and getting ready to set up a spot for night surveillance. I had an image intensification scope that I could use but it sucked a serious amount of power from the cadmium batteries, so it was an "only use if absolutely necessary" device. The bulk of the surveillance would be with my Mark One eyeball and ears and nose.

Close to last light, I heard the unmistakable sound of a couple of four-wheel drive vehicles on the other side of the airstrip on the road I had myself come down two days ago. The low-rumbling diesel motors were hard to track and when they stopped I had no real idea of exactly where they were. I used my binos to sweep the far side of the airstrip but saw nothing. The vehicles had not continued any further north because I would have seen them on the bend in the road into Mission Bay. They had to be due west of where I was, but what were they doing? It was no good speculating, so I concentrated on observation and deduction.

Thirty minutes after last light I heard one vehicle start up and watched its headlights as it started moving north towards the small muddy beach about a click and a half up the road. After a while, all I could see were the taillights, and I noticed the brake lights come on right near where I suspected a small boat like a tinnie, or a rubber ducky could make a landing. I changed to my telescope with a laser range finder and watched the shore. I saw the flare of a cigarette lighter on the beach. I swept the area north of the landing site and saw phosphorescence being whipped up by the bow wave of a small boat. If my briefing was as good as I hoped, then this would be the drugs coming ashore.

* * *

While I had been carefully circumnavigating the airstrip, another group of men had been out on Sudbury Reef under the guise of tourist scuba diving. Their dive boat carried all the markings of a legitimate dive operator, but they weren't diving for fish or sightseeing. I had not seen them while sweeping the area with my binoculars, but the afternoon sun and shimmering sea would have made it difficult for me to get a line on them anyway. They had been very busy recovering 200-litre drums packed with heroin and ecstasy tablets. In all, they had pulled up 20 drums and brought them back to shore where they had stored them under the close supervision of a couple of men who looked like they were on day release from Australia's toughest jail. This was a slick operation. The landing party had quickly set up a tent and were cutting the tops off the drums and unloading hundreds of packets of drugs wrapped in plastic to maintain a waterproof seal. Those packets were then being repackaged into cartons marked as agricultural chemicals. The three men were heavily armed, but their rifles and shotguns were out of sight and readily available. The only vehicle to come down the road had been a courier vehicle taking mail out to the Yarrabah Aboriginal Community, and it was highly unlikely they would have noticed the landing party in the scrub. By nightfall, the men were sitting on about 150 million dollars' worth of illicit drugs.

* * *

'Fucking mozzies!' Bart snarled as he slapped at the back of his neck. In the passenger seat, Kegs held a Big Jim torch with a red lens cover. As their vehicle drew closer to the bend in the road where they were to meet the boat party, Kegs said, 'Righto, slow it down to a crawl. They should be somewhere around here.' He opened the passenger door of the four-wheel drive and flicked on his torch and shone it in the direction of a road sign that indicated a right-hand curve ahead. Within seconds, the two saw a red torch flash three times in rapid succession.

'That's them. Drive up to that side road and watch we don't drive over any silly bastard. Turn the main headlights off,' Kegs said, trying to impress his sidekick. Bart Jackson grunted an acknowledgement and did as he was ordered. This was exciting stuff for the petty criminal, and he wanted to make a good impression because the pay for this job was better than anything he had pulled, including a couple of armed robberies in Brisbane a few years back.

*   *   *

I watched the vehicle drive off the road leading to Yarrabah and disappear out of sight into the bush. I could see brake lights come on and then nothing. I figured the crooks would now be transferring their booty into the vehicles for movement to the airstrip. It was time to get closer to the action. I shrugged into my backpack and headed off down the rise along a path I had made for myself that afternoon to facilitate my close recon. Within 15 minutes, I was on the other side of the airstrip opposite from where I thought the other vehicle may have stopped. The moon was now starting to come up and it was a biggie, perfect for night flying for anyone with the right skills.

Within half an hour, I heard two four-wheel drives heading up the track to the grass airstrip. They stopped about 150 metres from where I had positioned myself. *That's inconsiderate.* I wriggled backwards from my observation point and relocated to a point that was directly opposite where the vehicles were parked. I could make out at least four men and what was either a smaller crook or a woman. *Could it be the woman from the recon?* This was now getting interesting. I pulled my telescope out and switched on the long-range microphone. *I just love technology.* Yep, it was a woman and I was willing to bet it was the same one who had poked me in the back with a handgun. It wasn't great eavesdropping, but I could hear the woman giving orders and the noise of cartons being packed on the ground. Before long, one vehicle headed up the airstrip and was dropping small lights off at 100-metre intervals along both sides of the airstrip. The vehicle then did four laps up and down the airstrip to flatten the grass a little and probably check to make sure there were no obstacles hidden in the grass.

*   *   *

Carina Thuong pressed her ear closer into the headset of her radio and heard the pilot of the approaching aircraft ask if the strip was secure. She replied in the affirmative and gave the aviator the wind speed and direction and told him they were located at the western end of the airstrip. He acknowledged and began his approach. I slowly stood, taking care not to silhouette myself against the shrubs, to watch him line up over the ocean and quietly drop his machine onto the grass airstrip. Not a bad piece of night flying, even if he was a criminal.

For the next 30 minutes there was a flurry of activity as the Twin Otter was loaded with cartons in the cargo compartment and the main body of the fuselage. I took several photographs of the pilot, the ground crew and the woman who seemed to be calling all the shots. The aircraft registration numbers had been covered with a sheet of white plastic, and as the pilot walked around his machine, he stopped and peeled off the covering, revealing a set of standard aviation registration numbers. I managed to snap off a few shots of the rego number but had a feeling they would be fake anyway.

While I was intently surveilling the scene, I heard a noise behind me. A surge of adrenaline rushed through my system. I kept perfectly still as I lowered the camera to let it dangle gently from the lanyard around my neck. I felt for the Glock in my shoulder holster but kept myself still, trying to determine where the noise was coming from. I heard it again. A rustle of leaves and a shake of the undergrowth was now no more than 15 metres from my position. I was sure nobody had left the group on the airstrip. My ears were straining. I could hear my heart beating inside my chest. I began planning on how to drop and return fire if whoever it was began getting nasty. I drew the Glock out of the holster and cursed myself for not having put a round up the spout. Now I would have to cock the weapon before I could return fire, but that was of less importance at this very moment.

I lowered myself slowly down onto one knee and turned to face my attacker. More noise and rustling and then it hit me. The overwhelming stench of a feral pig rooting around in the undergrowth. It came into view and must have sensed I was close by. I could imagine its little squinty eyes searching for me, probably with intent on convincing me I should get out of his territory. The last thing I wanted right now was an argument with a feral pig, especially a boar with some serious canine equipment that could rip me apart. We stood about ten metres apart, staring at each other. I heard the Twin Otter start up and begin taxiing. I turned to look and see which direction he headed after take-off. The pig took half a dozen small steps towards me. What I wouldn't have given for a silencer right now. While the pilot revved his engine to check his revs, I cocked the Glock and took off the safety. I would have to shoot the bloody pig and then take my chances with being sprung by the nasties of the ground party. It was beginning to look very untidy.

The aircraft roared down the airstrip, but I knew the sound of my pistol would still bring attention to myself. Then almost as quickly as the pig had appeared, he moved off and back into the bush. I concentrated on the aircraft that turned south after clearing the end of the airstrip and then headed in a south-easterly direction, probably with intent on following the coastline to wherever they needed to redistribute their drugs. I moved to the other side of the tree I was using for cover to see what the crooks would do next.

*   *   *

Carina Thuong was on her radio.

'Viper, this is Rattlesnake, the buns are in the oven, over'. The HF radio was clear as she heard 'This is Rattlesnake. Good. Move to base. Out.' She turned to face the men who were leaning against her vehicle, drawing on cigarettes.

'Okay, mount up. Meet again in Townsville in two days' time. Make sure you wash your clothes thoroughly as soon as you get back. And drive carefully; don't go drawing attention to yourselves. Remember, you have been camping and fishing.' She then hissed, 'And keep those rifles well out of sight.' She turned and climbed into her vehicle and made ready to depart. 'Sure, Kreena,' Kegs responded, trying to sound like he was her second-in-command but not loud enough for her to hear. 'We'll be good boys, won't we fellas?' He smiled at the other men who were grinning like naughty schoolboys who had just sneaked a cigarette behind the school toilet block.

'I mean it,' she said, 'Fuck up one more time and it will be the end of you lot. Remember what happened to Stretch.'

Kegs involuntarily shuddered as he had an instant flashback to Stretch's head being blown apart by Franz Kudlov. Carina gave the men a look that would have melted stone. *They are such cretins.* She wondered how Zappia ever recruited men of such low intelligence and demeanour. They looked guilty before they even opened their foul mouths. But now her mission was to get back to Townsville and make sure the next phase of the operation was put in place.

*   *   *

As the vehicles began making their way off the grass airstrip, I pulled my satellite phone out of my backpack. It was set for coded burst transmission frequency hopping, and all I had to do was say that the goods were in the air and surveillance was ceasing. I also told the listener that I was heading back to Cairns. I gave the direction of the aircraft and the registration number and time of landing and take-off. I would have to make a full report when I got back, but now it was important to see if the aircraft could be tracked. I would love to have tried to plant a tracking device on the Otter, but there was absolutely no opportunity to get close enough undetected. It was now up to the airborne surveillance team who were well above us all at 35,000 feet in an RAAF P-8A Poseidon, trying to detect the Twin Otter amid a lot of civilian commercial traffic transiting up and down the eastern seaboard. I moved carefully back to my lying-up position and waited until first light. I wanted to make sure nobody was loitering in the area as a stay-behind party to catch people just like me.

The night passed uneventfully. The feral pig had moved on to greener and muddier pastures, and I listened to the bush awakening with the rays of sunlight and warmth returning to the soil. I collected my gear, carefully circled the vehicle, checked it out for booby traps before I climbed aboard and made my way back to the Bruce Highway. I stopped at a petrol station on my way back to Cairns, had a brew and checked my tail once again, but all was clear. Now, it was back to a full debrief, a lengthy surveillance report and get my digital imagery processed. It would be a long couple of days.

*   *   *

'And that was about it, Pete,' I offered as the four-hour debrief drew to a close.

'Good work, Bob,' he replied. 'Have you been able to get anything out of the photos you took?'

'I have and I did. Take a look at this shot and tell me what you reckon,' I asked as pushed the 8 x 10 colour prints across the table in my hotel room. 'Well, we can see that two of those blokes look like the mob that we are aware of and we suspected are working for Zappia,' he said slowly as he peered at the set of images that I had taken as the loading at the airstrip was underway.

'And what about that one?' I said, dropping a forefinger on an image of the woman with the long black hair. 'Does she look familiar?' I asked, then placing the photograph I had taken at the drug camp alongside it. 'Hard to say definitely,' he paused and stared intently at the images, 'but it sure looks like the same sheila,' he said. 'It wouldn't stand up in court but I reckon it is the same woman. The height must be about the same and the hair is the same.'

'She was definitely in charge of the loading of the plane.' I stood to get another cup of coffee from the kitchenette. 'Want a brew?' I asked.

'No mate, I have to be off. Good report, Bob, the boss will like all of this.'

'What happens now?' I asked.

'Well, we got a good lead on where the aircraft was headed but at this stage it is all being kept under a strict need-to-know basis. I think you can appreciate that, given the sieve that exists in headquarters,' he smirked.

'No worries. What jobs have you got for me next?'

'None at present,' Bryant responded, loading his briefcase and looking out the window through the venetian blinds to see if anyone was watching the room. 'Take a couple of days off and relax. It will be a few days before we have another op. What are you planning on doing?'

I thought about how much work had to be done to get the *Delfina* tidied up. Hopefully, the marina manager had been looking after her and not letting anyone on board while I was out of town. I also needed to get a berth lined up in the marina that was suitable for getting in and out of the harbour quickly.

'I'll probably take the *Delfina* for a run and make sure everything is tickety-boo and catch up with a few mates,' I said. *I might also see if Melanie is in town.*

'Good idea. Righto, catch you later,' Bryant said as he stepped out into the bright sunshine.

The *Delfina* was looking good, I went out into the Coral Sea for about an hour and put her through her paces. I was tying up again back at the marina when the marina manager, who I now knew as "Blue" because of his shock of red hair, came up and handed me an envelope.

'This came for you, Bob,' he said, handing a sealed white envelope down to me.

'Thanks, Blue. Any idea who dropped it off?' I asked.

'Some sheila on a bike, didn't leave her name,' he said over his shoulder as he walked back up to his office.

I went inside the cabin and opened the envelope. It read:

Saw you were back in town. We need to meet. I will pick you up at your motel at 10.30 a.m. tomorrow. Have enough gear for two days. Bring something for the hinterland. Melanie.

So, Melanie was keeping an eye on me.

Curiouser and curiouser.

I secured the *Delfina* and headed down to the Post Office to make sure I had no mail forwarded and headed back to my motel. I wondered what tomorrow would bring. One thing was sure: I had a lot of questions to ask and I sure wanted to lay eyes on that woman again.

R & R

I went for a run at about 6.30 a.m. After a couple of dozen laps at the rock pool I headed back to the motel for a shower. After enjoying a serious breakfast of eggs Benedict at the local coffee shop, I returned to my motel room and packed a bag to go away with Melanie for a few days. For back-up I also packed my sat phone, one of the Glocks, and a spare magazine. I took my camera in case we needed to ad lib my cover for anybody we might run into. After showering, I busied myself until around 10.15 a.m. and took my bag down to the motel foyer. I then walked outside, taking photographs of the surroundings while doing a sweep of the area to see if anyone was watching. It was all clear.

*   *   *

At 10.30 a.m. sharp, Melanie drove into the motel car park. I moved out and walked briskly across to her battered station wagon that had seen better days. I quickly opened the rear door, threw in the overnight bag, and noticed that the cargo compartment was packed with an Esky and cartons of groceries. A box with several wine bottles was visible near a bag that looked a lot like it had a camera tripod, or perhaps, a rifle inside. I climbed in beside Melanie and strapped in. She nodded at me with a prim smile and we smartly exited the car park. In a flurry of gravel, Melanie pulled out onto the Captain Cook Highway heading north. Not a word was said. *She must be playing the cover. Definitely got her game face on.* I decided to keep things cool. After ten minutes in light traffic, we turned west onto the Kennedy Highway heading for Kuranda.

We hadn't set eyes on each other since I had been in her apartment about two weeks before. Melanie looked across at me. I was more tanned now and I could see that she was pleasantly surprised by the ease with which I greeted her and looked into her eyes. I could see that something stirred deep inside her and it made her smile.

I turned sideways and looked at her neck. I had been thinking of kissing it as soon as I laid eyes on her from the foyer of the motel. But one never knew who was watching. It was imperative to maintain the cover, even on my "days off". Given that Melanie's apartment was under electronic surveillance, I could not discount physical surveillance by the nasties. As we motored along, I kept a watchful eye on the traffic and turned sideways in the front seat so I could cast a weather eye on the following traffic. Nothing caught my attention. I had to admit I was looking forward to this interlude, and I kept running my approach and tactics of how I would play the game over the next couple of days. I never really got far into this planning as various flashbacks of our brief moments together kept taking me off my track of concentration.

I recalled the way she arched her neck when we had last danced in the restaurant and thought how provocative a simple act like that could be. Other thoughts started cramming into my head, but I needed to clear my mind.

'Where are we headed?'

Melanie turned and smiled warmly at the question. 'Up into the hills,' she replied, 'I know a place that has great views and lots of wildlife … suitable for eco-tourism,' she added with a wry grin on her face. 'But to be honest, I wanted some time with you alone, so we could get to know each other a little better.'

My heart skipped a bit at the thought that she wanted to be with me … and alone.

'How did you find this place?' I asked, trying to maintain some composure.

'It belongs to a mate of my dad.' I noticed that Melanie now checked the rear vision mirror regularly.

Must be making sure we aren't being followed, or she is a very conscientious driver.

Pretending to look at the passing traffic as we headed into the hinterland, I studied her breasts. The seat belt cut down her modest cleavage. She said they were small, but they were "all hers", and unless I was mistaken, they showed a woman who was in damned fine shape. I was guilty of studying her legs frequently as she had moved around the *Delfina*, and I liked what I saw. Melanie was well toned, and her legs showed that she had done plenty of exercise to get into that shape. I was glad that I had retained a reasonable semblance of fitness since leaving the Army. Avoiding the fast foods, fried stuff, and my favourite ice creams had helped.

We were now out of civilisation and in the bush. I started to relax but noticed that Melanie was religiously checking her mirrors. Road works on the two-lane road, where excessive rain had caused some slips and rock falls, had caused delays, and the traffic was abysmal, but we chatted and the conversation flowed like a stream over rocks as it bubbled and swept us together. I joked and loved the way she smiled and sometimes chuckled at my pretty ordinary attempts at humour. The rainforest was now becoming taller and denser. It was nothing short of spectacular. Majestic was the word I liked to use in describing the bush in this area. The conversation dried up and we both went quiet as we made our way along the mountainous road climbing steadily up the side of the escarpment towards Kuranda. I kept quiet because the road did demand a driver's full attention, and it was a long way down if one screwed up.

I turned to look at the unfolding countryside that was jammed with all manner of magnificent trees and ferns, and when I turned back, I saw Melanie looking at me.

'What?' I asked with a smile on my face.

Melanie changed gear and accelerated up the steep climb towards our destination. 'You,' she answered with a slight smile that I realised had more power than the engine she was gunning, 'are a brave man to come on a weekend away with someone you have only known for a couple of weeks.'

I thought about the remark and agreed but said with a grin, 'I trust my inner soul and besides, I am bigger, faster and can always run away.'

She smiled at me again.

As we drove along a gravel road, I noticed Melanie sitting a little more upright in her seat. We passed a side road where she slowed the wagon and looked carefully at the road leading into a house in the near distance. She kept driving for a kilometre and then slowed and turned the vehicle around and started driving back down the road.

She is checking to make sure we aren't being followed. Just like doing a hook manoeuvre when occupying an ambush. I smiled inwardly. Back at the side road we had passed previously, Melanie stopped, got out to check the letterbox and scan the road for tyre marks. I smiled knowingly at her as she returned to the car and we swept up the gravel driveway into the cottage. It was almost noon. Once out of the vehicle, I turned and took in the magnificent views. The Coral Sea shimmered in the far distance and a haze made the lush verdant hills fade to a misty green. Large cloud banks were building down south, and an evening downpour was not out of the question. I admired the "cottage", as Melanie had described it, and thought how quaint that term was for a place in the Australian bush.

We began unloading the groceries and provisions out of her wagon. It brought strong flashbacks to the house my parents had once owned on the beach in New South Wales. Memories of the weekends I had shared with the family but had now lost came flooding back. I was feeling a little down so I moved outside to regather my emotions. Damn it! I thought I had moved on since Jenny and Annie had been taken from me so quickly and without warning. I did not have a day pass without thinking of them. *This may not be as easy as I thought it might be.*

I kept myself busy and enjoyed watching Melanie bustling around the kitchen, ordering me around and telling me where to put things. She began opening the windows to air the comfortable two-storey A-framed friendly little house. It was much more than I expected, imagining something along the lines of a bush shack with a porch, than this Oregon timbered cottage. I was impressed with the standard of maintenance for a holiday house, and noticed that there were no phones, no television, and a radio seemed to be the only means of mass communication in the residence. There was one admission to technology; a CD player sat on top of a buffet where glasses and china were housed. Bellbirds were ringing through the rainforest, giving the place a magical charm.

'You know this place well,' I said, as I stacked vegies into the fridge crisper.

'Since "Uncle" Harry lost his wife to cancer a few years ago, he rarely uses it.' She looked around the room with a wistful smile, 'and he said I could come up any time, and I do.' Melanie smiled while putting fruit into a bowl on the kitchen table. 'If I ever get enough money together, I would like to buy it from him, but until I get my master mariner's certificate, that's a pipe dream.'

I brought our overnight bags into the cottage. Now came the tricky part. I knew her bedroom was upstairs because she had described what it was like lying in bed – the loft was her "tree house," as I recalled.

She had described looking out over the rainforest canopy toward the sea. I made a beeline for the downstairs bedroom and dropped my bag in the room. I desperately didn't want to look as if she should expect me to share her bed just because we were sharing a weekend and a house. It was a strategy I hoped would show that I did not take her for granted. Melanie darted upstairs, telling me to do whatever I wanted while she changed. I felt like asking if I could come and watch but held my tongue at that dopey idea, and started unpacking my bag in the downstairs bedroom.

She called out, 'Get your walking gear on, I want to show you some of the rainforest.'

I quickly changed into a pair of runners. Melanie came bouncing down the stairs in her bushwalking attire that would have stopped traffic on the Cairns Esplanade.

'You know something, young lady, you sure know how to fill out a pair of shorts,' I smiled.

'Thank you, Skipper,' she smiled back, 'I think some mozzie repellent might be in order,' she added. She grabbed some fruit as we headed out the door. 'Lunch,' she said, tossing me an apple and a banana.

Melanie led the way down a well-used track that followed the ridge line heading east. I would stop regularly and take photographs of various species of fern and trees. Occasionally we could hear a distinctive bird sound and I would try to zoom in on it before it took cover. We came out onto a ledge of granite rock that hung above a vertical drop of almost 100 metres. The view was breathtaking. We stopped, and without a word spoken we both marvelled at the natural beauty that was laid out before us. As we stood close together, she brushed against my arm and I found her hand and gently squeezed it.

'And to think we get to see all of this … and for free,' I said quietly.

Melanie looked up at my face, 'Yep, Mother Nature at her best.'

We spent the next hour traversing along the ridgeline and then headed west down into a creek line where we drank from the crystal-clear waters of a fast-flowing creek. The tree ferns, birds nest plants, elkhorns and staghorns in the creek line were stunning. The water tinkled over the stones and provided a musical backdrop to the whip birds cracking the air with their calls.

Arriving back at the cottage, we had worked up a sweat climbing back up from the creek, and Melanie suggested it was time for a cold beer.

'No arguments from this side,' I offered.

'Good, grab a coldie while I tidy up,' Melanie shot back and headed up stairs.

If she is having a shower, she might need a hand. Nah, too crass. Stay cool, Robert.

When she returned we sat on the veranda of the cottage and chatted easily as we watched the light fade and the sounds of the bush go quiet.

'I love this time of day,' I said to no one in particular. 'I always used to enjoy this part of the day when I was in the Army, when you could finally put your feet up and let darkness envelop you.'

Melanie looked at me with her serious face on, 'do you miss the Army, Bob?'

'Not as much as I thought I would. I miss the blokes I used to work with more than the military itself.' I paused, thinking of Ian Taylor and a couple of good young soldiers my unit had lost in Afghanistan. 'Yeah, I think it is the people I miss the most. Bureaucracy and bullshit I can do without.' I smiled and raised my beer bottle, 'to absent friends.' We clinked our bottles together and I drew deeply on the cold beer.

'To absent friends,' Melanie repeated quietly and sipped on her beer.

A pregnant pause enveloped us as I turned to look Melanie square in the eye.

'I don't want to kill the moment,' I ventured, 'but can you tell me about those blokes I saw in your apartment the other day?'

Melanie sighed and said sombrely, 'I guess at some stage we were going to have to do this, but it is so very important that this stays between us.' I nodded, listening intently. 'I'm serious about this, Bob, one little slipup could be fatal here, and I am not being dramatic.'

'Got it,' I responded with my game face well and truly locked in.

'Okay, almost half a year ago we let it be known around Townsville and Cairns that I was the go-to person for places to work the reef for illegal fishing or diving.'

'Okay,' I said quietly, wondering where this was heading.

'Kegs and one of his mates came and saw me and made a proposition that I would show them on the charts where people could go and "fish" or "dive" without any interference or running into tourists.' Melanie shifted a little in her chair and added, 'they paid me money to show them where to go, and all I had to do was keep quiet.'

'What if you didn't?' I asked.

'Oh, they made it abundantly clear that I would be joining the fishes on the bottom of the Coral Sea if I spilled my guts,' Melanie smiled. 'And I knew they meant it.'

'Jesus Christ!' This was getting a little heavy. I leaned back in my chair.

'Don't worry, Bob,' Melanie said, touching my arm. 'I always had backup, and the best bit, I have it all on tape.' She smiled and sipped from her glass.

A moment of quietness then ensued as I took all of this in. Melanie's reply seemed to satisfy the question that had been bugging me since I had spied on the flat. It was time for a change of pace. I slapped my hands onto my knees.

'Right, then,' I said, standing as darkness started to envelop the veranda. 'Why don't you let me cook you dinner?'

'You were going to anyway,' Melanie smiled, 'barbecues are secret men's business and you showed you were dab hand on the *Delfina* a few times. There is some nice rib fillet that needs your handiwork. I'll whip a salad together and open that red wine that looks like it needs some attention.'

The alcohol had broken what little tension remained between us and the brief sunset and cooling evening allowed our conversation to flow.

The dinner was an easy affair. I cooked the steak on the barbecue and Melanie produced a simple but tasty salad that we washed down with the red wine. It was as if we had known each other for years instead of months, as we confided in each other's likes and dislikes in anything from food to movies, to people we had come across in our lives. After we had eaten, we went outside and sat on the veranda in the still of the evening, finishing what was left of our very nice bottle of merlot.

I now realised that my attraction to Melanie was being fulfilled. Yet I still had an inner doubt that I would be able to commit to anything even bordering on a lasting relationship. My thoughts earlier in the day as I was unpacking the car, had given me a stark and poignant reminder of my loss and bereavement that seemed a lifetime ago but was still hauntingly fresh. As I sat on the cane outdoor setting, listening to the music, Melanie moved towards me and, extending her hand, said in a voice that seemed huskier than usual, 'You don't have to sleep downstairs unless you want to.'

My heart skipped a beat. *If you don't want to.* Good God, I thought, a man would have to be made of clay not to want to share her bed. I knew Melanie had made a big decision and I admired her courage and pluck. She turned off the downstairs lights and locked the doors while I changed into my favourite silk robe. I brought it to indicate that nothing was being taken for granted. She smiled at the deep-blue silk dressing gown that was embroidered with golden dragons and started climbing the stairs to the loft. Again, I watched her shapely bottom as she ascended toward her bedroom.

This was the moment I was hoping would not be uncomfortable. I decided to let nature take its course and if everything worked, then all was well and good. I moved toward her and kissed her warm lips. Melanie kissed me back with a response that immediately felt its way to my groin. I gently kissed her neck and smiled and watched her back arch. Melanie's nipples began to harden, and as I looked down, I noticed the way they stood out against the cotton fabric of her top.

'Time for bed,' she said, and I almost yelled in agreement.

Melanie turned away and dropped her shorts and I saw the G-string that outlined her backside and almost lured me into pressing my body up against her. Instead, I moved towards the other side of the bed and dropped my gown to the floor. Melanie had turned down the bedside light, bathing the room in a faint glow. I dived under the top sheet. She turned towards me and I admired the shape of her slender figure and perky breasts as she walked towards the bed. Her pubic hair was trimmed into a small triangle, no doubt to accommodate her swim suits and the short shorts she sometimes wore. I noticed that she was muscled in the legs and arms but not overly so. She was in good shape.

Jesus, she's got a real six-pack there.

I made a mental note that I was going to have to get serious about getting into better shape.

Melanie's nipples were now rock hard, and I eagerly waited for her to join me. Melanie's legs quickly found themselves up against my thighs and she looked up into my face. I was smiling and had good reason. It had been a year since I had held a woman who seemed so warm and inviting. I moved my head towards her and kissed her gently on the lips.

Melanie pushed back with an urgency that indicated I should make myself more useful. I responded by moving my hand gently onto her breast and she shuddered as if a charge of electricity had gone through her body. I couldn't help but smile at her impulsive response and felt myself growing in anticipation of our union. I moved slightly and lowered my mouth over her firm breast. She moaned deep inside her throat as I gently nibbled and flicked my tongue over her nipples. I felt her hand moving towards my hardening manhood. I hoped she would not be disappointed.

I had grown as she held me in her hand. She could feel the throbbing of my cock as she snuggled up close. Melanie seemed surprised that my kisses were so gentle, given the expectation that a man of my background might be somewhat less inclined. She didn't have to wait long. In a single deft move, I slipped a pillow under her bottom and smiled knowingly.

Melanie's want matched my desire and I was relieved that she desired me as much as I wanted her. She held me tightly, wrapping her fingers around the base of my cock as I began penetrating her pussy. She gasped at the thickness of it. Later she would put her hand around her wrist and compare the similarity between her wrist and my shaft. It made her smile. I looked down at her face and she returned my gaze with what I hoped was a look of love. Her eyes were pleading with me to enter deeper and she moved her hips upward to make my entry easier. Slowly, I began to slide my cock deeper and then gently push in and out, almost leaving her before driving back into her again. Her backside was still on the pillow and I was able to almost reach the end of her vagina and occasionally she could feel my knob tickling the end of her love tunnel. For a solidly built man and weighing probably 100 kilos, she seemed like she could hardly feel my weight. She snuck a look to see me in a classic press-up position as I made love to her. Her look said, *Where have you been all of my life?*

I couldn't hold back any longer and my thrusts became more urgent, so she started kissing my ear and nibbling on my ear lobe as she felt my cock engorge and then a flood of warm semen as I came inside her. She noticed I had become very quiet. Slowly my penetrations and thrusts subsided. I pushed myself up off her breasts and said meekly, 'Sorry, but I think I have made a mess.'

We lay back on the rumpled bed, pleasantly exhausted, sexually satiated, not saying a word, but just looking at each other and smiling warmly. I had not felt this type of emotion for a very long time and I felt myself slipping into a melancholy state. I would have to stay alert and not let my guard down because I knew that out there, somewhere, were people who were willing to kill for what they wanted and to protect their criminal activities.

We drifted into an easy sleep, and I loved the way she spooned me during the night.

*　　*　　*

Always an early riser, I slipped out of bed and made myself useful, cleaning up in the kitchen as quietly as I could. I heard her soft footfall as she made her way down the stairs. She was wearing a T-shirt that did not completely cover her groin and I tried all I could to not stare at her pussy. She came up behind me and wrapped her arms around my waist.

'Could you do me a favour?' she asked coquettishly.

'Sure,' I responded, looking at her.

'Take me one more time before we have breakfast, would you?' She smiled as I quickly threw the tea towel onto the bench and followed her up the stairs into the loft.

As she took me into her arms she asked, 'And one more favour?'

'Yes ma'am,' I said, wondering what was coming next.

'When you do take me, don't fuck me, make love to me.'

'I can do that,' I smiled back and began to do just as she asked.

*   *   *

'How about a walk around the escarpment before brekky and you can show me the bush up there?' I offered, hoping she would not see this as a ruse to exit the love nest and avoid sentimental chit chat.

'Sure, that would be nice,' she said, bouncing out of bed with a total absence of modesty. 'I'll shower, get some gear on and be right with you.' I changed into fresh shorts and a shirt. I headed downstairs and did a quick sweep around the cottage to see if anyone had ventured near the building or around Melanie's vehicle during the night. It was all clear. *Well, at least we made a clean break from Cairns.*

We spent an hour bushwalking and chatting before returning to the cottage for breakfast. I cooked some bacon and eggs on the barbecue while Melanie got some toast going and brewed up a batch of coffee. As we sat down on the veranda and started wolfing down the food, I looked up and smiled at Melanie.

'What?' she asked, smiling.

'You,' I answered quietly, 'make me feel good again.'

'Why, haven't you felt good lately?'

'Not always,' I said, looking into her eyes. 'It has been a while since I felt like I do right now.'

'Steady, Skipper,' she laughed. 'Don't get all mushy on me.' But deep inside I knew that she felt pretty much the same. 'Has it been tough since your wife died?' she asked and I could see that she was hoping that this would get me to open up a little.

I cleared my throat and sipped on the aromatic coffee. 'Yep, it has.' I paused to keep my emotions in check, 'and to be honest with you, Melanie, I wasn't sure if I could feel the way I do right now without getting the guilts.'

She stood and walked around to my chair, tilted my head back, and kissed me ever so gently.

'I understand what you are saying, and I want you to know that I am glad you said yes to allowing me to kidnap you for the weekend.'

I smiled back at her as she sat back down, adding, 'My last conduct after capture course was nothing like this, I can assure you,' I said, remembering the torture that the Divisional Intelligence Unit had put me through when I was last in the regiment. 'Definitely not like this,' I smiled.

*   *   *

The return to Cairns was uneventful as we wound our way back south down the Kennedy Highway. Melanie suggested we should stop off in Kuranda for a late lunch, and we spent an hour or so mingling with the day trippers who had come up from Cairns on the scenic railway trip and who were now busily spending their money on souvenirs and the like. Melanie found a café with drop-dead views of the coastal hinterland and we just relaxed and soaked up the atmosphere. Every now and then we exchanged knowing looks at tourists from down south who were sporting red sunburn lines and dreadful floral printed shirts under hats they would never be seen dead in back in suburban Melbourne or Sydney.

As Melanie dropped me off at my motel, she squeezed my hand and said a simple 'thank you' and mouthed a kiss. I dragged my bag out of the back of the wagon and said a quiet, 'No, thank YOU, young lady, thank you.' I turned and walked quickly across the carpark and into the foyer, checking for messages from reception as I went. I wasn't looking forward to sleeping alone again, but I knew I would sleep damn well.

Bewick Island

I was just about to get out of bed when my AFP mobile phone rang. The voice was electronically disguised, but it was probably one of Bryant's men. All he said was 'Gladstone' and hung up. This was a code word that meant that I needed to get my arse down to the *Delfina* and put to sea before the next high tide. I rang the marina and arranged for the boat to be fully fuelled. I checked out of the motel and I decided to swing by Melanie's digs and say goodbye. I hoped it would be au revoir. I had my ready bag packed with my small armoury fully loaded and all the bits and pieces that would hopefully match any problem I was likely to encounter.

I stopped short of Melanie's apartment and swept the street for anyone loitering with intent. Nothing. I called her mobile and she answered quietly, 'Yes?'

'It's me,' I said hoping she would know who "me" would be.

'Hello me,' she said with her serious voice, 'What can I do for you?'

'I have to go out of town. Don't know for how long, or where at this stage, but I thought I would let you know that I wasn't running away.'

'Never thought you would, Skipper,' she replied, still in her quiet voice. 'Do you need a deckie?'

'As a matter of fact, I do. Are you available?' I asked hoping she would say yes.

'When can you pick me up?'

'I am sitting down the street.'

'Okay, don't hang around. I will join you at the marina in 15 minutes.'

'See you there,' I shot back, putting the Toyota into gear and cruised past her flat looking for any unusual activity or anyone loitering with intent as I did so.

*   *   *

There was a lot to do when I got to the marina. I put the vehicle in the long-term car park and checked in with the marina manager who seemed to be expecting me.

'G'day Bob,' he ventured, holding out an envelope, 'This was dropped off a few minutes ago. The bloke who left it said it was important you read it ASAP.'

'Thanks mate, I will,' I replied as I took the unopened manila envelope and walked down to the *Delfina*. I stopped and turned to ask him, 'Is she ready to go?'

'Sure is. Fully fuelled just like you wanted,' he said, giving me a thumbs up.

It was nice to have people you could rely on. I stepped onto the

Delfina, dropped my bags into the forward state room and sat down to read the contents of the envelope I figured had been left by Peter Bryant or one of his cronies.

In my briefings I had suggested the use of "one-time letter pads" where a pre-arranged code would be used to send and decipher messages. To the average person it looked like a series of scrambled numbers and letters in no particular order, but once a code was applied to the series of numbers and letters words appeared and the message could be unscrambled. We used the one-time letter pads in the regiment as a form of short term, but very safe security. I set about decoding the message. It took me five minutes to decode and double check my work.

It read:

B.M. Proceed to Princess Charlotte Bay. Conduct covert surveillance of Bewick Island on passage through to Pipon Island. Remain in that vicinity until contacted by sat phone in two days' time. P.B.

I went to the bridge and dragged out my charts of the area north of Cooktown. I had quite a trip ahead and was now very glad I had asked Melanie to join me. It would make staying alert easier and I could avoid long watches while at sea. The Coral Sea was no place to switch off or be tired, especially on the outer reefs. Another set of eyes and ears would be invaluable.

I heard an 'ahoy' and looked out onto the deck to see Melanie standing on the marina jetty with her duffel bag over her shoulder. She looked great.

'Ahoy to you, too,' I smiled back. 'Come aboard, we will be shoving off once I sort out getting some food brought on board.'

'Okay, where are we headed?' she asked while stowing her kit in the forward locker.

'I'll brief you once we get out of the harbour and underway, but for the moment we are headed for Cooktown.'

Melanie frowned. 'Cooktown? What the hell is in Cooktown?' she asked.

'My guess is crooks and criminals, and we are going to have to be on our toes,' I said with my game face on.

'Aye aye, Skipper,' she saluted as she started making a list of provisions we would need for our days at sea. 'Anything special you want on the shopping list?'

'Yeah, get some extra cans of stuff that we can eat cold if we have to in an emergency, and make sure our first aid kit is up to speed too, will you?' I replied as I started plotting our likely track up through the inner reef towards Lizard Island.

Melanie went ashore and started sorting out the groceries and other provisions. I checked that my scuba gear was all primed and ready to go if we needed it. I had the capacity to refill tanks on board but wanted to make sure nothing was left to chance. It was like getting ready to go on a patrol. Checking equipment, making sure everything was in working order, that all batteries were operating at full capacity and that all ammunition was serviceable. I went up to the bridge again and made sure the EPIRB was in working order and that my stash of flares was where it should be.

By the time I had done my readiness check, Melanie was back with a trolley full of groceries. We loaded the food on board, and I checked with the marina and told them that I was departing for Lizard Island and would be arriving in three days' time. I gave a radio check to the Coast Guard who acknowledged my departure and told me I could expect fair weather in close to shore, but there would be a medium swell running at two to two and half metres outside. We left the marina and harbour close to 10 a.m. It had been a busy morning. In all the readiness and preparation and checks, I felt that familiar surge of adrenaline that I always felt before going out to face an armed enemy. Even though most times we were not supposed to get entangled with our foe and simply conduct surveillance and report, it was still exciting to us as highly trained soldiers. Being as professional as one could possibly be was what being in Special Forces was all about, and I found that still gave me a buzz. I liked it.

We turned north once outside the harbour groyne and I set a course for Lizard Island. We had about 250 kilometres or 135 nautical miles to travel, and I wanted to cruise at about 15 knots to get my best fuel consumption. I didn't expect to get anywhere near there for at least ten hours which is what I wanted so we could anchor up in the dark and hopefully not draw too much attention to ourselves. I knew where I wanted to drop anchor on the northern coast of the island where most of the cruising yachts usually stayed. To anyone looking from the resort we would just be another couple living the dream and cruising through the Great Barrier Reef.

By mid-afternoon we were cruising along at a good speed and

taking turns to keep the *Delfina* on target. We had an autopilot, but I always like the Mark One eyeball to make sure things were going smoothly. Melanie rigged up a line to trawl aft and after only a short time she had jagged a serious kingfish that was destined for the dinner table. While we worked our way steadily north, I briefed her on what the mission was likely to be. I expected to get a call from Peter Bryant that would tell me what I could expect once I started sneaking around Bewick Island. I needed to know all the "W"s. Who, what, where, and why, and how many people were likely to be on this rock?

We took turns checking the radar, and apart from the odd cruiser anchored over a reef, there was very little happening on the Coral Sea this night. At around 6 p.m., Peter Bryant rang me on the sat phone and asked me to switch on my laptop. He was sending through a brief that would need decoding and warned me to spend at least an hour looking at what he was sending. When he finished, he asked how I was coping. I told him Melanie was with me and all I got back was a small 'oh'. Nothing else. He sounded concerned and I asked him if he had any problems with my crew. He said, no, but I should have told him of my manifest. I let it go through to the keeper. His final words were, 'Be careful, take nothing for granted and carry my protection.' That was his way of saying "go armed". I fully intended to after the last time I did a job for these characters.

As darkness enveloped the ocean, I switched on the running lights and we both manned the bridge. We arrived south of Bewick Island after a day of cruising along, trying to look like just another couple cruising the Great Barrier Reef. We had made good time in fairly compliant seas with a lazy swell of less than a metre. We pored over the charts, trying to see how we could get close enough for me to swim ashore and do some serious looking around. It was not going to be easy. The currents around the area were fairly strong, and I was starting to think of a drop-off north of the island and use the currents to bring me ashore. I would not use scuba as I was worried about how much air I would need and didn't want to be carrying big tanks for such a short swim.

* * *

Dropping the pick was not a problem. The bottom was reasonably rocky, and we soon had a good hold and swung with the wind. We waited to make sure it held, and I prepared to swim ashore. I had my waterproof backpack strapped tightly to me that held all the essentials; binos, two handguns, spare clips and some survival rations in case I got caught short and needed to lie low for a while. A small two-way radio would have been nice but would have easily given away my position if anyone with a scanner was listening out. I was applying my camouflage cream to blacken my face when Melanie sat down next to me.

'How long do you think you'll take?' she asked with a crease of a frown on her face.

'Not too long, I hope. The island is just over three square kilometres in size so unless I run into strife, probably one day, and I'll be back tomorrow night.' I tried to sound confident, but I had a nagging suspicion that given what happened to Squizzie, I needed to be careful. It had happened in Afghanistan when some locals tried to set us up by feeding misinformation on the whereabouts of the Taliban and we walked into trouble. We put an end to that trickery when always thereafter, we conducted a drone sweep prior to any ground movement. *One of those little suckers would be nice right now with some infra-red to flush out anyone sneaking around.*

'Be careful, Bob,' she smiled.

'Always careful ma'am. If anything turns to shit, I will throw up a red flare. If that happens, get the hell out of here and head back to Cooktown.' She nodded and gave me a peck on the cheek.

I slipped off the rear access deck, trying to make as little noise as possible. I adjusted my mask and was happy with my buoyancy. I started swimming breaststroke for what I thought would be a covered cove on the north-western tip where I knew there would be mangroves to cover my tracks.

Within 30 minutes, I had covered the 300 metres to the shore. The mangroves were thick and made life tough for a while, but I was glad to have the cover to allow me to ingress the island. I got my coveralls and sneakers out of my bag and repacked my gear and stashed my fins, snorkel, and mask. I marked a mangrove with a tear from my knife so I could recover my stuff when I needed to depart. I headed inland with the intent of scaling a small knoll about 200 metres distant and sweeping the area with my binos to see if the island had any guests. Theoretically, there should not have been anyone on this piece of dirt at all, as the charts showed it was part of the National Park, permission was required and there were no facilities anyhow. So why go there?

After climbing in and out of a few small creeks that contained low shrubs, I started heading south. Large basalt rocks the size of small cars appeared every now and then as if they had been scattered by some enormous hand. The scrub was low and thick and there were only large trees every now and then. I headed for the knoll using my compass because it was hard to navigate at times in the dense shrubbery. I moved slowly, stopping to listen every ten paces or so for about half a minute, but all I could hear was the whispering of the light breeze through the low bush. Moonlight started to shine as the clouds gave way to a half moon. This made my movement a little easier but definitely not faster. I still needed to move in the shadows where possible or look for cover as I made my way up the low hill.

It was close to midnight when I reached the spot where I could have a good look around the northern side of the island without having to cover too much ground on foot. I climbed up onto a large grey rock hoping I would not be silhouetted as I lay prone on the warm stone. There was a massive clay pan on the north-western side about a kilometre distant that reflected the moonlight and provided an easy reference for my sweep. I swept along the coastline, looking for tell-tale signs of campfires or lights of any description. I saw nothing. I wriggled around and started to sweep the southern sector where there was a reef about a click away and small white bubbling surf indicated where the shoals were located.

Then I saw it. About 500 metres off shore was a large motor

cruiser. It was larger than the *Delfina*, but strangely was showing no lights at all. I waited for the moon to reappear and sure enough it was at anchor. I zeroed in on the vessel and could see people on the aft deck. They were either night fishing or armed. I just didn't have the strength in my binos to pick out any weapons, but the way the people were moving indicated they were carrying something. I stayed on this boat as my primary target because they should have had their navigation lights on even while anchored off the reef, as it was in the main passage past the island. Most boats that size would have a mast head light and a stern light, but this craft had zip. They were either incompetent sailors or didn't want to be seen. My gut was telling me the latter. I now concentrated on where anyone from that vessel would have gone ashore. I swept the shoreline either side of the churning reef where a dinghy might have beached. Nothing. I continued sweeping slowly toward the western shore and stopped to rest my eyes. As I did so, the moon came out in all its glory and I saw a shiny reflective surface about 150 metres from a creek line. It was a rubber ducky. It was covered with branches to camouflage its presence. *More training required, fellas.*

It was time to find out where the people from the inflatable were camped. The questions going through my mind now were: are these people associated with the Zappia drug cartel? Or are they just illegally fishing in the National Park? If they are nasties, was I expected? If so, what was their aim – kill or capture? If they were bad guys, how the hell did they know I would be here, or was it just a coincidence that they were up to no good? Lots of questions and not too many answers at this stage. In the back of my mind I was hoping that Melanie was maintaining a watch and would not be caught by surprise if they started heading towards her. I double checked my flares to make sure they were handy.

My sweep through the binos showed that if there was a surprise party waiting for me it would be near the obvious spot where someone would try and come ashore near the clay pan. I had over a kilometre to travel to make the eastern side of the objective. I was sure anyone wanting to ambush me would be on the western side on a small ridge line that had a good overwatch of the area. I slipped off the rock and set my wrist compass for 270 mils to bring me out close to the fringe of the clay pan. I felt like I was back on ops again and trying to detect the bloody Taliban who used local villages to hide their weapons and stores north of Tarin Kowt before making a strike against the Allies.

I moved northwest at my normal pace with listening stops and found that my sense of alertness had gone up a notch or two. The adrenaline had kicked in as I moved steadily towards the clay pan. I was forced into moving at a crouch at times as the scrub thinned out. I tried to move when the clouds reduced the moonlight as they scudded past silently above. Around 2 a.m. I was where I wanted to be and moved forward to the edge of the clay pan on my guts. To stand would have been inviting a response I really didn't want. I smelt cigarette smoke. It wafted across and I knew that at least one person was somewhere on the other side of the empty grey-white stretch of dirt. I got my binos out and started sweeping the higher ground directly in front of me about 600 metres distant. I was looking for anything that would give me an indication of how many people lay in wait and their intent.

The air was suddenly very still. I strained to listen and then heard the unmistakable sound of a squelch on a VHF radio. It is a sound like "ssshhhtt" and indicates that whoever has their radio on doesn't want others to know about it. The moon came out again, and I swept the area above the ridgeline hoping to see a radio antenna. Nothing. I did a quick appreciation and decided that I would close up on the other side of the clay pan by traversing to the southern side. I had very little option as the northern side was too open and I would be easily seen and outlined by the reflective surface of the clay. This was going to get tricky. A diversion would have been nice, but the cupboard was bare. I would just have to be very careful.

Closing in on a target whose exact location is unknown is fraught with danger, and it is very much a case of hastening slowly. But intelligence was on my side because I was halfway around and I saw the muted glow of a cigarette. Whoever was up on this hill was a dedicated smoker. Finally, it gave me a reference point to aim for and I moved further south to be behind my target. I hadn't gone more than 50 metres when I crossed over their footpath through the low scrub. My basic tracking skills indicated that there were at least two individuals. I propped and very carefully slipped off my backpack and extracted my NVG. Now that I was closer to my target, I would have a better chance of seeing who or what I was up against. I was mindful of the fact that not too long ago I was doing this and got caught from behind, so I moved very cautiously.

My world had now gone green as I adjusted my vision to the goggles. My quarry was now easily seen. Two blokes, backs against a tree and one cradling what looked like a high-powered rifle. The other guy had what looked like an AK-47 in his lap. From their position it was if they were expecting someone to come strolling across the clay pan. *Perhaps it wasn't me they were expecting?* I crawled closer to see if I could pick up any conversation. It took me almost an hour to cover 100 metres, but now I could even smell the stale body odour of the waiting duo. *Jesus, these two could do with a shower.* I was now less than 15 metres from the pair in a small depression in the ground. My Glock was cocked and ready by my side.

'Fuck me, Kegs, how long are we gonna wait in this shithole?'

'Until the slope says we can leave,' hissed Kegs. 'Keep ya fuckin' voice down will ya? Carina says we can expect some snoop to come onto this rock sometime today and we are gonna be ready for the sucker.'

'What makes you so sure he is gonna turn up?' asked Bart, trying but failing to mute his hoarse voice with a stage whisper.

'All I know is that the Russian said we can expect company,' and Kegs leaned in closer to Bart and hissed, 'and he doesn't sail around the ocean on a bloody hunch.'

'Still reckon it's a waste of fuckin' time. Why don't we just waste him in town? It'd be a lot bloody easier.'

Kegs turned with a look of disdain at his fellow conspirator. 'Because out here there's no fuckin' evidence, you clown! We nail 'im, chuck 'im in the briny, and the sharks or crocs will dispose of the remains. Too easy.' Kegs smiled to himself. He thought that when he popped the other copper called Taylor that there would be no evidence, but the tides had swept his body into a place he couldn't follow.

I had heard enough. This was an ambush and these two jokers were out to get me. It was time I took my leave and prepared to exfiltrate back to the *Delfina*. I was going to have to retrace my steps to avoid being sprung. It would take me at least two hours and dawn would be in three. It was going to be tight.

The Office

I clambered back aboard the *Delfina* just as the first rays of sunshine were striking the white hull of our boat. Melanie helped drag me onto the rear diving deck.

'Jesus, Bob,' she uttered as she hauled me up on board. 'You look stuffed.' She had a concerned look on her face.

'I am. The current was pretty strong coming back with the outgoing tide. Get the pick up and start getting us out of here. We've got to move asap.' I crashed back onto the deck. I wasn't stuffed, I was bloody exhausted. The tides that swept around Bewick Island were treacherous and it took a lot of effort to get back. I estimated I had swum four clicks just to go 500 metres.

I heard Melanie start the auxiliary motor to pull the anchor up as she kicked over the motors of the *Delfina*. I moved to the bridge and took the wheel as Melanie signalled me with a thumbs up from the bow that the anchor was safely secured. I made a heading of due east, using the cover of the island to aid our egress, and then took a long swig on a water bottle.

'Are you okay?'

'Yeah, just buggered from a tough swim,' I smiled back. 'We're heading for Cooktown, so drag down the charts so we can plot a course, will you?'

'Sure, but I thought we were heading for Princess Charlotte Bay. What did you find?' she asked as she secured the chart to the navigation table.

'Change of plan.'

She looked at me with expectancy written all over her face.

'Well, for a start I was expected. And for good measure I think they hoped to kill me to boot.'

'What!' Melanie exclaimed with her eyes narrowing. 'How can that be? Who was there? How many of them?' she shot off in rapid succession.

'Let me run through how it went,' I replied and gave her a blow by blow description of the recce that took about ten minutes. I left nothing out.

'Christ, you mean they were expecting us?'

'It sure looks like it, but I have a feeling they think I was arriving this morning. That's why I want to head north-east and then north to make sure they can't track us,' I said, looking back over my shoulder to the fast disappearing Bewick Island. 'Once outside the Reef we will beetle on down past Lizard Island and then swing back into Cooktown.' Melanie swung around with the binos to her eyes and scanned the ocean in our wake.

'Nothing so far,' she said, joining me back at the nav table.

'I'm going down to have a shower and clean up. Steer 90 degrees for the next hour, then 60 until we get to the outer reef, and then we will head due south. I reckon we are about 10 hours from Cooktown. And don't answer the sat phone until we sort this shit out.'

'Got it,' she called back as I went below.

By the time I was back on the bridge, Melanie had cooked up some eggs and bacon. I wolfed them down like there was no tomorrow. I was still a bit hyperglycaemic from the adrenaline overdose of the night before.

'Bit hungry, big boy?' she asked with a wide grin.

'Yeah, excitement does that to me,' I came back with a cheeky grin.

I picked up the binos and scanned the ocean behind us as Melanie maintained our easterly heading. All I could detect was a large yacht to the southwest and nothing else. My concern was the cartel cruiser could eventually run us down and we had nowhere near the speed or the firepower to then duke it out with the crooks.

'It seems we have a few unanswered questions we need to resolve, and pretty smartly by the sound of it,' Melanie stated in her official voice.

'Yes, we sure do.'

We then listed all of the people who knew we were heading to Bewick Island. Somehow, the Russian and his cronies were expecting us. We gave no indication to anyone that we were headed for Bewick Island. Melanie could not recall Kegs mentioning it recently or even hearing it from him in the past few months. It was always a suspicious site owing to the fact that it was uninhabited – or supposed to be. As far as most people were concerned, we were heading north up the coast. I relieved Melanie at the helm and changed course to due south. The *Delfina* was pushing along at a steady speed without chewing through too much fuel. I was feeling we had been very lucky: me not to get sprung on Bewick Island, and Melanie and the *Delfina* not to get captured.

Melanie was sitting with her elbows on the table and her head in her hands.

'Methinks there is a rat somewhere on the ship,' she eventually exhaled as she leaned back against the seat. 'And I think it's in the AFP. Nobody else knew where we were going, and in fact you were ordered to go there.'

'What, are you saying that Peter Bryant is a mole?' I asked. 'Nah, I don't think so. I am usually a pretty good judge of character and I don't think he is the kind of bloke to set us up.' I hoped I sounded positive, but my brain was running through all the conversations I had recently had with Bryant trying to find a weakness, a slip, anything to indicate treachery. I came up empty.

'Well, it must be someone else in the Ops cell,' Melanie retorted, with a perplexed look on her face.

'Yeah, but who?'

We lapsed into silence, trying to figure out who was the bad apple in the barrel.

Melanie broke the silence with, 'I think we should go off the grid for a while and wait and see who contacts us.'

I didn't have much else to offer except, 'You know, Melanie; I am not a spook and have never been trained as a spook. I have always been the guy to secure an outcome or remove a threat. This is a bit out of my league with intrigue and sneaky peek stuff. I will bow to your suggestions.' I stood at the helm waiting for a response.

Melanie came and stood by my side as we pushed our way through the sparkling sea. It seemed incongruous that we could have all this madness occurring in such an idyllic setting.

'It *has* to be someone close to Bryant – either above or below,' she offered.

'Or … on his level,' I added. 'But how in the hell do we find out who it is? We just can't ring up and ask, "Hey, who is the bad guy down there in the organised crime section", can we?'

'Not really. I think we are going to have to do some more snooping around before we can put questions to anyone,' she responded. 'Perhaps we need to get cunning ourselves and set a trap.' *That's appropriate: a trap to catch a rat.*

I thought about her last statement and wondered what she would have in mind.

'In the meantime, just how are we going to go "off the grid", young lady?' I asked.

'For a start, we need to find somewhere to put the *Delfina* where she won't be found,' Melanie offered.

'That could be tricky.'

'Not if you pay enough hush money to the right people, especially those looking to minimise their taxable income,' she smiled wickedly.

*   *   *

Melanie spent the next half an hour tracking down some guys who worked for National Parks around Cooktown. She arranged that they should meet us near a bridge that passed over the Annan River the next day around 10 a.m. I had no charts of the river and expressed my concern.

'It's alright Skipper, trust your first mate,' she smiled.

We skirted around Cooktown to avoid anyone seeing our vessel, but by now we were also getting low on fuel.

'Thought of that,' Melanie smirked. 'We will have to do some heavy lifting, but it will be fixed.'

I wondered what the hell she had in mind, but I was busy pushing us along at best possible speed. It was now late afternoon and I didn't want to go poking up an unchartered creek in the middle of the night.

Melanie outlined her hastily prepared contingency plan. We would go to an RV where her "friends" would help us disguise the *Delfina*, help us refuel and provide security for a couple of days while we sorted out what to do next. We would tell all and sundry that I had mechanical difficulties and would return to Cairns, but it would take several days. We were really flying by the seat of our pants now.

*   *   *

The sat phone went off just as we dropped anchor a couple of nautical miles from Annan Creek estuary. It was Peter Bryant.

'Where are you, mate?' he asked with concern in his voice. 'Are you in Princess Charlotte Bay yet?'

'Nope. Had a pretty serious problem with my power plant and am returning to Cairns. Should be there in a couple of days,' I said, trying to sound genuine.

'Okay. Did you get to your objective?'

'Negative on all counts,' I said, trying to maintain security.

'Roger, keep me informed. Let me know when you get safely to port. Out.'

Melanie looked across the table at me and asked, 'Do you think he bought it?'

'Dunno. He didn't sound anything other than concerned as to our welfare.'

'You know, whoever is after you, is probably also the same person that had Taylor killed.'

'Yeah, I know, and that worries me,' I mused. 'After overhearing what Kegs had said on Bewick Island about removing Taylor, it is starting to add up, because from all accounts the Russian and his cronies were in on that as well.'

'Well, let's turn in, it has been a long day and we have to come up with some clever cunning plan soon,' Melanie said as she headed for the forward state room.

*   *   *

We were up early the next morning and after breakfast carefully nudged our way up Annan Creek. It was deserted, not even mosquitos would come up here. We chugged along slowly with Melanie keeping a watch over the bow to make sure we didn't find a sandbank although my depth sounder kept telling me it had several metres of water under the hull. After an hour or so, Melanie signalled for me to pull over to an old jetty that looked like it would fall into the water at any moment.

'We're here,' she shouted, and we prepared to moor alongside the decrepit structure.

'How the hell do you know about this place?' I asked.

'Did a job up here a couple of years back,' she said, scanning the riverbank as if expecting someone to appear.

I cut the motors and all we heard was the lapping of the river. Before long, a faded red flat-bed truck came into view. I could only see the top of the cabin as the grass was so long beside the river. The truck stopped and two men in National Parks uniforms climbed out.

'G'day, Mel,' one yelled.

'Hi, Greg,' she called back, 'Come and meet the skipper.'

The two solidly built men walked down the rickety jetty, obviously trusting it to hold their combined weights. I stood on the edge of the quarterdeck and asked them aboard.

Melanie did the introductions.

'Bob, this is Barry and Greg.' We exchanged giddays and shook hands. Barry stood about 6 feet tall in the old measurement and probably weighed about 110 kilos. He had the look about him that said *don't screw me around or I will rip your head off and piss in the hole. Probably a rugby forward, I would guess.* Greg was a bit lighter in build but looked really fit and had a well-tanned complexion. His nose was straight, and his hair was reasonably short in an almost crew-cut style. *Looks like he can handle himself as well, probably a distance runner methinks.*

'Understand you need someone to look after your boat, Skipper,' Barry asked.

'I do?'

'Yep, sure you do, Bob,' he replied, smiling at Melanie knowingly.

Melanie joined in, adding 'While we go into town and poke around, Barry and Greg here are going to do some "remodelling" while we are away, and fill her up with fuel.'

Melanie could see the look of distrust in my eyes and quickly jumped back in with an explanation.

'Barry and Greg do work for our agency from time to time, so they know the rules,' Melanie winked. 'They also have enough firepower to not only kill crocs around here but repel boarders as well.'

'I see,' I responded.

Melanie stood directly in front of me and said in her serious voice. 'You are going to have to trust me on this, Bob. I can't say too much but not everyone who works for us has a big AFP badge tattooed on their forehead.'

'I see ...,' I murmured, trying not to sound too suspicious.

The two men smiled at Melanie's attempt at black humour.

'We know the drill, Skipper. We'll look after things while you are away. Take our truck because it's a good cover.' He slipped a piece of paper into my hand. 'Here is a joint you can stay at just outside town where you should be undisturbed. Mel knows the layout,' Greg joined in, nodding to Melanie as he spoke.

We spent the next hour wheeling 200 litre-drums of dieso down to the boat where the guys set up a pump and started refuelling the *Delfina*. I looked in apprehension at a couple of boxes of tools and assorted equipment that could have dismantled the *Titanic*. We discussed our outline plan of trying to determine who was who in the zoo in Cooktown, and how we could move around. There were spare uniforms for us to wear while in town to help us blend in, and the Dry season tourist trade would help us blend into the people moving around town.

We agreed to RV back at the *Delfina* in a couple of days, drew up a couple of contingency plans and packed for a few days serious recon in town that was about a 30-minutes' drive away. The guys were intending to remove the flying bridge and lower the look of the superstructure, throw in some paint lines, and generally remove the signature look of a 60-foot Vitech Flybridge cabin cruiser. Just as we were about to climb into the red Isuzu truck Pete asked, 'What do you wanna call your new boat?' I looked at him, swivelled to look at Melanie and she shot back, *The Office*. I nodded and we headed for the truck.

Cooktown

Melanie threw our gear into the back of the truck and drove out through the kunai grass, heading for the road into Cooktown. The drive was uneventful apart from some Grey Nomads driving their bloody caravans too close to each other and making passing a chore — if not almost impossible. The tenth van that I came upon had the occupants' names on a neat sign in the rear window. I rang Elsie and Ray on their CB radio that had the frequency plastered across the back of the van and asked them to drive a little further apart and expecting an 'Agro' response, instead I got a very professional 'roger out' from Elsie. *I bet your old man is an ex-Army bugger.*

We got into the outskirts of Cooktown just before noon and headed off down a road that took us towards the airport. I had been to this little town — probably best described as an outpost — years before on a big training exercise, and nothing much seemed to have changed in 15 years. We crossed the Endeavour River and were heading out past the end of the town airstrip when we found the dirt road we were looking for and drove slowly down towards the house that would be home for a couple of days. We stopped a couple of hundred metres short, and I got out of the passenger side without shutting the door. I told Melanie to give me 10 minutes and then drive up to the house. She nodded, and her eyes widened when she saw me tuck my Glock into the waistband of my shorts and pull my shirt over the top. 'Expecting trouble?' she queried.

'The way things are going, I am not taking any more chances.'

Keeping behind any cover I could find, I headed off into the light bush to come around the property from the rear to ensure we weren't walking — or driving — into any trap.

I quickly made my way around the outbuildings of a shed and a decrepit dunny that looked like it should have been demolished years ago. There were no vehicles or motorbikes around that I could see. There were no tyre tracks or footprints in the dirt and loose gravel around the back yard. I closed up behind the rear steps of the house that was a typical high-set Queenslander. I waited under the rear of the wooden house near a laundry and listened for Melanie's arrival.

The truck pulled up and I heard Melanie climb the front stairs. She knocked on the door and I then heard her footfalls as she walked steadily through the house. The back flyscreen door opened and Melanie called down 'All clear'. We did a quick search of the house. I checked each doorway as we entered a room to clear for wires or booby traps. Nothing. Melanie looked for stores and food while I searched for surveillance and listening devices. Again, nothing on all fronts. We would need some food and basic essentials for a couple of days.

'We can go down to Morton's Store near the airstrip to get some stuff,' Melanie offered.

'Sounds like a plan. Let's put our stuff somewhere secure in case we have uninvited guests while we are away.'

I made a stash of my second handgun and ammo in the shed and Melanie put together a grab bag in case we had to leg it in a hurry. We jumped back in the truck and headed towards town. We passed the end of the airstrip and I saw an Army chopper on the refuelling apron. We drove up to the store and stopped in the gravel parking area. Outside the wooden store there was an empty Army Land Rover and a young digger demolishing a pie. He was too intent on stuffing the pie into his mouth to say hello as we walked up the low stairs into the shop. Inside what was basically a small general store, was an Army pilot resplendent in powder-blue beret, ordering a coffee and a hamburger. We nodded greetings as the lady behind the counter took his order and told him to make himself comfortable while she got his food ready. Melanie busied herself walking around the set of well-stocked shelves, grabbing supplies and filling a plastic basket with food.

I looked out the window as another four-wheel drive pulled up in a cloud of dust and an elderly woman who obviously had some serious business to attend to stormed up the stairs and burst in through the fly-screened door. She was on a mission and of that there was no doubt.

'Ah, just the bugger I want to speak to,' she thundered in a voice that took me by surprise. She sounded like an army sergeant bellowing parade ground orders. And all of this coming from a female who barely stood 170 centimetres tall. She was tough and wiry, and her hands were on her hips of her faded jeans. 'The mob at the airport told me you'd be down here.'

'I'm sorry, ma'am,' the male pilot replied, looking a bit perplexed. 'What seems to be the trouble?'

'You, in your bloody aeroplanes using my airstrip at all hours of the bloody night, without so much as a "by your leave" … that's my problem young fella,' she thundered, legs akimbo and looking like she was about to take a shotgun to the aviator.

'I am not sure what you are talking about. Where is your property, ma'am?' The pilot started pulling a map out of his flying suit trouser pocket and walked over to a coffee table and spread the map out.

'Just here,' she snapped as she stabbed the map with a gnarled and weather-beaten finger that looked like it had done its fair share of hard work. 'Just north of the Lion's Den. Our property is called Bamboo,' she said as she straightened and fixed the pilot with a steely glare.

'Well, I'm sorry about that, but we haven't been on your airstrip and we would have no need to. I am doing communications checks for the exercise later this year and I do not need to land on any airstrip unless we need to get a land clearance, or wish to speak to the manager or the owners,' he said quietly but firmly, hoping she would be satisfied.

'Bullshit! You just don't wanna get into any strife for not asking permission,' she shot back.

The pilot was being very much aware that he was now in the spotlight as his driver had re-entered the shop. Two more customers and the shopkeeper's wife had all gathered to listen in to the altercation.

'Tell me, ma'am,' the pilot asked as he folded up his map and took out his log book, 'When did you say your airstrip was being used?'

'Last Tuesday night … well after midnight, and the Friday before that … and a couple of days before that. All in the middle of the bloody night! I know youse Army blokes have been up here looking around for that big thing you got goin' later this year,' she added accusingly, with eyes glaring into the young captain's eyes. 'So, what's the story?' she asked.

The pilot referred to his notebook and said calmly, 'Well, Mrs …?'

'It's **Ms** and it's **Betty**,' she snapped back sternly.

'Well, Betty,' the handsome young pilot said as he flipped open his log book, 'We don't usually fly at night on the sort of jobs we are doing because we have limited night flying equipment, and I am the only pilot. So, I am usually not able to fly at night except in an emergency. The other thing is, last Tuesday we were up in Coen for the night and didn't return to Cooktown until Wednesday afternoon.' He offered the logbook for Betty to peruse. She pulled a pair of glasses out of her shirt pocket and stared down at the place where the pilot was indicating.

Betty's eyes narrowed and her stance softened.

'Tell me, Betty, what did the aircraft sound like when it took off?' the pilot asked with what he knew was going to be his trump card.

'Like any small plane around here,' she said adding, 'Like the ones the crop dusters use.'

'Ah,' he offered with a slight smile crossing his face. 'Well, the Army is only using a chopper around this area at the moment,' he replied, replacing his logbook. 'It must have been someone else. Perhaps you should let the police in Cooktown know,' he finished.

'Yeah, righto. Okay. Sorry about that young fella. I'll let Tim know.' Betty offered her hand in a conciliatory handshake and left the store.

The crowd dispersed as the issue dissolved into silence and the pilot took his hamburger and coffee and left with his driver.

Melanie was looking at me to see my reaction and I gave her the nod to join me out the front.

We caught up with the pilot as he was sitting on a bench seat under the large mango tree out the front of the shop, tucking into his hamburger.

'G'day, mate,' I offered. 'Couldn't help but overhear Betty inside before. What are you Army blokes doing up here?'

'We are proving our comms for a big multi-nation exercise later this year and we want to make sure we can grab the best frequencies for safety and aircraft coordination,' he said matter-of-factly in his best official sounding voice. He nodded towards the shop saying, 'We don't need to fly at night, and I haven't got the kit for it anyway. And ... I would not use someone's strip without asking unless it was an emergency.'

'Okay, thanks.' I said trying to sound like an inquisitive tourist. 'What sort of a chopper do you fly?'

'A Bell Jet Ranger,' he said, 'We call it a Kiowa. Looks like the choppers the TV stations have'.

'Oh yeah, I know. Thanks mate,' and we headed back inside.

After paying for the groceries and grabbing what would have to have been one of the best burgers on the east coast of Australia, we headed back to the house. Just after we turned off, we slowed to see if anyone had driven over the small stick I had placed on the track. Nothing.

*　　*　　*

After unpacking our groceries, we agreed that we should head into town and see how things were. Melanie had a few old contacts and thought she might be able to find out from the local Shire Council guys where Betty's property was so we could check out the strip. We headed off into town, resetting our improvised security checks, and Melanie was scrolling through her mobile phone.

'Drop me at the Cooktown Shire council building and I'll catch up with you at the Top pub,' she said, checking the side mirrors and making sure we were not being followed once out on the main road into town. The truck's aircon was busted and we had the windows down, trying to get some cool air into the vehicle cabin. It had to be 38 degrees Celsius and 70 per cent humidity outside.

'Okay. I'll just hang around the main bar and see what I can pick up from the locals,' I responded. 'This is like fishing without any bait on the hook.'

'I know, but it's the best we can do until we make the *Delfina* disappear,' she replied, looking at me with a shrug of hoping for the best.

I stopped the truck short of the Council building so it might not be noticed, and Melanie headed off with her well-tanned legs under her denim shorts looking as good as ever. I parked around the back of the Imperial Hotel and walked around the wide wooden veranda and into the main bar. It was distinctly cooler inside, with fans lazily rotating under a very high ceiling. Fishing memorabilia and happy snaps of fisher folk holding enormous reef fish were hung haphazardly around the walls. *They sure like fishing up these ways.* I ordered a middy of beer from the barmaid who looked like a refugee from World

Championship Wrestling, and sat on a stool. She grabbed a chilled glass out of the bar fridge and pulled a XXXX draught beer. There were about a dozen locals, mostly men wearing hats, sitting quietly talking among themselves. Three younger men were playing pool in an area off to the side of the bar. No one looked out of place. I pulled out a map as if I was a tourist checking where I should be heading next. A couple of men along the bar looked at me and smiled to each other knowingly, probably thinking, *another city slicker on his big four-wheel drive adventure.* Both were wearing tattered rugby league supporters' T-shirts. One had a Broncos Power's beer sponsor on it, and it had to be at least 20 years old. The odd thing though was he was wearing a pair of old army ankle boots. Not the normal footwear in the land of the flip flop or thong one normally sees in the tropics.

I looked up and then along at the two men and asked, 'Are you blokes from around here?'

'Yup,' one replied as he sipped from his glass. 'What, are you lost or something, mate?' he said with a slight snigger.

'Nah,' I said, sliding off my stool and walking up and placing myself between them and spreading the map on the bar. 'I just wanted to see where I could do some white-water rafting.' I was hoping that by kicking my old cover story back in I might get some good oil on who was who in the zoo in Cooktown.

'Yeah?' my new chums chimed back in. 'When are you looking to do that?'

I had a feeling these two men were looking for some extra work and/ or a cash opportunity to supplement their normal income.

'Probably once the Wet is over next year. The company I work for wants to start cashing in on young Japanese kids who would fly into Cairns and then do their big jungle adventure,' I said, trying to sound like I did this sort of stuff every day.

I looked down at Bronco's ankle boots and said, 'Where the hell did you get those ABs?'

'I get 'em from a disposal store in Cairns. Can't beat a good pair of boots,' he stated proudly.

His mate chimed in, 'Silly bastard only wears those clodhoppers, that's why we call him Boots.'

'What's this down here?' I asked, pointing at what looked like an airstrip south of Black Mountain.

'Ah ... that's an old World War Two bomber strip,' the younger bloke in a Cronulla Sharks T-shirt said, peering down where I had my finger pointed.

'Is it still serviceable?' I asked, looking at other places on the map to avoid looking too interested. 'I always have to have an emergency evacuation plan for the tourists in case they go a gutser,' I said nonchalantly.

'Yeah, it's part of old Betty's property, although I think the Council mow it for her because she hasn't got a slasher.'

'Okay, and what about rivers and creeks I could use for rafting?' I said, maintaining the cover story.

'Not a lot really, you need to go higher up onto the plateau to get some serious water,' the fellow in the Broncos T-shirt replied. He obviously knew the ground around Cooktown.

As we continued looking at places on the map, Melanie walked into the bar. The conversation stopped abruptly as my two new mates ogled Melanie's toned body.

'Hi, fellas,' she quipped as she looked down at the map. 'Hey, Bob, are we ready to go?'

'Sure,' I said, 'These fellas were just pointing out some places where we could do the rafting,' hoping she would pick up on my lead.

'Oh, good,' she shot back, 'I have found a place for us to stay while we check out the sites,' as she dragged me away from the bar and toward the veranda.

Outside Melanie stepped closer to me and said in a hushed sotto voice through clenched teeth, 'We've gotta move … now!'

We made our way to the rear of the hotel and drove to the lookout above the town. We got out as if to check the view and I asked, 'What's the go?'

Melanie spread the map on the bonnet of the truck and said, 'Well, I know where Betty lives.'

'Yeah, down near the old airstrip at Helenvale,' I put in. Melanie looked at me in a manner that indicated I should shut up until she finished. So I did.

'Right, and it is used by a few locals who have light aircraft and travel down to Cairns, but the usage is quite low.' She pulled a notebook out of her denim shorts, adding, 'But, Betty has a lease on it and she is able to charge maintenance and so on for the emergency lighting and general tidiness of the hangars. I spoke to the lady that manages leases and so on around town and she said that light aircraft use in the area has gone up a notch in the last year, and the folk at Cooktown are not amused because they are not using the CASA facility.'

'Can't blame them, that way they avoid paying landing fees,' I quickly put in.

'Yes, but they are also not talking to the air traffic control or filing flight plans,' Melanie said, 'And the Civil Aviation guys are not happy about it either.'

'Sounds like someone is using the strip at Betty's place to make illicit flights,' I opined.

'Sure does, but I also picked up that some "foreigners" have been around lately, and they haven't been too friendly.'

'Is that so?' I asked.

'Yep, and they have acquired a piece of Australia just off-shore,' she checked her notebook quickly, 'called Blackbird Patches, which National Parks off-loaded several years ago because the endangered species there all got wiped out by a mysterious virus.'

'I see.'

'From what I could glean from my friends in Council, no-one is welcome on Blackbird Patches and the occupants of this little rock value their privacy greatly.'

'Hmmm. Perhaps we should pay them a visit?' I asked, looking at Melanie's map where she had circled Blackbird Patches. 'What's on this intriguing little island?'

'Not much from what I could gather. It has water, a jetty, a cabin or two but really pretty basic. The girl who looks after the rates said that they never see the owners, but everything is always paid on time from an account overseas.'

I pored over the map looking at Blackbird Patches which was due east of Cooktown and about forty nautical miles off shore. It was a speck on the chart and probably only 25 hectares in size. Not that big really, and not too many places to hide anything.

'Whoever owns it has done some work on the place, because a landing craft ferried a lot of stores over there six or seven months ago and something serious was being built. Whatever it was has never been inspected because the owners maintain the "work is in progress", and no-one in town is pushing the envelope.' Melanie finished with one raised eyebrow. 'My friend thinks the Shire inspector has been paid not to ask too many questions.'

'Anything else?' I asked.

'Yep. I think I saw one of the crooks that was in Cairns. I'm pretty sure it was Kegs.'

'Oh, Christ! If he sees us, we're dead,' I said quietly. 'Was anyone with him?'

'Couldn't see or pick that up. I was more worried about him seeing me to be honest,' she said apologetically.

'Of course, and you're not easy to miss, young lady,' I said, climbing back into the truck. 'Let's get back to the house and make a plan.'

* * *

Back at the safe house we made a coffee and started trying to connect the dots. If someone on the inside, actually in the AFP Ops cell, had tipped off the crooks, then that would explain why they were expecting me on Bewick Island. The fact that someone was flying out of airstrips at night in a light aircraft had all the hallmarks of what I had recced back in Gordonvale months ago; close to an ingress from off shore, an unmonitored strip capable of handling light aircraft of considerable size – and in the middle of bloody nowhere.

I tried to think of who was working in the Ops cell when things had started to go sour. There was Peter Bryant, my handler who I just couldn't imagine being a bad apple — and I liked him. Then we had the boss Superintendent Ballantyne, and he was as straight as a dye — and I liked him. And then the AONA; add in Frank Benning, ex-army and someone I thought was shifty – and I didn't like him. Was it all too easy? What about Melanie? I saw her in Townsville with the bad guys, but Peter Bryant vouches for her and says she is okay. Her story of her association with them sounded very plausible, but then I might have had the rose-coloured glasses on as well, given our time up on the Tableland together. What if there was more than one mole? *Christ, there's enough money to keep everyone happy in this drug trade.*

Melanie interrupted my thought process with 'A penny for your thoughts, Skipper.'

I looked up from the notes I had scribbled down and the links connecting everyone, and I must have had a guilty look in my eye.

'Yeah, I am just trying to see where the weak link might be.'

'And?'

'Well, apart from me, everyone is capable of being crooked,' I said, trying to sound light-hearted.

'Oh really, and what puts **you** in the clear, Mister Squeaky Clean?' she retorted, looking just a trifle wounded.

'Good God, Mel, I am stumped on this. How the hell can we sort out the wheat from the chaff?'

'Who do you suspect the most … and if my name comes into this, I will cut your balls off, Bob McTaggart,' she said quietly, but her words were dripping with menace. *I think she means it.*

'Well, since Taylor was murdered, there has been one bloke in the picture who I haven't got a lot of information on … and I just can't warm to him.'

'Who's that?'

'The guy from ONA , you know, the ex-army major. Frank Benning.'

'I think I only ever met him once in Canberra,' Melanie mused. 'What makes you think it is him?'

'Just a gut feeling, I guess,' I shrugged.

'I like gut feelings,' Melanie said as she put the kettle on the stove. 'Why don't we set him up for a fall?'

'And how would we do that?' I asked.

'Give him something that nobody else knows about and see if we get a bite.' She shrugged.

'Okay …' I paused, trying to think how we could possibly arrange a trap.

'Let's say we leak something into the system but only he is the sole recipient?'

'Okay …'

'I'll get his mobile number from Ops on the pretence of something else and scatter some burley on the water,' Melanie said thoughtfully.

'And we'll wait and see if the fish take the bait,' I added, staying in the simile mode.

'Why don't we drop something like we know where the stuff is being flown out from and if that's the case, he'll tell the Russian and then he'll send the goons to sort it out.'

'Right, and the only way the Russian would know and react is if he gets something from Benning,' I finished.

'As long as Benning doesn't tell anyone else,' Melanie said with a concerned look crossing her face. 'That could be the tricky part.' She paused. 'Because if he is clean, and tells someone else what is going on, then we are back to square one.'

'What if we put a "need to know" marker on the text and for his eyes only?' I asked.

'That could work.'

*   *   *

We spent the afternoon assembling a list of scenarios that we could put into a message for Benning's phone. There were a set of message markers that most operators used to identify the veracity of a message including code words or phrases. Melanie contacted Canberra, asking to speak to another section, saying her phone had been damaged and she had lost her address book. It took some smooth talking, but she eventually got Benning's work mobile. It was starting to come together. We knew it would take a day or two for things to gel, so we decided to head back to the *Delfina* to do a covert recce of Blackbird Patches and take it from there. Melanie rang the guys on the boat, and they said we could come and collect the boat first thing in the morning.

I used the satellite phone to send a message to Benning, knowing he would identify the phone number as coming from me. The text message read:

P.B. Change of plans. Have discovered egress for shipments. In Cairns and will be in Cooktown and gather intel for next couple of days. Lost boat in fire after engine explosion. Not suspicious. Have arranged ground transport through old boy net. RV at safe house in one week. Wait out. BM

Now all we hoped was that Benning thought the message was for Peter Bryant and that he would alert the Russian and set the train in motion. We also hoped that he thought we no longer had a boat and the risk of us looking at Blackbird Patches was now minimal. Hopefully, they would let their guard down and I could get to see what was happening offshore.

I needed some gear from in town so the next morning we drove in and found a store where I could get some lightweight camping rations for emergency use. Around 11 a.m., I dropped into the pub and sure enough my two mates from the previous day were there holding up the bar. We exchanged greetings and they asked how my recce was going and I said I had mixed joy and avoided any direct answers. Then the Broncos T-shirt asked, 'You don't have a boat with ya, do ya?'

'Why?'

'Cause there's a fella goin' around town offerin' big bucks to anyone who has seen his stolen boat,' he replied, taking a swig from his chilled glass. I noticed his mate was watching me closely.

'Nah. The only boats we use are for rafting,' I said. 'What sort of boat is it?'

'Big fucker, about a 60-footer. Got a wog name … Desa something.' His mate chimed in, '*Delfina*, got a fly-bridge and everything.'

I tried to sound interested and asked, 'How much is he offering?'

'Fifty grand!'

'Jesus!' I whistled. Now I was impressed that the Russian was keen to get his hands on Melanie and me. 'Must be some boat.'

'Yeah, the bloke wants his boat back really bad. He said that whoever took it is dead meat if they catch 'im.'

'I bet. Jeez, for fifty grand, he must be keen. If I see it, who do I tell?'

As quick as a flash the two drinking buddies said, 'Come and tell us and we'll make sure he knows.'

I looked at the two cheesy-grinning half-drunken bar flies and thought, *Yeah right, and there goes my reward … and my life.*

'Well, I don't think I am likely to see a boat up a white-water river, but I'll keep my eye out,' and turned and left the bar. Melanie picked me up near the Post Office where she had been gossiping with the lady in the local souvenir shop to see what else she could find out. I almost didn't recognise her in a large floppy straw hat and sunnies.

'What's the go?' she asked as I climbed into the truck.

'The crooks are onto us, I think. They are asking about the *Delfina* and telling the locals it is a stolen boat.'

'They must know we are around somewhere,' she said. 'Glad we are giving the old girl a make-over.'

'It didn't take long for Benning to push the panic button either,' I added. 'The sooner we find out what is on Blackbird Patches the better,' I said. 'Have we got access to any long arms around here? A rifle to give us a standoff capability might come in handy, methinks.'

'I am glad you asked that question, Skipper,' Melanie smiled back, looking like a cat that had just swallowed a canary.

*   *   *

Back at the farmhouse I followed Melanie down to one of the sheds, and after moving a few empty boxes around, uncovered a trunk buried in the dirt floor. It was an arms cache similar to ones I had seen in Afghanistan where the locals used to hide their weapons when the Allies would rumble through, looking for dissidents.

I took out a .308 Remington 700P rifle which I had last seen being used in our SAS sniper section training in Perth. I was impressed. This was a sniper rifle used around the world because of its toughness, reliability, and ease of maintenance. There was a waterproof bag next to it and what looked like a seven-power scope.

'We keep these at most of our safe houses, just in case,' Melanie said, taking the weapon out and passing me a cleaning kit. 'Will this do?'

'It's bolt action but I reckon it will be just what we need. Have you ever fired one of these?'

'I did on Majura Range down in Canberra, during orientation,' she replied. 'Why?'

'Because you are going to be my fire support if things get ugly on the island. I will need you to stay on the boat and be the cavalry if I get into strife.'

'I thought it would be better if I was with you on Blackbird?' she asked.

'No use both of us getting jammed. Someone needs to be able to hit the toe if the other gets caught.'

Melanie looked at me with a quizzical look on her face. 'You know, you are sounding awfully negative about this, Bob.'

'Yep, and that's because we don't have any detailed maps of the island; we don't know what security they might have deployed, and we don't know how many people are on this bit of dirt. In fact, we know bugger all. To be honest Mel, we are going in blind and on this kind of recce our chances of success are only 50-50.'

She looked at me with a concerned look on her face. 'Shouldn't we enlist the help of someone else then? What about Greg and Barry?'

'I was going to get those two fellas keep an eye out at Betty's strip,' I said. 'They could give us early warning if something starts getting heavy.'

'Righto, let's get this beast ready for action and grab some dinner,' Melanie threw back. 'I'll ring Greg and tell him we will be down tomorrow after first light.'

*   *   *

We took turns during the night, doing two-hour shifts to maintain a lookout, and apart from some seriously noisy possums who sounded like they were wearing hob-nailed boots and doing line dancing on the corrugated iron roof, all was quiet. I had set some trip wires with cans on the stairs but nothing eventuated. I would have liked to have passed the night away in more pleasurable pursuits, but this definitely wasn't the time nor the place. At least our safe house was secure.

We packed our stores for the return to the *Delfina,* and after tidying up the safe house and removing any visible trace of our presence, we set off. I drove the red truck and Melanie maintained a lookout for any tail. The main road was relatively free of traffic and only the occasional four-wheel drive passed us heading into town.

We bumped our way down the dirt track through the long grass to the jetty. Greg and Barry were sitting on the jetty next to a boat that was totally unrecognisable. I climbed out of the cabin and stood on the rickety wharf and must have looked like a stunned mullet.

Melanie was first to speak. 'You alright, Skipper?'

'Christ,' I said, 'Where's my boat gone?' It was incredible. Tied up in front of me was a boat that looked like any of the dozens of game fishing boats along the east coast. Just bigger.

The two boat renovators stood up; arms folded, and looked very happy with themselves. 'Yeah, sorry about that, Bob,' Barry said, 'we had to chop the flybridge off and make up a few portholes to give the impression of a Bertram 60 or something like that. We put a stripe along the side to make it look flatter, and Greg painted on some portholes to change the front end. We used some material from the flybridge to put a mock weather station on the front. Welcome to *The Office*.'

'Thanks guys, I think,' I uttered quietly. I was shattered. My beloved boat had been chopped and channelled and done over. 'The only good thing — I guess — is that now we have a cover for the next phase of the op.'

Melanie briefed the guys on what had gone down in town and the search for the *Delfina*. They all agreed that what we had done was timely. Melanie also told them about the plan to recce Blackbird Patches and things went quiet.

'You sure you want to do that, Bob?' Greg asked. 'These blokes sound like they don't muck around with strangers. We heard on the local grapevine that they had armed security guards on the island.'

'I have run into them before,' I said. 'They are not Special Forces types and I think I can get the drop on them.'

'I bloody hope so, mate, because reinforcements are a long way south of here,' Barry put in. 'What about getting a Terrorist Assault Group from the Army up here on the grounds of a terrorist threat?' he asked.

'If we do call in a TAG it will show our hand straight away and the birds will have well and truly flown,' Melanie said bluntly, 'Besides, we are pretty sure there's a bad apple in the barrel and we want to catch the bastard. I'm sure they will call in the Special Ops Team. They don't stick out like the TAG tends to these days.'

'Let's get our gear stowed on board and run through the plan for the next 48 hours,' I said. 'We've got some contingency planning to sort out.'

'I bet we do,' Greg offered, 'This will not be a walk in the park.'

*   *   *

We spent the majority of the morning thrashing out plans for doing the boat recce of the Blackbird Patches, getting ashore, and extracting. Barry and Greg were no mugs when it came to sorting out how they would overwatch the airstrip and had plans for how to disable any aircraft venturing in after dark. They would also "borrow" some flares from the marina and make sure they had good comms with the *Delfina*/*Office* and Melanie while we were at sea. It was decided that the creek was our RV if things turned to shit and failing that, the safe house outside Cooktown. Barry and Greg had access to some serious rifles from the National Parks rangers who always carried large bore weaponry in case of crocodiles, rogue buffalo or pig attacks.

Things were about to get interesting.

Blackbird Patches

I spent the early afternoon studying the charts around Blackbird Patches and checked the currents and tidal flow for that evening. It wouldn't be a cakewalk but it was going to be easier than my last swim. We set off down the creek with the goal of getting within a kilometre or so at last light, making identification of who we were or where we were anchored difficult. I wanted to be west of the target so that anyone looking our way would only get a silhouette and not see too much else. We would leave the running lights off and only turn them on if someone came near.

As we approached our laying-up position, I went through the plan with Melanie one more time. 'Okay, so if I am not back on board by 5 a.m.?'

'I will weigh anchor and move two clicks to the south of the island,' she shot back.

'And?'

'And wait until 5 a.m. the next day,' she said somewhat forlornly.

'If I am not back by the second RV time?' I continued, checking our notes.

'Weigh anchor and head back to Cairns and radio Peter Bryant,' she answered stiffly.

'What if someone approaches while you are laying up?' I asked.

'I will tell them I am with James Cook University and doing reef soundings and checking for Crown of Thorns starfish infestation,' she answered with a slight smile.

'Right, and if things look untidy?' I questioned.

'Jettison the anchor and hit the toe – as you put it,' she answered firmly, looking me in the eyes.

'Fine, Mel. It's important that if anyone does approach you, you have the motor running so you can shoot and scoot. This switch here,' I pointed to a red button on the console to the right of the running light switch, 'will unleash the capstan. We will lose the pick and chain, but it will make us a tonne lighter. It will give you a standing start and they won't be expecting it. Stay in the main channel and get on the blower with a distress call and tell whoever is on the frequency that you have seen people looking like terrorists acting suspiciously. That will bring them running.' I looked at Melanie as I finished. 'Questions?'

'Nope.'

Things went quiet and I double-checked my gear for a scuba swim to shore. I couldn't risk being seen on the surface and I was hoping that the currents at 15 metres would not be as severe in deeper water.

I checked my wrist compass and dropped over the side once it got dark. I could feel my heart beating in my chest. I liked that. It kept me on my toes, and my adrenaline levels were pumping. *Just like the old days.* The water was cooler than I expected, and I pumped my legs steadily as I headed towards what I hoped would be a deserted strip of sand near a thin point of land. I was banking on a shoal being near the beach and using it as cover while I made my way through the shallower waters.

Around 7.30 p.m. I felt the water getting warmer and I could sense the surge of shallow water above me. I surfaced and could make out the outline of my destination. I headed for the lee side on the south. I slowly rotated to make sure there were no other boats and could barely make out the *Delfina*. I couldn't bring myself to call her *The Office*. The moon was not yet up, and Melanie was keeping the boat in the dark and had no lights showing. *So far so good.*

Luckily, the bottom was a mixture of sand and small rocky coral outcrops. I swam in less than half a metre of water until I had the rocky point next to me. I stood and slowly got my bearings. I heard nothing but the lapping of very small waves on the gritty sand. There was no wind to speak of. I would have to be very careful moving around. I stowed my scuba gear in a small depression next to a shrubby tree and noted a large cabbage tree palm about 10 metres distant that was leaning to the southwest. That would be my emergency RV point.

I shrugged out of my wetsuit and opened my waterproof holdall that had been clipped to my chest. I took out my night vision goggles and utility belt that carried one pistol holster. I never liked shoulder holsters because they impeded my arms in a fight and if I needed to do some serious climbing in a hurry. I fastened my leg holster and secured a second pistol. I had loaded both weapons prior to leaving the *Delfina*. I checked the safety catch on both guns and put my backpack on. I had enough goodies to get me out of trouble if things went pear-shaped.

The evening air was milder than I expected. With almost no wind it was as quiet as a church. I was hoping it would stay that way. I knelt down on one knee next to a scraggly acacia bush and waited for my night vision to kick in. I didn't want to use my goggles until I really had to and wanted to save the batteries. The ground was rocky but firm under foot. It was easy moving quietly, and I started heading for the only piece of high ground I could see. After 15 minutes of picking my way through low scrub, I stopped on a smooth bare rock about the size of a tennis court. I sat down and began to slowly sweep the area below me as methodically as I could. I always carried a telescope lens that gave good distance, but you paid the price with a limited field of vision. I started searching the ground closest to me at around 250 metres distant. I swept from left to right and then went out another 250 metres until I started to lose clarity. It was on the third sweep that something caught my eye.

It looked like light was shining upwards from a hole in the ground or from a subterranean vent or some such device. The light was muted and not very strong, but it was definitely man-made. I stood to get another perspective and was now sure that light was coming out of the ground. It was time to take a closer look. I looked back towards the *Delfina* but could not make out the shape of the boat in the inky blackness of the water. The moon would be coming up in about four hours, so I wanted to make best use of the darkness. I hadn't gone more than 50 metres towards my objective when ambient light reflected off what looked like a pipe sticking out of the ground. It had a chimney pot type cover, and I could smell something like industrial cleaner. I carefully lowered myself onto the ground next to the pipe to get a better sniff at the air, and then heard the unmistakable sound of human voices — albeit muted and distorted. It had to be an air vent. I was lucky I hadn't tripped over the bloody thing but now noticed that there was a pile of light grey dirt not more than three metres away. Obviously the spoil from the air vent hole.

I now needed to find out how many more vents there were to get an idea of what I was dealing with here. *How organised were these people and what the hell were they doing under here?* I now located the source of the light coming out of the ground. The trapdoor to the stairs leading down into what was obviously an underground chamber of some sort had not been closed properly. I skirted around the entrance and after another five minutes found another air vent. From the look of it this was a pretty big hole in the ground. I couldn't find where the spoil was hidden, but it may very well have been removed totally from the site. From my reckoning I was now confronted with an underground chamber about 25 metres square. *Big enough for a drug lab or a processing area for anything else illegal.* This was no amateur operation. My early warning light was now full on in the back of my head, and I figured there had to be some sort of security. One doesn't go to all this trouble and hope nobody drops in unexpectedly. It was time to just lay low and wait and see what happens. I made my way back to where I found the first vent and found a little copse of low bushes in which to lay in wait. The air was getting a little cooler and a very light wind was starting to blow. Occasionally, the sound of voices would peak as the wind shifted slightly. From the pitch and tone of the voices, there were at least three or four people below me.

Surveillance can often be as boring as bat shit, and countless hours spent just waiting for the target to make a move, even if it is simply hanging out the washing, which can tell you how many others are inside a house. I swept the area north of the lab towards the only structure on the island but saw nothing. I started making up a plan for heading down to the cabin and sheds near the jetty. There was a dry creek line that seemed to head that way that would give me a covered ingress, and I thought that now would be the time to use my goggles to make sure I didn't walk into any early warning devices or, worse still – any crooks.

The light source suddenly changed to red and the trapdoor swung open and two men emerged from the chamber. They were no more than ten metres from my hidey hole. I heard one walk across the gravelly soil and then the unmistakable sound of him having a piss, punctuated with a loud fart. The other male sniggered and said in a low guttural voice,

'Glad you didn't do that down there or the bitch would have killed you.'

'Golden rule, Kegs. Never fart in the lab.'

Christ, this bloke Kegs gets around. He was always popping up whenever stuff was being moved around by the mob. It was now all starting to come together. Whoever Kegs was working for was the mastermind behind the drops of drugs at sea. And now, here we had what was starting to look like a methamphetamine lab of some sort. There was no shortage of clients for the stuff known as "ice". From what I had heard from the narcs in the AFP, getting hooked on ice was more or less a death sentence, and they considered it a greater threat to society than heroin.

The fatter of the two men than cupped his hands around the end of a cigarette and lit up. He had his back to me, and I couldn't get a look at his face. The second male who had relieved himself lit his smoke off the one held by the bloke called Kegs.

'How long before we get off this fuckin' rock do ya reckon?'

'Dunno, Bart, but it must be soon 'cause Franz reckons the Feds are getting close, and we have enough shit for a plane load.'

'How the fuck does he know that?' Bart asked, while turning to look straight at me. I hoped he couldn't see anything that would give my position away.

'He has mates in the right places,' Kegs said while grinding his smoke out on the ground with his boot. 'C'mon, back to work before Madam Lash jumps out and rips our nuts off.'

The two men hovered over the trap door, knocked sharply twice and then a pause before knocking again three times. The trapdoor opened and red light emanated from the chamber. The two men disappeared into the underground lab, and this time the door was closed properly. I was in pitch blackness again. I waited for five minutes before standing to take off my backpack and get out my NVG. I strapped the goggles on, adjusted the head straps and moved towards the small gully that I hoped would lead down to the cabins by the jetty.

My world was now shades of green as various shrubs and trees reflected varying degrees of heat. The image intensification allowed me to make out the terrain, but I still had to move slowly as I made my way down the dry creek bed. I was now in low ground and dominated by ground some ten metres above me. I never liked moving like this, but sometimes you had no option in order to avoid detection. After 20 minutes I was in open ground and I started looking for cover as I made out a cabin with a light on inside. The adjoining shed, some 20 metres away, was in total darkness. The cabin looked like a two- or three-bedroom affair with a veranda on which were several folding chairs and a small table.

I decided to skirt around the cabins and shed and do a tight circuit to see if there were any early warning devices or other surprises. I checked my holster for the readying assurance my handgun was available. The goggles gave me a great advantage. I caught a glimpse of someone inside the cabin with what looked like a coffee mug in his paw. He seemed to be talking to someone else who was hidden from view. So far, I had three or possibly four nasties up on the hill and at least another two down here. I came up behind the shed and looked through a dirty window but could see nothing of interest. It appeared to be full of drums and cartons. The shed door facing the cabin had a padlock on the barrel bolt. *Something of value must be in here.*

No sooner had I moved back into the shadow of the shed than I heard the cabin front door swing open. The footfall signalled the tread of a man wearing leather boots. I saw the flash of a cigarette lighter and heard the footsteps walk to the end on the veranda. I pressed up against the wall of the shed and waited for more footsteps. I quickly moved to the flank of the cabin to get a look at the male who had come outside for a smoke. Not only was it a heavily built male, he had a machine pistol of some sort slung across his chest. *Now things are getting serious.* I needed to get a closer look in the cabin but would need to wait for the gorilla with the Uzi — or whatever it was — to go back inside.

I waited and hoped he wasn't going to sit on the veranda. *I could be here for hours.* Then I heard him slap at a mosquito on his neck. That pushed him back inside. I made my move. I came up on the rear of the cabin and carefully made my way around to where the kitchen was located. I could see two men sitting at a table and the one with his back to me was wearing a shoulder holster. What was scarier was that the end of the table had boxes of all manner of ammunition stacked on it, indicating there were several weapon types somewhere on the premises, and I was now seriously outgunned. *Time for me to leave.*

I made my egress back up the gully. I had to move carefully, not knowing whether or not Kegs or his mate were out having a cigarette. I called in to check on the lab that was still hard at work and noticed the smell of chlorine or some other chemical was even stronger. The voices were even more muted, indicating they might have been wearing masks. I decided to head back to the boat. Just as I started to make my move, I heard loud noise from the direction of the cabin and lights go on around the cabin and shed. Suddenly, three or four men came bolting out of the rear of the cabin. Something was up, and from the noise they were making it was not good. I dropped back over the ridge line off the big bald rock and saw four people come out of the chamber with torches and start heading down toward the cabin.

I arrived back at my gear on the beach where I had come ashore. The moon was now starting to rise and I could see the *Delfina* still in location. The running lights were still off, indicating nothing was amiss. I stowed my gear in my backpack, climbed back into my cold wet suit, got the scuba sorted and started swimming back. I swam just below the surface to allow me to surface occasionally and sweep the area. I was only 50 metres from our boat when I bumped into a heavy object in the water. It gave me a start and I pulled up instantly. It was a fully clothed male body. There was no immediate indication of cause of death. My heart gave a leap and I dived down to five metres and pushed hard towards the boat. I decided to tie my gear to the anchor rope and get on board with just my diving knife for support. I didn't like it, but I didn't have a lot of options. Shits were trumps, and I had a poor hand to play with.

Escape and Evasion

I tied my gear onto the forward anchor chain and quietly swam using small breast strokes toward the forward porthole so I could get some purchase to lever myself up onto the deck. This was going to be tricky. I waited about a minute to see if I could hear any movement on board and then made my move. I lay prone and very still on the deck, now cursing the light of the moon. After a short time, I made my way toward the bridge. There were charts all over the floor and a quick check of the radio gear showed it had been seriously smashed. *Someone doesn't want me to call for help.*

I made my way into the forward cabin area and the place had been trashed. No sign of Melanie but there was blood smeared on many of the cupboards and on the bulkhead. I touched the blood and it was still sticky. Whoever had bled here had only done so in the last four to five hours at most. I made my way down into the engine room after unlocking the access hatch and was relieved to see the propulsion units weren't disabled. I had plans of action screaming through my head. I went forward again to the hatch where my emergency equipment was hidden and retrieved a sat phone and a loaded handgun. I continued searching for signs of Melanie but was coming up empty.

Had they grabbed her? Answer: Most probably. Would they have killed her? Answer: Only if she fought to the death or refused to talk. If they hadn't got her, where was she? Answer: Probably on Blackbird Patches somewhere. Likelihood? Slim.

I tried to stay calm and rationally go through my courses of action. What worried me was the dead guy in the water. I decided to bring him on board and see if I could deduce anything from his person. I moved onto the rear access deck and searched around for the body. I saw it about 15 metres from the rear of the boat and slipped back into the water without making any splash and swam towards him. I grabbed his jacket and started towing him toward *The Office*. I started thinking about how much effort had been put into disguising the *Delfina*. That vessel was now well and truly out of the picture. Things were starting to get just a little bit untidy.

Damn! That subterfuge didn't work one little bit. These guys were onto us the moment we left Cooktown. For crooks they sure had good intel.

I struggled a little to drag the heavy soggy body onto the diving deck. It was starting to get light. Secretly, I was hoping Melanie was on shore and watching me, but deep down I knew it was wishful thinking. *This would be another good woman lost to me if they've wasted her.* It was starting to get light. I moved forward and recovered my scuba gear and backpack that had been tied to the anchor chain. I started assembling all of my weaponry in various parts of *The Office* so I had firepower within easy reach wherever I went.

I checked my watch, it was almost 5.45 a.m. I went back to the rear deck and started stripping the body. He was an ugly sucker. His nose was smashed, and he had a contusion on the side of his neck. No bullet holes, but from the way his head was flopping around I figured his neck had been broken. Underneath his jacket were a cotton shirt and a shoulder holster that would have held a reasonably large handgun or possibly a small machine pistol. He had no other ID on him. A packet of cigarettes, a lighter, and a spare clip of ammo in a twelve round magazine that looked like it had come off a Browning or a Colt pistol. He had prison tattoos on his hands and forearms and a few scars showing someone had once sliced him open and not for any normal surgical procedure. He had been around.

As I searched for clues as to who this dead guy was, I caught a glimpse of a flash of light like someone was watching me with binos from the rise above the beach where I had been last night. I quickly got my binos out and saw someone in jeans and a shirt carrying a long-barrelled weapon, talking on a radio or mobile phone. *Time to skedaddle, Bob.*

I dashed to the wheelhouse and activated the emergency capstan button that immediately released the chain and anchor from the front of *The Office*. I hit the start button and the twin Detroit diesels roared to life. *Thank you, God.* I pushed the power controls hard down and headed northeast out into the open water of the inner reef, heading licketty split for Cooktown. I set my heading and grabbed the sat phone with the intent to let Peter Bryant know that things had gone seriously pear-shaped and that we had a person missing. I thought it best to use veiled speech in case we were being monitored but the way things had been unravelling, I seriously wondered if that was a waste of effort. *The Office* surged beautifully over the oily early morning waters of the Coral Sea. I kept looking back over my shoulder to see if anyone was in hot pursuit and hoped that I would be able to maintain my lead on whoever was after me.

After only 15 minutes, I saw the landmass south of Cooktown start to appear and was heavily concentrating on my heading when a flare suddenly shot across the bow of *The Office*. It startled me because the only thing I could see in front of me was a low cay that wasn't marked on my charts and was only a metre above the high-water mark. I pushed the throttles forward and slowed, thinking that someone close by was signalling for help. In the bright morning light, I saw a figure standing on the cay waving for help. I again powered down and slowed to about ten knots as I approached the cay. My heart leaped when I saw it was Melanie. She pointed for me to come into the cay from the western side, and as I shut down and drifted into the shore, I saw a small tinnie half submerged sitting on the sandy bottom. I slowly turned *The Office* around and pushed toward Melanie, stern first. I wanted her to climb quickly onto the back access deck so we could get the hell out of there. She yelled for me to give her a hand and I then realised she had a passenger. He was in just as bad a shape as the one covered in a tarpaulin on the rear deck that I had so recently recovered and searched.

'Gimme a hand, Bob, I've got a body here'. She had business written all over her drawn face. Melanie looked well and truly strung out. I quickly jumped into the shallow water, and together we lifted the body out of the tinnie and onto the rear access deck.

It was not a time for small talk and we quickly dragged the inert male onto the deck. I dashed back up to the wheelhouse to get us going again while Melanie headed down into the galley. She re-emerged a minute or so later with a bottle of water in her hand. She came up close to me and gave me a hug.

'Boy, was I glad to see you,' she said in between gulps of water.

'Me too girl, me too,' I responded, looking down into her troubled eyes. I took up my driving position, throttled up and headed off at best speed toward Annan Creek. It was time to go into emergency mode.

She sat down at the chart table and let out a big sigh.

'Jesus, Bob, what the hell is going on here?' she asked imploringly.

'Well, my recce on Blackbird Patches shows that these crooks have a serious drug lab operation and they have a bunch of thugs armed to the teeth.' I paused and looked back at her again. 'But what happened to you? I heard a ruckus on the island and when I came back to *The Office*, I bumped into that guy under the tarp.'

Melanie took another swig from the water bottle and leaned forward in her seat. 'Yeah, well I'm afraid they got the drop on me back there,' she said quietly. 'I was keeping watch and heard a bump against the starboard side. I looked over and saw that tinnie we left back there on the cay. There was a guy in it wanting to know who I was. Next thing I had a gun shoved in the back of my neck, probably by that bloke we just loaded onto the boat. His mate had come up alongside behind me and I hadn't heard a thing. Well, one thing led to another and we wrestled around a bit and while I was doing that, his mate came on board and started smashing the radios. I kicked him in the head and then the neck and he fell over the side. His mate came at me,' she paused to take another swig from her water bottle, 'but I was able to disable him.'

I had listened in utter fascination but had to ask, 'Oh, and just how did you "disable" him?'

'Stabbed him with a biro in the eye,' she said with a slight smile on her face.

'Oh,' was all I could manage.

'Yeah, so I figured that whoever these guys were, they were not very friendly, and I would get out of there. I made a quick decision to take their boat with me so it would buy us some time. It also meant you might have some transport as well. I hoped like Christ that you would head back to the RV or head towards Cooktown, so I hid behind the cay hoping you would come past. I grabbed a flare off our boat to grab your attention,' she said with a determined look in her eyes.

'Well done and a bloody good idea,' I replied.

'What now?'

'I'm thinking we need to get back on land and get some bloody help ASAP,' I said. 'Problem is, we have a rat in the ranks, and someone is tipping these clowns off about what we are up to.' Melanie looked down at her feet and nodded her head. 'I don't know if they knew that *The Office* was once the *Delfina* but they sure as hell knew we were coming, or they treat anyone near Blackbird Patches as their enemy.'

'I agree. Have we got any comms?' Melanie asked.

'Yep, there's a sat phone under the compass housing. I reckon we should let Greg and Barry know we need reinforcements and to get the heavy artillery ready.'

'On it,' she snapped back and disappeared aft to see if she could get a signal.

I swept the sea behind us, but nothing was following us. I wondered what the crooks on the island were thinking with their tinnie gone and two of their mates missing in action. Hopefully, the tinnie was their way of getting on board their own cruiser. That problem might slow their reaction down a bit at least.

Melanie came up the ladder onto the bridge. She was slowly recovering but still had an edge about her.

'How long did it take him to die?' I asked, nodding towards the body she had searched.

'Too long,' she said with what I thought sounded like menace in her voice. 'The bastard had a second weapon and nearly took my head off … but his aim was skew-whiff,' she retorted.

I couldn't help it. I let out a large guffaw and turned to see she was quietly sniggering as well.

'Come here,' I said and held her with one arm. She looked up at my face and smiled warmly.

'Thanks, Skipper,' she said as she squeezed my arm. Silence descended on us while we made good progress towards Cooktown. The coastline was now clearly visible, and we could make out prominent land features.

'Head up the creek where Greg and Barry worked on the boat. We'll have less of an audience if we come in the back door.'

'Good idea, Mel,' I said. 'We'll make a tactician out of you yet.'

'Hope so, I've got the killing squared away … it seems,' she said, casting a look behind us towards Blackbird Patches. 'How long till we reach the jetty?'

I looked down at the chart. 'Probably be there by three or four this arvo.' Why don't you go down and whip us up a feed, First Mate?' I said, trying to bring a normalcy to what had been a harrowing night for everyone.

'Will do. I'm famished.'

Melanie dived down into the galley and I could hear her clattering among the pots and pans.

Suddenly she popped back up and reached behind her jeans' waistband. 'Nearly forgot to give you this,' she said, as she put a Colt .44 pistol into my hand.

'I reckon it belonged to the guy with the broken neck,' I mused.

'Yep, the other gun went in the drink when we were fighting in the tinnie.'

'I'll put it with our growing armoury.' I realised that we now had four handguns, but all of different calibres. We didn't have much ammunition, so any firefight we got into would be short, sharp and very close range.

Melanie was back in the galley and she yelled out, 'Once we get to the safe house, we'll be able to up the ante.'

'Right. I just hope Greg and Barry have stayed out of trouble.'

'They'll be okay,' Melanie shot back. 'There was nothing doing at the airstrip. They said they would meet us at the old jetty.'

I breathed a sigh of relief but now had to come up with a plan. I couldn't help but think that there was a high probability that an ambush was on the cards. If someone in Canberra knew what we were up to, then things were going to get even more untidy. Somehow, we had to take out the bad guys but make sure we could uncover who the bad apple in the barrel was … and who he or she worked for. Whatever we did, we had to get ourselves re-armed because at present we were under-gunned, under-manned and operating on minimal intelligence, with any plans we came up with being fed to our opposition.

*   *   *

We made Annan Creek around 3 p.m. and I slowly made headway up the creek, keeping to one side of the main channel so I could do a quick about face if required. We motored up to the jetty and started tying up when we heard the truck driven by Greg and Barry approaching.

'You meet them,' I said, 'I'll cover you from the forward hatch in case there's a set-up.'

'Okay,' Mel said, tucking a handgun into the back of her jeans and pulling her shirt over her waist.

Greg and Barry stopped their truck and Greg climbed up onto the rear tray to cast an eye over the surrounding scrub.

'Hi guys,' Barry called out. 'Wanna lift into town?'

'Sure do,' Melanie called back while giving me the thumbs up sign.

I went down into the engine room and immobilised the starter and then locked the engine compartment. I gathered our weapons and made my way up onto the aft deck.

'Glad to see you, fellas,' I said, shaking hands all round. 'Things have got a bit ugly. We've got two bodies here and no death certificate.'

Greg and Barry moved forward and looked under the tarps.

'That's the dude who was going around Cooktown offering a reward for the *Delfina* a few weeks ago,' he said. 'He doesn't look too flash with that biro hanging out of his eye.'

'Don't look at me,' I said as the two agents then turned towards Melanie.

'You okay, Mel?'

'I'm fine,' she snapped. 'Women can eliminate threats too, you know.'

'Yeah, yeah, we know, it's just …,' Barry's voice trailed off as Greg gave him the signal to zip it.

'What's the plan?' asked Greg.

'To be honest, fellas, we're winging it from here on.' I gave them a short brief on how we suspected we had been betrayed and that there was a high possibility it was someone in head office where our operations were formulated.

'Any idea who the rat is?' asked Barry.

'Not a clue at this stage. I have a feeling that now that the crooks on Blackbird Patches have realised they may have been compromised, someone is going to come after us before we get too far away, and by the look of it they could have considerable resources.'

'I suggest we get back to the safe house and get ourselves geared up for a small war,' suggested Barry.

'My thoughts exactly, mate. I reckon we need another set of wheels as well. Travelling on the back of a truck is not exactly covert ops,' I said as I threw my backpack up into the truck.

'Jump in the front, Mel,' Greg said, 'Bob and I will ride shotgun in the back. When we get close to the house, we will sweep the area and make sure we are not walking into trouble.'

'Sounds like a plan. Let's go,' I said as I cocked my two handguns and put them back in the backpack.

'Ahh, before we do that,' Barry started and throwing his head towards the rear of the boat, 'what about these two? Can't leave 'em here, they'll get flyblown and make a right mess of the diving deck.'

'True,' I said. 'Trouble is, if we take them back to Cooktown and hand them over to the local coppers, everybody and his dog will know about it and we'll be toast.' I paused thinking of what few options we had left.

'It'll take a while to dig a hole,' offered Greg.

'Yeah, and we need to be well off a track,' added Barry.

'Feed 'em to the crocs, Bob,' Mel stated matter-of-factly. 'They're bad guys and no bastard will report them missing anyway.'

It was not exactly by the book or following the law, but we were in a bit of a jam.

'Okay, tip them into the creek,' I said, wondering if this was going to jeopardise my standing with my employers. Melanie interrupted my train of thought.

'Hang on a minute. Get your phone and take a photo of them first. It will help if we ever get to file a report on this mess.'

'Good idea, Mel.' And I busied myself taking photos of the bodies next to the deck hook to give size comparisons, and shots of their faces front-on and profile.

Greg and Barry took care of stripping the bodies and weighing them down so that they wouldn't resurface before becoming lunch for the local salties. Melanie and I gathered our kit and checked the boat for any clues we might have left behind. She gave the rear deck one last sluice of water to get rid of any blood or traces of what had been lying on the deck. We all headed for the truck. Barry opened the door of the cabin and handed a 12-gauge shotgun to Greg.

I looked at the weapon and he said matter of factly, 'We get big rats at the house sometimes.'

*   *   *

We pulled up on the side road within sight of the safe house and Greg and I made a quick plan to sweep down each side of the entrance road, check for recent signs and once clear, we would signal Barry and Mel to come in.

After 30 minutes, we had finished our clearing patrol and made our way onto the veranda and waved to Barry to come in. We were now in the big league.

Setting the Bait

Greg set about making coffee for everyone while I sat down and started preparing a set of "orders" that I could put to the group about how and what we were going to do next. We needed a plan, an outline of how we were going to stave off what was now looking like a determined attempt to halt any AFP operations against this drug cartel. The fact that the nasties had boarded *The Office* and tried to silence if not kill Melanie. The biggie was they were prepared to shoot and ask questions later, and this had upped the ante considerably. In the back of my mind was that they had murdered Ian Taylor in cold blood.

Barry came in from the shed out back and smiled at the group sitting around the kitchen table. 'Well, our armoury is still intact, including the stashes, and I did a pretty good look around and nobody has been snooping under the house or setting bugs or booby traps.'

'Good,' I replied and swept my gaze around the group. 'If you all agree I will make up a set of plans so we can sort out our next course of action.' There were nods all round as everyone sipped their coffee.

'Before we do that, I reckon we need to pool what info we have so far on the crooks so we can counter their likely moves.'

Melanie chimed in with 'And don't we need to set up this prick who nearly got me killed?'

'Yep, and we are fairly certain it is Benning, but somehow we have got to get him to show his hand.'

'Who is Benning?' asked Barry.

Before I could reply Melanie came back with 'He is an arsehole in Canberra who is from the ONA but has been working with the AFP.'

'Right,' I added, 'and when we went out to Blackbird Patches, I more or less got confirmation that the crooks knew I was coming and one of them — who I suspect was Kegs — was blabbing on about how they had someone on the inside.'

'Hang on, waddya mean you heard someone "blabbing on" about someone in the AFP?' queried Barry, whose eyes had widened just a little.

'I heard them when I was on Blackbird,' I said, finishing my coffee. 'They were about 10 metres away, there was no wind. I could hear everything he said.'

The two men looked at each other and one raised his eyebrows as a mark of respect and a look on his face that said ten metres? *This bloke has got his shit together.*

'Okay, mate, I reckon you ought to be the bloke who now leads this merry group. Waddya reckon, Mel?'

Melanie had been watching the reactions of the two field agents and turned to look me in the eye. 'I think the time has come when we know we are going to get into some heavy hitting, and Bob is probably the best person to take charge.' She kept her poker face on and there was not a hint of anything other than co-workers trying to sort their shit out.

'Fine by me.' I stood and stretched and said, 'Why don't we regroup in about an hour and come armed with everything you know about what has gone down and who is who in the zoo so we can start to put a plan together?'

Barry and Greg stood and started making their way out to the back veranda. 'Righto, we are gonna clean all of the weapons and make sure everything is tickety-boo.'

I needed to know a bit more about our new team members and I pumped Melanie for some details so I would have some idea what Barry and Greg would be capable of when push came to shove. I needn't have worried because they were both former commandos in the Army Reserve who had seen action in Iraq in the early days, and Barry had also done a tour in Afghanistan. As Melanie related, 'They had their shit all in one sock.' She had the utmost faith in them to be able to handle things if and when it got ugly. I was somewhat relieved because I had worked as a cadre with the commandos in Melbourne. I very quickly found out that they were as capable as any blokes from my regiment. I stood to go and retrieve my notebook from my backpack. As I headed out to the back room, I leaned down and kissed Melanie lightly on the top of the head.

'That's for not getting killed yesterday.' She rose quickly, grabbed my shoulder and swung me toward her and kissed me hard on the lips. 'When this shit is all sorted, you are gonna be in a lot of trouble, Skipper.'

'Good trouble or bad trouble?'

'Oooh, good trouble,' she said, smiling wickedly as she gathered the coffee cups and headed for the sink.

'Can't wait.' *C'mon Bob, concentrate on the task at hand. Fun and games later.* I went and got my notebook and started to go through my situation enemy paragraph for my outline plan.

*   *   *

I was about to start pulling all of the intel we had together when I remembered a thing from my army days about knowing your men, knowing their strengths and weaknesses. It was easier in the Regiment with our five-man patrols because we were all so highly cross-trained that we could do each other's jobs if push came to shove. I knew bugger all about Greg and Barry. It was time to find out and confirm what Melanie had given me on the two men.

They were in the shed and were stripping, cleaning and assembling our small armoury.

'Looks like you two blokes know your way around weapons,' I offered, hoping they would give me some background.

'Yeah,' said Greg. 'Barry and I were lunchtime commandos back in Melbourne a few years back and served with 2 Commando Regiment.'

Barry added, 'We went out to Swan Island a few times to get some time up using gats we might run across in Iraq.' He was deftly pulling apart a Glock as if he had done it a million times.

'Oh, so you were in the Reserve and went to Iraq,' I asked, picking up one of the rifles and checking its safety.

'Yep, we both did a couple of tours, and I did one in the Ghan, and then when we came back home, we both realised that working for Telstra and the bank was no longer our bag.' Barry looked at Greg as confirmation and grinned, 'We then were asked by a bloke in Customs if we would like to work as field agents but in reality we would be working for National Parks and Wildlife as a cover.'

Sounds familiar, doesn't it, Bob?

'And that's how we met Mel,' Greg said.

There was a pause as I studied their sun-tanned faces.

'You just wanna know if we can cut the mustard, don't ya, Bob?' asked Barry.

'To be honest guys, I do. I really don't know much about you apart from the fact that you are good welders and can destroy a perfectly good boat in quick smart time.' I smiled back at them.

They both grinned and Barry looked me straight in the eyes. 'Don't worry, Skipper, we can shoot and scoot with the best of 'em, and we won't let you down.'

Greg looked at me and said with a lop-sided grin, 'This prick here can shoot the eyebrows off a fly, and I can blow up anything your little heart desires.'

'Ta. Thanks fellas,' and I turned and went back to the house. I felt a lot better knowing I had two highly trained soldiers – well, ex-soldiers, but commandos – at our backs. I was starting to feel a whole lot better.

*   *   *

I spent about an hour pulling together everything I could think of about our adversaries. How many would there likely to be? What type of weaponry did they have that I hadn't seen? How were they getting around town? Where would they most likely be set up as a base? How was Benning getting his info to them? Jesus, I knew less than I thought I did, and there were more holes in my plan than in a piece of Swiss cheese. The only thing left that I could do was draw the enemy out into ground of our choosing and hope we hadn't been compromised somewhere along the way.

We gathered for lunch that Melanie had whipped together, and I asked everyone to bring a notebook and pencil to our meeting. I didn't want to call it an orders group just yet, I was still fishing for ideas.

'Okay guys,' I said, hoping I sounded like I knew what I was on about. 'This is gonna be more of a planning session at this stage because I am a great believer that one person doesn't have all the good ideas. What I would like to do is run an outline plan past you and then open it up to questions, comments or whatever. Do not hold back, okay?' They all nodded silently. I looked around the group and they all had their game faces on.

'Right then. The first thing we talk about is the enemy. We know they are onto Mel and me and they knew what the *Delfina* looked like, but hopefully they have no idea what *The Office* looks like because both of the crooks who saw it are no longer with us.' I smiled slightly, looking at Melanie who was not showing any emotion whatsoever.

I continued, 'Sooner or later, they are going to ask around and put two and two together and come looking for us. On the minus side for them, I am guessing that their major weakness will be poor field craft and battle craft. They are really just thugs with guns and use brute force to do whatever it is they want to achieve. I have seen them in the field, and they are pretty slack when it comes to security, so I am hoping that also is the case for their minor tactics. I reckon our best course of action is to get them onto ground of OUR choosing where we can dictate what goes down.' Greg and Barry were nodding their heads and Melanie was just looking at me with a strange look on her face.

Melanie shot in, 'What about that bastard Benning?'

'Yep, Mel, we have to somehow draw him into the play.'

'What's gonna do that?' asked Barry.

I swept my gaze around the group looking for agreeance. 'Let's face it. These crooks are into this for the seriously big bucks that are out there. We are talking millions — if not tens of millions of dollars. They are prepared to kill for their reward.' I paused and let it sink in. 'So, if we put their money or their drugs at risk it will force their hand.' I waited for a response from anyone.

'How can we do that, Bob?' Greg asked. 'We know they've got drugs on Blackbird Patches and we know they fly shit out of some of the local airstrips, but how are we gonna know which one to hit?'

It was a good question, but I had thought about the fact that the gang would need to keep a lower profile than usual, seeing as how Melanie and I had disrupted their activities a few times already.

'Okay, what is the airstrip around here that gives the greatest privacy; the one that nobody is likely to use?' I asked.

'That would have to be Betty's place down south of Black Mountain,' said Greg, pointing to it on the map laid out in front of us.

'So, what are we gonna do, knock off a shipment and see what happens?' asked Mel, not sounding too convinced.

'I was thinking along those lines, but we need to drag Benning into this somehow.' I was starting to have some ideas formulating off the top of my head. 'We have to convince him that he is about to either lose a shipment or lose the money …'

'Or lose his cover,' added Mel, now smiling just a little.

'Yep, and if we can somehow get them all in the one place – or on the road to one place – we might have a chance of getting it done.' I looked at the group who now had their eyes on the map. 'One thing we cannot afford to do is get civvies involved. We need to minimise the collateral damage. This little op has no official backing and if it goes pear-shaped, we are all for the high jump.'

Yeah, but with a rotten apple in the barrel what other recourse do we have?' asked Barry.

'Not a lot mate, not a lot,' I said, hoping that brainstorming might throw up some ideas.

I was met with a deafening silence. After half a minute or so I started, 'What if I draw Benning up here on the pretext that I have found the gang's hideout and we need back up?' I offered.

'Or what if you said you were about to uncover their stash of drugs?' Melanie chimed in.

'Or both?' added Greg.

'Yeah, that way we would be bound to get a bite,' I mused. 'First things first, let's find out if they are sniffing around Betty's airstrip. We are going to need another set of wheels, guys,' I asked, looking at Greg and Barry.

'No sweat, Skipper, leave it with us. I will get a work vehicle and go down and see Betty on the pretext of feral pigs or some such shit and have a look around,' Greg said confidently. 'Barry will bring the four-wheel drive back here.'

'Okay, it's starting to sound like a plan. We've got a couple of two-ways in the bag in the shed. Make sure they are working, and let's use call signs that will give us cover.'

'Copy. How about one two three four? KISS it, I say,' said Greg. 'Bob will be one, Barry will be two, Mel will be three and I will be four.'

'Works for me,' I said. 'Let's get going. Minimise the traffic, and once you have the radios working let's set up the code word "shot duck" for flicking to an alternate frequency. Barry and Greg looked at each other and smiled.

'What?' I asked.

'You wouldn't believe it, but we had a similar code word in Iraq, except is was "fucked duck",' Barry said, chuckling as they walked out.

*   *   *

I sat wondering what ruse I might use to draw Benning up north. We HAD to find out if he was the shit in the sandwich. Nothing else we were thinking of doing would work unless we removed the threat that gave the nasties early warning of our plans or movements. It was like fighting with one hand tied behind your back. After 30 minutes, I drew up a message I would send to Benning. I had to get him believing I was sending it to Peter Bryant and wanted to run it past the team. It read:

> P.B. Looks like we have uncovered the hidden goodies. We are in the safe house outside of C'Town on the southside of Keatings Lagoon. We will wait for your arrival before we move on the target. B.M.

A round table meeting agreed that we should send the message and prepare for the arrival of Benning and most probably a bunch of goons along with him. There weren't too many properties around where we were holed up, and it wouldn't take long for anyone with some serious nous to figure out where we were staying. We reckoned that two things were likely to happen and we needed a course of action for both. I reminded the team that a plan was simply a course of action from which we would most probably have to adjust, and I asked everyone to use their initiative. If they thought things weren't right, they probably weren't, and they should act accordingly.

We surmised that Benning would probably want to come up to Cooktown and oversee our demise because he wouldn't want any loose ends. On the other hand, if he was a gutless sort, he just might tell whoever was leading the gang to come out to the safe house and kill us all and try and keep himself at arm's length. We had to prepare for both contingencies. I was secretly hoping that Benning would show himself and have an ambush of his own up his sleeve. At best we might have three days to get ready for action; at worst it could be within 24 hours. For once, the tyranny of distance in Far North Queensland was working in our favour. We needed to set a basic trap, knock off as many bad guys as we could, and develop and improve that basic trap as time went on. We would have to move quickly.

It was essential to have two vehicles for a hasty withdrawal, so Greg and Barry headed off into town with a shopping list I had prepared. Greg was tasked with procuring and preparing a serious amount of explosive charges that we would need to either eliminate our opposition or help extricate us from a bad situation. Barry was going to get us some more ammunition from some "mates" he had in town. No names, no pack drill.

*   *   *

Just before sunset, Greg and Barry reappeared with a well-worn four-wheel drive that hadn't had a wash in quite a while. The Toyota Land Cruiser looked like any other off-road vehicle one saw around Far North Queensland. After unloading their supplies, I called the group together and ran through what I hoped would be a set of orders that we could operate from and adjust if things turned pear-shaped. Melanie had cups of coffee on the kitchen table and everyone sat down with their notebooks and pencils. *Ready, class?*

'Okay, guys, here is the plan. Let me run through the outline plan and, if possible, save your questions until I have finished.' They all looked at me like kids about to get a serving of their favourite ice cream.

I started my plan by giving a rundown of the "enemy". I spoke of Kegs and what he looked like, his mate Bart who was tall and skinny and not too bright. I mentioned the Asian woman with the long black hair and my best guess of their overall strength, their weaponry, and the fact that they were not going to play nice and would break any rules that civilised society could expect when it came to prisoners.

I paused and looked at the two men who had been jotting notes and listening intently. Melanie had made a few notes but was watching me like a hawk.

'Next, our mission.' I was using the army model for orders because it was easy to follow and I knew it backwards, as would Greg and Barry. It also made sure I didn't miss anything that should be covered.

'Our mission is to kill or capture whoever comes down the road to the house.' All eyes were on me now. I now deviated a little from the strict army code of orders. 'This is where we need to be flexible, guys. If Benning swans in by himself, we will have to give him the benefit of the doubt. We just can't waste him on sight, although I know some people who would like to do that.' I glanced across at Melanie who was scowling and not returning my gaze.

'Right. Tasks. Melanie, you will be my cover inside the house if Benning rocks up by himself. If he looks like shooting me or inflicting harm on me in some way, shoot the man dead.'

'Got it,' she replied tersely.

'Barry, you are to set command detonated explosive charges along the track and in the house driveway where somebody might stop and park. You are also to recon an egress route for a hasty withdrawal if we need to bug out. If shooting breaks out, if we find ourselves in a serious firefight, you are to cover us with fire and prepare for a rapid withdrawal. The roof of the shed will probably be your best possie.'

'Copy, Skipper,' he said sternly.

'Greg, you will have the sniper rifle. I want you to find yourself a good position from where to cover the road up to the house so you can take out anyone trying to flank the house and remove any threat. That hillock about 150 metres down the track on the southern side only gives you a couple of metres height but it is better than nothing and has good cover from view.'

'Right, Bob,' he said, making notes as he spoke.

'As you can see, we have to prepare for two options. One is that Benning shows up and tries to bluff his way through this and convince me he is a good guy. The other is that he realises his cover is blown and needs to silence Mel and I. Hopefully, he will not be aware that Barry and Greg are loitering with intent.' Both men smiled at each other.

'My thinking is that if the goons show up, they will come in hard and try to smoke us out with either firepower or some other means. We will need to be ready for both options. We will need to establish a killing ground for our ambush far enough out to avoid being hemmed in and caught in the house.' The group all nodded in agreeance.

I paused and took a swig of coffee.

'Okay, Actions on anything and everything. Action on contact is to return fire, but watch your ammo. Single shot over 100 metres and double tap inside 25. If the bad guys make it off the track, we have to drop them before they can outflank us around the house. The last thing we want is to be caught up here and easily smoked out.' Barry and Greg nodded. 'Action on withdrawal. Those that can will head to the Land Cruiser and we will RV on the western side of the caravan park at the Lion's Den Hotel south of here. That RV will remain open for 60 minutes from the time we withdraw from here. The secondary RV will be Betty's homestead but behind the main shed, not the house. That RV will remain open for three hours. After that, head back to *The Office*, but be sure you are not followed. I will give you the start-up instructions for the boat after these orders.'

I let that all sink in and continued.

'Logistics. Everyone is to have a backpack with some rations, spare ammo, your spare batteries, a torch if you have one and anything that will make up a first aid kit from the stores the guys brought back from town. Once the shit hits the fan, have that backpack on so you cut and run.' Everyone was nodding.

'Okay, comms. Make sure you all have a couple of spare batteries. If we are split up, we will have a sched on the hour and half hour. Be careful what you say and make sure you know who you are talking to. To verify the receiver ask them if call sign 5 is on air and you will soon know if we have been compromised.'

I finished the last of my now tepid coffee and said, 'Guys, this is really taking a chance here. We are not sure if Benning will take the bait, and we don't know the size of the gang that might turn up. But we have little choice in the matter. Our security has been compromised and we will have to suck it and see. Righto, check your notes and I will take questions in a minute.'

The group all studied their notebooks and I readied myself to see what holes I had in my plan.

Barry asked, 'Boss, do want me to set any charges that Greg might use to extricate himself?'

'Good point, Barry. Yep, give Greg a couple of slabs that he can use if he has to bug out.'

Greg smiled and said, 'That was gonna be my question. I am out on that hillock by myself and I will need to head south into the creek line if I am to egress out of there without getting my bum shot off.'

'My thoughts exactly, Greg' I replied, 'If you do have to extract, head south in the tree line for as long as you can and we will try and hook up on the main road. If not, stay in cover and keep heading down to the Lion's Den pub.

'Roger.'

'Melanie?' I asked, looking at her.

'Nup, Skipper, I think you have covered it all. Oh, except when do reckon this will all start?'

'No idea, Mel, but I want us to be ready by mid-morning tomorrow. Benning has probably got the means to get himself up from Canberra at relatively short notice. That "start time" is my guesstimate on Benning tipping off the crooks and them figuring out where we might be. It's 30 clicks into town and they will have to ask around to find out where our likely safe house is. Yeah, so be ready to go by 10 am. Everyone okay with that?' A chorus of agreeance greeted my question and Barry then stood and said, 'Well, this calls for a beer. We brought some back and we might as well have one to soothe our nerves.'

'Okay, fellas, but I want you to also set up a roster for sentry tonight.'

'Spoken like a true sergeant,' shot back Greg with a grin on his dial.

It was going to be a long night and a busy couple of hours in the morning.

A Gathering Storm

The cold cloudy late July weather wrapped around Frank Benning's Canberra office building as he sat contemplating his next move. He now had two messages from Bob McTaggart that somehow had been sent to him in error. It looked like McTaggart was well and truly onto the ring that was operating in the Cooktown area. Benning's very lucrative cash cow was now seriously under threat. He needed to know a few things before he could make a move that wouldn't compromise his extremely delicate position. How much did Peter Bryant and Ballantyne know, and what was the current state of play? Benning always figured that to stay on the front foot was critical to success and keeping your opponent off guard, so he decided to pay the AFP Ops Room a visit, but he would need to see Bryant to get in.

Peter Bryant knocked on his Superintendent's door frame. Superintendent Ballantyne looked up, 'Yes, Pete?'

'Benning's on his way over. He reckons that radio chatter is increasing, and he wants to know what we know.'

Ballantyne went back to his papers and said dismissively, 'Sure, let that gumshoe know what is going on, but don't give him anything current, and I mean in the last few days.'

'That won't be hard,' Bryant responded, 'haven't heard from McTaggart in almost ten days. He's been off the air totally.'

'What, no scheds?' asked Ballantyne.

'Nope, we had a call-if-you-must arrangement, and he hasn't rung in.' Bryant turned and headed back to his desk littered with files marked Confidential and AFP Eyes Only.

Benning was ushered into Peter Bryant's office that adjoined the Ops Room.

'Frank.'

'Peter.' There was no warmth in either greeting.

'What can I do for you, Frank?'

'As I said on the phone, we have had an increase in chatter up north of Cairns with an emphasis on call signs that aren't related to aircraft or shipping movements. And it definitely doesn't sound like barramundi poachers.' Benning paused, trying to keep his voice calm and not show any sign of the incredible tension he could feel in his chest. 'Just wondered if your people had come across anything unusual in the last week or so?' He walked so he could gain a view of the Ops map on the wall. It was too far away for him to make out anything of significance.

'Nope. In fact, it has been very quiet for us. We haven't had a peep out of our operatives north of the Tropic of Capricorn, to be honest,' he said while scanning Benning's face for any tells.

Frank Benning's heart skipped a tiny beat as he realised that the messages he was getting were meant for Peter Bryant after all. At least he had confirmed that piece of intelligence.

'Ah, oh well. Never mind. I will tell our sig analysts to keep looking, maybe something will turn up.' He started to walk out but paused and asked, 'Is there any way I could have a look at your Ops map? Ours don't seem to carry as much topo detail as yours do.'

'Sure, help yourself. We can give you the map series if you want to order from the Survey guys in Bonegilla.'

'Great. Okay, I'll get out of your hair,' and he headed towards the map on the far wall. He quickly cast his gaze over the area of Cooktown but tried not to appear too obvious. The only thing that caught his eye was a blue pin on the map south of Cooktown. It was better than nothing.

*   *   *

Benning scuttled back to his car, cursing the chilly damp day that was now mizzling a fine damp blanket of moisture on him as he hurried along. He retrieved a satellite phone from the glove box and rang Franz Nesbitt. He was glad that their phones were encrypted because the Defence Signals Directorate would be all over them in a flash.

'Nesbitt.'

'Franz, it's Frank. I have a problem.'

'YOU have a problem? Fuck me Frank, we ALL have a fucking problem.'

'What do you mean?' asked Benning, dreading something nasty coming his way.

'Well, for a start, two of our guys are missing from the island and so is one of our tinnies.' Nesbitt screeched down the phone. He was working hard to contain himself ever since Kudlov had threatened to kill the next person who screwed up.

'What happened?' asked Frank, hoping to lift the fog of uncertainty on what was quickly becoming a disaster.

'How the fuck should we know?' yelled Nesbitt. 'They went out to patrol around the island and never came back.'

'Was it bad weather or what?' asked Benning.

'Nuh, calm as buggery. They just vanished.'

'Maybe a croc got 'em,' Frank said hopefully.

'Not out there. Too far for salties. They have gone, and no trace of their bloody tinnie.'

Benning heard Nesbitt sigh into his phone. 'Anyway, what is YOUR problem Benning?' Nesbitt threw back at the agent.

'I think that the AFP have an agent in the Cooktown area, and he is onto the operation.' He didn't want to give too much away at this stage as his priority was self-preservation.

'Jesus Christ! Waddya mean "onto the operation", Frank? What the fuck is going on down there? We are on the brink of shipping out almost half a ton of shit in the next few days and you are now telling me we could be compromised? Kudlov will not be fuckin' happy, Frank.' Nesbitt wiped his brow as he could feel tension rising in his body. His core temperature had suddenly spiked.

'Listen, don't sweat it. I am on my way up to Cooktown to see if I can neutralise the threat. In the meantime, tell Kudlov I am on my way up and to start looking for a house south of Cooktown that might contain the Feds. But Franz …'

'What?'

'Be careful. These guys know how to look after themselves. They are not local coppers. Expect serious opposition.'

'Yeah, yeah. Just get your shiny arse up here, Frank, and sort this crap out.' Nesbitt stabbed the phone hard with his stubby finger to end the call and walked around in a tight circle muttering 'Fuck, fuck, fuck, faaarck!'

His next phone call was to Carina who he needed to gather the troops.

*   *   *

'What else did he say, Franz?' Kudlov peered over his sunglasses and leered at a young woman in a very brief bikini sunbathing by the pool in front of his luxury villa in Cairns.

'He said he was coming up to Cooktown to neutralise the threat,' Franz offered meekly over the phone.

'That jerk couldn't neutralise fuckin' Switzerland!' He swivelled on his sun lounger and sat up. 'Okay, okay. Tell you vot ve are gonna do. Leave a few men on the island and get everybody together in Cooktown as soon as you can.'

'Already on it, Boss.'

'Really, Franz? At times you amaze me zat you can actually plan-afuckin-head.'

Franz stood statue-like, waiting for more orders to be barked at him.

"I vill fly up the day after tomorrow to make sure that effery ting goes good for the fly out. Get as much ice off the island as possible and get it ready to go.'

'Right, Boss.'

'Franz, do not let this screw up or I will get very, veery angry.'

'Right, Boss.'

Kudlov snapped his fingers and a thick set man appeared by his side. 'Tell the pilot I want to fly to Cooktown the day after tomorrow and tell everyone to pack. We are going for a few days. Make sure we take all our ammo.' He looked intently at the thug doing his bidding, 'And I mean ALL the ammo, okay?'

'Yes, sir, Mr Kudlov,' and the lackey disappeared to do his employer's bidding. He was excited about going to Cooktown because he would get to ride in the Lear jet. The job had its perks.

* * *

Peter Bryant was going over his notes on who was working the drug scene north of Rockhampton when his intercom buzzed.

'Bryant.'

'Reception, Sarg, you have a visitor who needs to speak to you in the secure facility.'

'Sure, who is it?' Bryant asked, his curiosity triggered by the request to meet with someone in a room that not too many people knew about.

'He said to tell you … Pronto Eee-wart. Well … at least that's how he pronounced it,' said the bemused security officer on the ground floor.

Bryant smiled to himself. Ewart Chase was a former Army Signals Corps officer who had commanded a regular Army signals squadron and then, after completing the SAS cadre course, was moved into the 152 Signal Squadron, the SAS Regiment's own dedicated signals unit. Chase was now working in the Defence Signals Directorate, and they had worked together on a few operations mainly pointing their noses towards "our northern neighbours", as Chase so diplomatically put it on several occasions. As Peter Bryant made his way down to the secure bunker, he wondered what had dragged Ewart across town to speak one on one.

An AFP security officer was standing with the DSD operations officer near the entrance to the facility.

'Didn't know you knew about our secret squirrel room, Ewart,' Bryant said with a friendly grin on his face as they walked down to the elevator to head underground.

'We spooks know everything, Pete. You know that.'

'Yeah, so you keep telling me. How ya been, mate?'

'Not bad. But I think I am gonna fuck up your day.'

Bryant entered the code to the secure bunker into the lock and after shedding the security detail they entered the room. It was often used as an operations room when security levels needed to be ramped up. The communications into and out of the security bunker were far above those levels of security normally expected on operations with government departments. The walls were covered with maps, but all had plain white covers draped over them.

They sat opposite each other at a large desk. 'So, what have you got to tell me that needs all this secrecy?'

'Well, you know how we always have a DSD cell operating up on the Cape York Peninsula?'

'Mm hmm,' Bryant nodded. Now his interest was now really piqued.

'Well, we have been picking up some interesting stuff for the last couple of days. The kids up north were following coded transmissions that were bouncing around the Cairns and Cooktown areas, and then last Monday they all went clear.'

'What, deliberately sent in clear?'

'Nup, whoever was using the encrypted devices forgot to re-code their sets at the end of the month. Either that or they have somehow flicked off their crypto key. Common dog fuck, really. Any decent operator would know that and be ready for the coding change.'

'So, who is it?'

'Mate, you not gonna like this, but someone is on to one of your blokes operating in the area around Cooktown. Chase looked at Bryant's frowning face. 'And let's just say they have murderous intent.'

'Christ, do you know who?'

'All we could deduce was that the intended target had a boat called the *Delfina*, his name was McTaggart and they wanted to rub him out.'

Bryant sat back in his chair.

'You all right, Pete?'

'No, I'm not bloody alright.'

Peter Bryant then gave Ewart Chase a run-down on the operation that Bob was conducting, but he also said that he hadn't heard from his operator for over a week.

'Any idea who these nasties are?' he asked.

'We've got some idea. One is a bloke with a seriously heavy Russian accent, and we believe his surname is Kudlov. He has been talking to a bloke called Nesbitt, and from the tone in Kudlov's voice, Nesbitt has screwed up and Kudlov is calling all the shots. My int section reckons they know who this Kudlov is because they picked up a message a year ago off the coast when you were chasing people dropping drugs offshore.'

Bryant nodded, his mind now racing as to how he could reach McTaggart and keep him out of harm's way.

'But the zinger, Pete, is that someone here in Canberra has been tipping off Kudlov and Nesbitt ... although we are not 100 per cent sure who that is. The one thing we do know is that he is called Frank and our best guess is he is in ONA, or a department closely aligned with that.'

'How do you figure that?'

'Well, without going all tech on you, when we found out the gist of the messages we got our people down here to get off their shiny-arsed backsides and put some RDF on sat phones using the frequency that had gone clear and bingo!'

'Christ, how did you swing the money to push that through?'

'Wasn't too hard. Our initial assessment was based on the fact that this mob were using call signs, veiled speech and encrypted phones. Mix that in with the accents, the threats and it was starting to look like a terrorist group raising money for their nasty little campaigns against us infidels.'

'Okay.' Bryant was bemused at how federal agencies could push their goalposts around when they really needed them.

Chase continued, 'We narrowed down which office he was in, got his photo from the clearance files and then followed him. We noticed he would move away from his office and make sat phone calls from the car park. Got some feelthy pictures if you wanna see 'em,' he said with a lop-sided smirk on his face.

Chase pushed a large brown envelope across the desk towards Peter Bryant who dove into a manila folder and pulled out half-a-dozen 8 x 6 glossy photographs.

'Frank fucking Benning,' he said with disgust dripping off every word.

'Ah, so you know the gent?'

'Now it all makes sense,' Bryant sighed and slumped back into his chair. He explained the operation in Townsville that had extended north to Cairns and then Cooktown and some offshore islands. When he recalled the death of Ian Taylor in mysterious circumstances, Ewart Chase grimaced.

'What, what is it?' Bryant asked, looking closely at Chase.

'When we were recording some of the transmissions there was an oblique reference to killing a diver,' he said softly.

'Jesus H Christ!'

'What can I do to help now, mate?'

'Please stay on those people and keep me in the loop on anything about going after a bloke called Bob McTaggart. He doesn't know it yet, but he is in deep shit … or about to be.'

*　　*　　*

Franz Nesbitt was feeling the heat and not just from the warm tropical sun of Cairns. He was on the phone to Carina Thuong.

'Kreena, I need you to get a few blokes together and collect Frank Benning from Cooktown airport at 5.15 tomorrow afternoon. Make sure you keep it low key. I don't want anyone pickin' up on who we are or what we are doing.'

'Okay, Franz,' Carina responded, wondering why Frank Benning was coming all the way from Canberra to Cooktown and seemingly breaking cover. 'Is there a problem I should be aware of?' she asked, hoping to shed some light onto this sudden development. Things had gone a bit pear-shaped when two of the guys on Blackbird Patches seemingly vanished into thin air.

'Nuthin' for you to worry about at this stage. You just get Benning into the motel and give him whatever he wants.'

'Okay. Got it. Will he need a car?'

'That's for him to decide. Let me know when you've picked him up.' He rang off, wondering what Benning would be doing to "neutralise the threat". In the meantime, he had two of his men driving down the main road out of Cooktown looking for vehicles or people out of place that didn't fit in or looked like Feds.

*   *   *

Cooktown airport is not much more than a flash shed with some palm trees out the front. There is no control tower, no hangars, and a few light aircraft tied down on the apron. Any maintenance for aircraft is done in Cairns and refuelling is not encouraged. The regular airline flying in and out was Hinterland Aviation. Flying twin-engined Cessnas, they had a monopoly on flights for people who needed to get north of Cairns.

Frank Benning waited for his suitcase to be unloaded from the cargo compartment in the nose of the Cessna 404. He felt as if he was wrapped in a warm wet blanket as he stood on the apron in the bright but now fading sunshine. Soon it would be dark, and the heat would begin to go out of the clear sky. He gathered his bag and started walking towards the airport terminal shed. He saw Carina Thuong, accompanied by two males who looked like refugees from a bikie gang in downtown Sydney.

'Carina,' Benning offered as he handed his suitcase to one of the men who he knew was called Kegs.

'Frank,' Carina gave back with no trace of emotion on her face whatsoever. Benning always thought she was a cold bitch, and this greeting reinforced the belief.

'Do you need a car?' she asked matter-of-factly, 'Cause if you do, we can pick one up tomorrow in town.'

'Not sure at this stage, I am hoping for some more information, but there's a good chance we will need a four-wheel drive or a decent large sedan.'

'Copy,' she shot back as they began exiting the small car park.

*   *   *

As they pulled out in their four-wheel drive, they drove past the local police sergeant Tim Brophy who was picking up his daughter who was up for the school holidays. Tim was out of uniform and using his private car. Carina and Benning drove past him but Sergeant Brophy had already noted the licence plate and the fact that an Asian woman and two goons had collected a bloke who looked like the mug shot that he had received from his headquarters with a privacy marking of Confidential. Rarely did anything of this nature cross his desk, and he immediately entered the rego number of the car into his note pad. He would need to drop his daughter off and head straight back into the office and get on the phone to Brisbane, given the urgency of the matter.

After ringing Brisbane, Tim Brophy was given the mobile number of Peter Bryant from the AFP. Things were ramping up for the local copper for whom a big day out was chucking a few drunks into the old shipping container at the rear of their police station and kicking them out the next morning. That and a few search and rescues for Grey Nomads who had got themselves bushed was usually the norm in this remote part of Queensland.

Brophy was on the phone to Peter Bryant who had returned to his office after the Brisbane AFP office had alerted him that things were moving after his alert went out for the people of interest in the Daintree operations.

'Agent Bryant,' he said down the phone.

'Ah, g'day mate, its Sergeant Tim Brophy from Cooktown here.'

'G'day, Tim,' Bryant responded, dropping any formality with the country copper, 'What have you got for me?'

'Well, I was out at Cooktown airport and I saw the bloke called Benning you had an alert for … and he was being picked by this Asian sheila and with her were a couple of goons who definitely weren't tourists.'

'Did you get a lead on where they were headed?' Peter Bryant asked hopefully.

'Nah mate, I couldn't. I had my daughter with me that I was picking up from the same flight Benning arrived on.' He added as his reason for not following up, 'I was in civvies in my own car and not really set up for shadowing a couple of crooks.'

Peter Bryant smiled to himself as the sergeant went on to explain that he had managed to track the licence plate and car ownership to a company owned by Marcos Kudlov who he had also discovered was an occasional visitor to the area and had some business interests locally.

'That's great work, Sergeant,' Bryant said sincerely. 'I need you to be able to talk to me directly from now on because we are on a short fuse here. I will talk to my super and get the clearances for that, but rest assured we will be okay for direct comms.'

'Okey doke.'

'Tim, I have to tell you that we have a bad apple in the barrel so I must ask that what I am about to tell you is on a need-to-know basis, and we need to keep this as tight as possible.'

Brophy straightened in his chair. 'Got it,' he shot back.

Peter Bryant then spent ten minutes giving Sergeant Tim Brophy the essentials of the operation; the fact that several murders had already taken place; that the gang was armed and very dangerous, and that they would be fighting for millions of dollars' worth of drugs and they would take no prisoners. Bryant walked straight into Superintendent Ballantyne's office and stated that their team should now move to the Brisbane office as things were ramping up faster than expected.

*   *   *

Tim Brophy sat back in his chair and started scouring the map for likely places that might be holding a gang of criminals and the most likely place for flying illicit cargo out of the area. Having served in Cooktown twice in his 20-year career, he had a good feel for who was who in the zoo. He decided that first thing in the morning, he would get Cairns to give him the flight manifests for all incoming aircraft. He would get his clerk to ring around all of the real estate agents and see who had let out houses recently and to whom and for how long. Then, he and his senior constable would take a drive down towards the Lion's Den and drop in and visit Betty Humphries who had spoken of people flying off her airstrip in the past without permission. It was going to be a busy day, and he would be spending very little time with his teenage daughter. The fishing trip out to the reef that he had promised would have to be on hold.

*   *   *

Carina pulled into the large house on the outskirts of Cooktown that Franz Nesbitt had hired for a couple of months while they moved the ice they were manufacturing on Blackbird Patches further south. She led Benning into the front rooms that served as a meeting and planning room for the gang.

'Hello, Frank,' Nesbitt offered without offering a handshake.

'Franz,' Benning replied sternly. 'Did you have any luck tracing the Feds safe house?'

'The boys spent a bit of time driving down the Mulligan Highway and Shriptons Flat Road, and we reckon they are holed up near Springvale Station about an hour south of here. There are a few old homesteads that have been vacated owing to the downturn in beef exports and the crunch on barra fishing. Some of the locals said there were a couple of blokes staying in this place,' Nesbitt pointed a stubby finger at the map on the table, 'and they are not locals.'

'How far down the track did you say?'

'About an hour. Only one way in from what we can see and off the main drag so we can keep things quiet, if need be.' Franz smirked at what he thought was a nice play on words.

After a day of travelling and changing planes three times, Benning was not in the mood for sarcasm.

'Okay, have we got a laptop here so we can Google the area?' Benning asked, looking around the untidy room.

'I've got one,' Carina offered, and she moved towards her bedroom at the rear of the house.

'Waddya got in mind, Frank?' Nesbitt asked.

'Well, from what you have told me, it lines up with what I saw on a map in Canberra.' Benning paused, not wanting to give too much away. 'I am thinking we get everyone we can, and we go down and pay a visit to whoever is on that property and eliminate the threat to our operation.'

'Eliminate?' asked Kegs who had been standing behind the table and listening to his bosses' plans.

'Yeah, Kegs, eliminate,' snarled Franz, 'That means we kill the fuckers.'

'Right,' said Kegs quietly.

'We're gonna need another vehicle,' Carina said as she stepped forward to examine the map. 'I reckon you will need a four-wheel drive to carry the heavier weaponry, a sedan to do the initial approach and gain early intel, and a third vehicle for cut off and backup.' All the men in the room looked at the woman with a new respect as she offered up a quick plan of action that covered all the bases for shutting down the Federal agency now threatening their criminal livelihoods.

Franz Nesbitt stepped back and said, 'The boss is flying in tomorrow with some more muscle and we will have to run this past him, but I think he will like it.'

The impending presence of Marcos Kudlov brought a strange quietness to the room. Everyone in the room knew what a vicious animal the man could be and knew of his reputation for dealing with those who crossed his path or failed to meet his expectations. There was a pregnant pause to the proceedings as each person dealt with their own thoughts on having the master criminal present. Things were now getting serious.

Benning looked directly at Carina, cleared his throat and said, 'Sounds like a plan. You travel with me tomorrow in the sedan and we will look like tourists or potential property investors if it turns out that the Feds aren't there. No need to blow our cover unnecessarily.' Carina nodded and opened her laptop to get a satellite image of the property and see what the ground surrounding it looked like.

Franz gathered his soldiers around him and started detailing who would be travelling in what vehicle. He wanted all the ammunition they could muster to be distributed, and he tasked Kegs and Bart with getting another four-wheel drive from the local car rental agency in town. They would depart their house at 10 a.m. sharp. Carina would have her radio to give Franz and the backup team the go ahead once they determined who was at the homestead. Now all they had to do was get their boss to give them the nod.

The Trap is Sprung

Barry adjusted his position up on the roof of the shed. He had found an old tarpaulin to protect his body as he lay prone on the scorching hot corrugated iron roof. He had a good field of fire down the 500-metre-long dirt gravel road that led to the farmhouse where Bob and Melanie lay in wait. The grass was almost a metre high each side of the road and provided good cover from view but little else. Thankfully, there were few trees that blocked his line of sight. Greg was covering down the road and would provide a good cut off if anyone managed to escape the ambush killing ground.

Bob was at the front window of the house on the veranda that had been enclosed to provide extra bedroom space for whoever had lived in the farmhouse. The windows were a series of glass louvres, most of which were still intact but needed to be open to see clearly. He had a good view of the road and could just make out an indentation in the grass where Greg was laying in his sniper hide on a small hillock about 175 metres from the farmhouse on the south side of the road. He was thinking through his courses of action and was glad of his position because he wouldn't have to cross over open ground to bug out in a hurry.

Melanie was in a room adjacent to the kitchen and could see Bob's back and also had a limited view down the entrance road. The temperature inside the weatherboard house was starting to rise to what would be a normal day in this part of the country in the Dry season. The humidity was hovering around 70 per cent and the temperature would climb from a low of 19 degrees Celsius and peak around 27 degrees. Just another day in paradise. Melanie was wondering what Benning was likely to do when confronted and exposed for the criminal that she was sure he was.

Greg was happy with his sniper position. He could see the top of the shed where he knew Barry was in hiding with his explosive charges and had a good elevated firing position. He was happy with his and Barry's endeavours overnight when they had managed to fashion improvised explosive devices out of an old disc plough and had fitted plastic explosive laced with all manner of metal debris found in the shed including old nails, nuts and bolts. They had drawn on their training from the commando regiment in fashioning these nasty pieces of work and were sure that they would do the job most effectively when required. Even if they didn't maim or kill anyone, the charges would create a reasonable amount of panic and confusion once they went off and hopefully disorient any would-be aggressors in their ambush site.

*   *   *

The day slowly wore on. It was late morning and that time when the thought that the task is all a waste of time and effort starts to sneak its way into the brain. Bob was beginning to think they had been too confident. *Have I misread my opponent? Are they onto our ambush plan and trying to outflank us?* Suddenly, a black Land Cruiser drew up at the front gate. Bob had closed it so they could all get eyes on whoever alighted to open the steel mesh gate.

Benning looked down the entrance road and could see the rear end of a red truck to the right of the farmhouse. This was now the time to bring this shit to an end, he thought.

'Get out, open the gate and leave it wide open,' he said to his passenger.

Through his rifle scope Bob could see it was Benning in the driver's seat. Then a woman alighted and moved to open the gate. It was the same Asian woman he had seen in the camp and then on the airstrip. Benning had finally shown his hand.

'Heads up, guys, its Benning and that Asian woman. Go straight to Plan B. Let's try and nail this bastard when he gets to the house.'

'Two, copy, out.'

'Four, copy, out.'

'Got him,' said Melanie from her position near the kitchen. Bob smiled at the precision in her voice. *Calm as a cucumber is that girl.*

'Get a rifle, Melanie, I have a feeling this is gonna get untidy,' Bob said without turning around.

Melanie moved to the back room to recover the last of the long arms they had in their armoury.

Frank Benning made as if he was on the phone as he sat near the front gate. As soon as he saw Kudlov's two vehicle convoy behind him come over a rise about 250 metres distant, he started down the dirt entrance road. It had been a stroke of luck being told by a local that the bloke from the eco tours company was using a red truck. The "tour fella" was now staying in the old farmhouse that the Fishers used to own before they had to move to Cairns when their daughter contracted Ross River Fever. *A stroke of luck indeed,* Benning thought to himself. He got back in his vehicle and texted to Kudlov:

At front gate on right of road. Close on me now.

 Kudlov texted back:

15 seconds.

Bob was watching Benning's every movement through his scope. Benning tore down the driveway at best speed, and in a cloud of dust alighted from his hire car. Bob was totally focussed on Benning and did not see the next two vehicles rapidly enter the farm road and push hard down towards the house behind Benning. *If anything can fuck up in an ambush – it will.*

Bob was staring intently as Benning's vehicle came down the track. Bob's mobile phone went off. He looked at it on the table next to his position alongside his spare magazines. *I don't believe it, Christ not now!* It was Peter Bryant. Bob pushed the speaker button and went back to his firing position to keep focused on the approaching Benning.

'Yeah, Pete.'

'Bob, you need to know that Frank Benning is the rotten apple we've been looking for.'

'Yeah, I figured that out already Pete. Look mate, I'll have to call you back, things are a bit busy here right now.'

Barry watched intently as he saw Benning and then two more vehicles come charging down the track. Barry had placed his charges to prevent an egress from the house because they wanted Benning inside with Bob and Melanie. Greg heard the two vehicles come thundering down the gravel road and saw the occupants were carrying automatic weapons. He decided the time had come to spring the trap. As he prepared to fire, he heard Bob on the radio say in a calm voice, 'Four this is One, hit it.'

As the first of Kudlov's vehicles drew level with his primary IED, Greg initiated the device and a massive explosion rent the air. A large grey, brown and black cloud of smoke erupted skyward. The blast of the improvised claymore mine slammed into the side of the vehicle and fatally wounded the driver who was hit just above the ear by a large bolt that penetrated his skull. He lost control of his vehicle and it slid into the monsoon drain on the side of the track and toppled slowly onto its side. The occupants were all concussed as five kilos of high explosive shattered the warm moist air.

*   *   *

Before Bob had a chance to hang up the phone a massive explosion rent the air as Greg fired his first charge. Immediately afterwards small arms fire started cracking. Peter Bryant listened in amazement as what sounded like a small war started coming over his phone. He left it on as Bob had still not hung up. He spun around at the desk in his Brisbane office and yelled at his staff,

'Get me the Special Ops Team team in Townsville and organise flights to Cairns ASAP. Warn out the aviation unit in Townsville to be prepared to move 20 pax to Cooktown within an hour.' Peter Bryant now realised that what he mistook for nothing happening from McTaggart was most probably self-imposed radio silence.

* * *

Kudlov screamed at his driver to stop his vehicle, fearing they were driving into an ambush much like he himself had experienced in Bosnia a decade before. He watched intently from behind the door of his four-wheel drive as he saw Kegs half stand next to his vehicle to shoot at the farmhouse and heard a crack whistle past his ear and saw Kegs spin violently as a round slammed into his right shoulder and then drop to the ground. This was the key for Kudlov realising that things were getting out of hand, and that there were more Feds here than they were anticipating. He moved in a half-crouch to the rear of his vehicle and pulled several anti-armour weapons out of the back compartment. He knew that these M72 light anti-tank weapons would come in handy one day. He pulled open the rocket launcher, flipped up the sights and took aim at the left front of the building where he had seen a muzzle flash. His eye then caught movement on the roof of the shed.

Bob watched with some surprise as the first claymore was set off. He knew the boys had rigged up some charges but was not expecting that. He concentrated on who was going to exit the vehicle. As he did, he missed seeing Benning pull up almost under the high-set farmhouse and enter the building through the rear stairs. Barry was intent on acquiring a target near the overturned vehicle as the surviving occupants were now spraying the farmhouse with automatic fire. Barry saw one man in camouflage clothing move around the rear of the overturned vehicle to check on Kegs and took the opportunity to fire a single round from his .308 Winchester. Designed as a big game hunting rifle, it made short work of the man as the bullet ripped into his chest, tore through his lungs and exited out his back, leaving him with a sucking chest wound. He would die in agony two minutes later.

Carina was guarding the Land Cruiser and could hear Barry engaging the convoy on the entrance road. She fired a burst from her Uzi up into the shed roof in an attempt to get whoever was up there to show themselves. Up on the roof, Barry heard the clattering of bullets tearing through the corrugated iron sheeting only a metre from his firing position. He wished he had brought something heavier up than the tarp he was laying on.

Melanie was peering down the road, trying to get some idea of what was going on. She could hear Bob engaging the lead vehicle that had been forced off the road. Bob was on the other side of a thin fibro partition that had made an extra bedroom on the veranda. Bullets were slamming into the glass louvres and shattering and spraying secondary shrapnel in all directions. She had never been in a firefight like this before and she could feel her pulse rate lift dramatically. She failed to hear Benning come up behind her and felt everything go black as a Taser charge ripped through her system. She collapsed onto the ground and Benning pulled her backwards along the floor towards the rear doorway. The sound of the gun battle was deafening as dozens of bullets started ripping across the wall behind him. Fearing for his own life, Benning dragged the unconscious Melanie down the back stairs towards his vehicle.

Barry drew himself up to see where Benning was headed and to see if he could engage him or at least blow one of the claymore charges to prevent him leaving the ambush. It was a fatal mistake. Kudlov saw Barry's silhouette and fired his missile at the shed roofline, hoping to hit slightly below the barge board. Bob watched as Kudlov fired the LAW and instinctively ducked thinking the rocket was headed his way. He heard an enormous explosion as the rocket slammed into the gable of the shed and blew the lid off the shed and killed Barry instantly as his body was shredded with torn corrugated iron. Kudlov smiled at his work and returned to the vehicle to get another rocket.

Bart had finally extricated himself from the overturned vehicle. He crawled around the side to see Kegs lying in a pool of blood. He immediately started firing indiscriminately into the house. He had never had any military training, but he knew his way around shotguns and automatic rifles. It took him a while to realise that he was the only one from his vehicle still capable of returning fire. He heard the rocket scream past his head and turned to see Kudlov grinning as the rocket detonated with a massive blast. He half stood and started making his way towards the second vehicle still parked on the road. Franz Nesbitt and another thug were each side of Kudlov and heavily engaging the farmhouse. Kudlov screamed at them to 'kill the motherfuckers.'

Franz had been in some gang warfare in his time, but this was something out of this world. They had expended almost three 30 round magazines each from their Kalashnikovs and the high-pitched chattering of their weapons was creating a continuous din of battle. Bob had moved to a different firing position and turned every now and then to see where Melanie was because another barrel firing down range would be really handy. He called at her to come forward but got no response. He was busy trying to acquire targets near the second vehicle and was increasingly concerned as Greg was now cut off from the farmhouse as the goons started circling toward the northern side of the building. Franz Nesbitt crossed the road and dived into the monsoon drain and was climbing out of it when Greg put a round into the side of his head almost removing half of his scalp. It was a risky shot because now the other two men would know that he was close by.

Kudlov resumed his firing position with a new M72 anti-tank rocket. He popped open the tube and squinted through the sights and concentrated on putting this rocket into the left front of the building. Just as he applied pressure to squeeze the trigger, a large calibre rifle round slammed into the car door next to his head causing him to flinch as the rocket sped on its way.

Bob thought he may have hit Kudlov as he saw him take cover and then saw the tell-tale cloud of dark brown smoke with a black centre as the LAW rocket headed straight for the farmhouse. Bob instinctively hit the deck and took cover behind the overturned dining table. With a thunderous roar the rocket slammed into the corner of the building bringing down half of the room he was sheltering inside. *Time to get outta here, Bob, old son.*

Bob now realised that shits were trumps. Barry had seemingly gone down when the rocket slammed into the shed that was now partly on fire. Melanie was missing and he could not raise her on the radio. Bob was now on the two way.

'Four this One, Shot Duck over.'

'One this Four, Fucked Duck, out.' Even in dire straits, the ex-commando could find time for a little humour.

*   *   *

Benning dragged Melanie most unceremoniously down the stairs by her hair toward his Land Cruiser and screamed at Carina who was now covered in debris from the burning shed. She heard Benning yelling to help him drag Melanie into the back of the Land Cruiser. He told her to sit in the back and cover their exit as he accelerated away from the farmhouse and headed off through the bush, intending to link up with the main road. Melanie lay slumped unconscious in the back compartment of the four-wheel drive. She started to slowly waken and was trying to focus on what she could see and hear. She saw Carina and started to move when all went black again as Carina pistol-whipped her across the temple and she slipped back violently into unconsciousness.

'Everything alright, Carina?' asked Benning as he heard the unmistakable smack of metal into skin and bone. It was a sound one never forgot.

'It is now,' she said without any emotion whatsoever. 'Where are we headed?'

'I need to regroup, so we will head down towards the Lion's Den and see what we can figure out.'

Carina's jaw tightened as she absorbed the fact that her investment in what should have been a very lucrative venture was now going very badly indeed. Her faith in the villains she had consorted with almost two years ago was fading as fast as the afternoon light.

*　　*　　*

Back on the road into the farmhouse, Kudlov saw Nesbitt go down. It was time to cut and run because the Feds had a superior firing position. He yelled at his remaining soldier Bart to get his arse into the vehicle and get it turned around and pick him up as they left the property. Not wanting to hear what Kudlov was screaming at him, Bart ran towards the four-wheel drive, threw his weapon into the front seat and drove down towards the house, executed a brilliant U-turn in a massive cloud of orange and brown dust and headed back toward Kudlov crouching in the drain beside the track.

'Go, fuckin' go. Get the fark outta here,' screamed Kudlov.

The young criminal floored the four-wheel drive and headed towards the farm gate.

Greg was about to start moving off his small hillock and saw the vehicle departing. He fired his two remaining claymores that would most probably not disable the vehicle but would at least dissuade the occupants from returning to re-engage. The IEDs went off and shrapnel rent the air. It was not a good day for the young driver as he caught an ugly piece of what had once been the end of chisel in his neck and he started bleeding profusely. Bart couldn't talk as his windpipe had been lacerated and his larynx partly destroyed.

Kudlov continually yelled at his lackey to drive faster but Bart was rapidly losing consciousness through loss of blood. Kudlov looked across at the driver and realised he was going to have to drive. The vehicle was slowing. He was no longer under accurate small-arms fire and reached across and stopped the vehicle. He got out, went around to the driver's side and pushed the young man into the passenger seat. He drove the remaining 100 metres to the front gate. Realising that someone would see the smoke and flames from the burning shed he would have to drive south towards the Lion's Den where he suspected Benning must have gone when he saw his four-wheel drive crashing through the light scrub south of the farmhouse. He was a great help. Not.

* * *

Greg started crawling on his guts through the long grass. He hoped his last claymores had done some damage. He now had to head for the

RV. He kept low in the light scrub. *Christ, what a day.* He wondered what had happened to Barry, but his thoughts were not good. He thought he saw Barry's body flying through the air when the LAW rocket smashed into the roof.

Bob was on the radio. 'Four this One, we need to RV. Meet me near the track south of the cattle ramp.'

'This is One, I am on my way. Give me five.'

'Roger out.'

Bob had grabbed his go bag and all of the spare ammunition he could gather. He saw Melanie's rifle on the floor in the kitchen and drag marks that showed she hadn't gone of her own accord. He slung her rifle and was now positioned in long grass and standing in the back tray of the red truck, close to a cattle loading ramp. He was scanning the road that was 50 metres distant and searching the grass each side of his position for sign of movement.

The two-way burst into life.

'One this Four, I am 25 metres to your six o'clock.'

'Roger, close now.'

Greg emerged from the long grass and moved quickly up to the truck and threw his backpack into the tray. Bob got down and stood next to the ex-commando and saw the look of a warrior in his earnest face.

'Barry bought it when that rocket hit the shed,' Bob said matter-of-factly but aware that the news was going to hit Greg hard.

'Yeah, I figured that, poor bastard. What now, boss?'

'Well, I am pretty sure Benning has grabbed Melanie.'

Greg's eyes widened a little and then narrowed. 'Okay.'

'He must have got her when the shit really started because I didn't hear a bloody thing.' Bob looked over Greg's shoulder at the burning buildings. 'This place will be crawling with people soon.' He took in the burning shed, the smouldering farmhouse that would probably ignite soon, and a small grass fire near the road. 'Yeah, there'll be firies, coppers, locals, you name it. I didn't see Benning head north, so I put my money on him having the same RV as us.'

'The Lion's Den caravan park?' Greg asked.

'Yep, it is the only way you can hook around this place and get back to Cooktown.'

'I saw the nasties head off that way after they pulled back to the main road. We could be heading into more trouble here, Bob.'

'Yeah, I know. But we have gotta get that bastard Benning and that Asian sheila before they do something nasty to Melanie.'

'Reckon they will use her as a hostage?' Greg asked while checking his rifle magazine.

'Wouldn't put it past him, but this is not really my cup of tea, mate. I don't normally converse with people I am shooting at.'

Greg smiled knowingly, 'Yep, give me the Taliban anytime.'

'C'mon, let's go get Melanie back.'

'And Greg?'

'Yeah, mate?'

'No prisoners, eh?'

'No prisoners.'

The two men climbed into the truck and drove out onto the road heading south to the Lion's Den.

* * *

Melanie came to as the Land Cruiser drew up into the caravan park camping area. She kept her eyes closed. Her hands were tied behind her back and her wrists felt like they were cuffed with plastic zip ties. Her head was throbbing unmercifully from the hit across her head with Carina's pistol. She overheard Frank Benning on his mobile phone leaving a message to whoever he was calling.

'I am at the Lion's Den car park. Meet up with me now. We have gotta sort this shit out NOW!'

Melanie heard what she believed was a mild form of panic in Frank Benning's voice. She moved her hands slowly to her waist band and to her horror could not feel the Glock pistol she had tucked into her jeans. *Must have come out while that bastard was dragging me down the stairs,* she thought with a wry look on her bruised face.

She then heard a female voice, 'What are we going to do with this woman?'

'I am a great believer in always having a fall-back position, Carina.' Benning smiled thinly. 'If everything goes pear-shaped, we will have a bargaining chip to get us onto that Lear jet that Marcos Kudlov likes gallivanting around in.'

Carina offered nothing in response. Her thoughts were on how she would escape and evade if it looked like they were going to be forced into capture. Her Plan B would be to cut and run into the bush because she knew she had the skills to survive in the tropical bush. She hadn't expected the firefight they had just survived. Nor did she think that Benning was as merciless as she first thought. He had finally shown some backbone in the 18 months that she was aware that he existed.

Melanie maintained her still position in the back of the Land Cruiser. *Carina. Aah, that must be the woman that Bob kept referring to from his past run-in with the gang.* Melanie made a mental note to give Carina a really good smack in the face the next time she had her hands free to atone for the massive headache she now suffered. She had to work on a way to get her hands free and get her hands on a weapon of any sort. It was not going to be easy as the zip ties were quite tight. She hoped that sweat would help her ease out of the cuffs but so far, nothing was moving.

*   *   *

Bob's mobile phone rang as he pulled off the main road onto a bush track about 500 metres from the Lion's Den Hotel.

'G'day, Pete,' Bob said quietly into phone.

'What the fuck is going on, mate?' Peter Bryant asked.

'Well, it's a long story but I figured that someone close to us on the op was selling us out.'

'Go on.'

'So, I set a trap and our mate Frank fell into it.'

'It sounded like fucking war was going on up there, Bob. Is everyone okay?'

'No, not really, mate. One of the local AFP guys here was killed when you rang. They pulled out the heavy artillery and we are in the middle of a real shit fight here at present.'

'I see.'

'Yeah, and it gets worse. That bastard Benning has grabbed Melanie as a hostage and legged it out of where we were hoping to grab him. He must have called in a few favours from that gang you were warning me about. There's been a bit of blood spilt and we could do with a hand right now.' Bob looked across at Greg who was nodding and smiling slightly at the understatements he had just heard.

'Christ, any idea where Benning is right now?'

'I think he has headed south of here towards a place called the Lion's Den. I wouldn't be surprised if they are regrouping and thinking of coming back to the place where we had been hiding up, but I have had to abandon that site. I am now going after Benning and try to get Melanie before someone gets desperate.'

'Righto, you're the man on the ground. I have warned out the Special Ops Team in Townsville, but they will not be in Cooktown before dark. I am on my way up with another team of Armed Offenders guys and we will be there around 8 o'clock tonight.' Peter Bryant paused, trying to think of something to assist Bob McTaggart.

'Okay, Pete. I am off on a recce at the Lion's Den shortly. I'll keep you posted. Get someone to secure the place that is currently a bit of a mess. One of our guys is in the ruins of the shed.'

Bob sent the grid coordinates through to Bryant as a text message while Greg loaded some magazines for Bob's rifle.

'Have you got a handgun, mate?' Greg asked.

'Yeah, I've got the Glock and three mags. I've got an idea on how we might be able to flush out these pricks. I want you to drop me about 500 short of the Lion's Den and then drive past the pub and caravan park at best speed. I want anyone in the Lion's Den to think we have headed into town and chasing them. I just hope the bastard Benning is there. Stop about half a click south, hide the truck and delay any bastard trying to link up with Benning or nail him if he gets away before I get there.'

'Got it,' Greg replied with a stern grin on his face "I love it when a plan comes together.'

Let's hope so mate, let's hope so.

*　*　*

Kudlov was studying the map on the bloodied front seat of his four-wheel drive. A text message said he had missed a call from Benning. He listened to the excited voice of the crooked agent and smiled to himself. *You wouldn't have lasted a month in the war back home, you pussy.* He would have to get rid of this agent once he had sorted out who it was trying to kill him back at the farmhouse. *Just like old times, eh Marcos?*

Kudlov had gone about half a kilometre down the road and Bart, slumped in the passenger seat, was still gurgling blood. He pulled up a side road and drove for about a minute so he wouldn't be seen from the highway. He stopped near a small creek crossing, got out and went to the passenger door. He searched Bart's clothes for ID or anything that would tie him to Kudlov or their operation. He dragged the goon from the car and unceremoniously shoved the fatally wounded man into the long grass. Bart wouldn't be found for three days when pigs would start gnawing at his remains.

CHAPTER 21

The Last Dance

The two men were quiet as Greg drove the red truck south down the bitumen road leading toward the Lion's Den Hotel and caravan park. They were definitely no longer inconspicuous with their vehicle now scarred with bullet holes from the panicky spraying of automatic fire by Kudlov's thugs. Greg slowed to a stop as Bob climbed down and looked back down the road to make sure the way was clear.

'Righto, Greg. Set yourself up south of the car park area and listen out on the two-way. If it all turns to shit and you don't hear from me, ring this number and ask for Peter Bryant. He's the AFP guy I have been working with.' Bob handed him a card that Greg slipped into his shirt pocket.

Greg looked down into Bob's face and saw nothing but steely resolve. 'Got it.'

Bob pulled his backpack on, thumped on the door signalling he was off and headed into the thick bush. Greg engaged the low gears as quickly as he could and sped off toward the Lion's Den. *Not a bad plan old mate, let's hope they fall for it and get sloppy.*

Bob moved quickly through the underbrush that was entangled with vines. It was not easy going but nothing he hadn't encountered before. Several times he had to skirt around large clumps of dense foliage that were just too thick to penetrate. *At least I have got some cover from view here, I just need to figure out some way to get up close and personal.*

*   *   *

Benning sat fidgeting with his handgun in the front of the car. He was running various scenarios through his head on how he could resurrect this operation. Priority one was to get the enormous stash that the gang had accumulated and get out of this godforsaken place and away free. Any chance of returning to Canberra was shot, as was his former life. He had to make it work because from now on he would be a wanted man, with no income and his Government pension was well and truly gone. *Welcome to the dark side, Frank, old fella.*

Carina had gone to the toilet as an excuse to scout the area and check around for any sign of a follow-up group. When it came to tactics, security, and just plain old common dog-fuck, she had realised very quickly that Frank Benning was next to useless. She returned to the vehicle and opened the rear door of the Land Cruiser to check on Melanie who was still lying curled up, and now gagged with a filthy rag. Melanie looked up at Carina with a pleading look in her eyes trying to ask to go to the toilet.

'What are we gonna do with this bitch?' Carina asked.

'Hang onto her for insurance until we sort this shit out,' Benning snapped back while checking his mobile phone for messages.

Melanie could sense that once this "shit was sorted out" she could very well be a useless commodity and end up dead – at best. She started to wriggle and move around and started making noises through the gag. Carina took her Glock out and put it to Melanie's head and said through gritted teeth, 'Make one loud noise and I will put a hole in your pretty little skull.' She then savagely pulled the gag out of Melanie's mouth.

'I just want to go to the toilet, I'm busting,' she pleaded to anyone, trying to sound as helpless as she could. 'I don't want any trouble, I'm just a Quarantine Officer who was asked to help out. I don't want any trouble … please, please can I go to the toilet, I promise I won't run away.'

Benning looked at Melanie who was trying to cross her legs.

'No chance, bitch,' Carina said with a smirk on her face. 'Piss in your pants.'

Melanie looked aghast. 'No, I need to go to the toilet and do a Number Two,' she said, trying her very best to appear harmless and helpless all at the same time.

'Oh, for Christ's sake!' Benning snarled, 'Take her down to the dunnies and let her have a crap. Keep a good eye on her.'

Carina dragged Melanie out of the Land Cruiser and ushered her quickly through the long grass towards the toilet block on the edge of the caravan park. She kept herself between Melanie and anyone likely to be looking their way.

'Make one move to escape and I will shoot you down,' Carina hissed.

*　　*　　*

Bob was now on the verge of the caravan park and camping area. The place had about a dozen campers in tents and a smattering of smaller caravans. It was typical of the tourist season that was now drawing to an end with the oncoming Wet. He moved purposefully along the edge of the park staying about ten metres in the scrub line to avoid being seen. He was now at the southernmost end of the mown reserve and had still not seen Benning's dark four-wheel drive. *Jesus, I hope I haven't misread this bastard. Maybe he has legged it all the way back into town. Nah, he would want to tie up loose ends. I wonder how many other goons they've got with them.*

Bob's mind was racing through probabilities and possibilities when he saw the Land Cruiser in the shade of some larger trees about 150 metres distant. Benning has parked away from everyone else, obviously waiting for reinforcements, he thought to himself. He needed to find a suitable spot to take a well-aimed shot and remove the most obvious threat to Melanie. He had to be very careful not to be spotted. He started a slow and methodical approach to a large copse of thick shrubs he could use for cover.

*　　*　　*

Greg had moved the red truck into the bush down an old access road once used for logging. He was now in thick scrub with a clear view down the road, giving him at least 150 metres of fire zone. He settled down with a spare magazine in his side trouser pocket and the two-way radio now clipped to his belt.

'One this is Four; in position, over,' Greg said quietly into the two-way mouthpiece.

'Four this One; roger out.' The two ex-soldiers kept it short and simple.

It would now be a waiting game, and he was hoping that Bob could somehow get Melanie out of this jam. He practised sighting on an imaginary target 100 metres away and set his sights at that distance.

*   *   *

Marcos Kudlov had just got off the phone to his pilot and told him to have the Lear jet loaded with everything that his boys could stuff into it and to meet him at the airstrip that everyone called "Betty's". Kudlov was banking on the fact that they could carry almost three tonnes of cargo with just him and the pilot. There would not be any room in the aircraft for people like Benning. It was time to cut and run, regroup, and set up somewhere else.

Benning jumped as the phone went off on the front seat beside him.

'Frank, dis is Kudlov. I am on my way down to Lion's Den. Vere are you?' he barked.

'I'm at the far south end … not far from the toilet block.' He replied as he looked around, hoping to see Carina and the woman he had allowed to go to the toilet.

'Okay, I vill be dere soon. Ve are gonna sort dis shit out!' he snarled into the phone before throwing it back onto the seat of his hire car. In his mind, sorting "this shit out" was eliminating anyone and everyone that could tie him to the firefight and the operation as a whole. It was time to clean house.

*   *   *

Carina was herding Melanie toward the cement block toilet block. They entered the ladies' toilet and Carina pushed Melanie towards a cubicle. Melanie turned keeping her head down and studying Carina's feet. She needed an opportunity to get this nasty woman off balance. She looked up and saw Carina now holding a flick knife that had suddenly appeared. *Oh shit, she is gonna do me in right here and now!*

Carina smiled maliciously, 'Nah, I am not going to kill you … yet. Turn around.'

Melanie did as she was told and felt Carina slice through her zip ties. She turned to face Carina who now had her pistol pointed directly at her face.

'Get in there and do your business. Leave the door open,' she hissed.

'What if somebody comes?' Melanie asked in a timid and pleading manner while looking around the toilet.

'That will be your bad luck. Now get in there!'

Melanie now wished she still had her handgun that had fallen out of her jeans when she was abducted. *Looks like we are going to Plan B, Melanie old girl.*

Melanie sat down on the pedestal and urinated while Carina stood looking out of the high window in the toilet washroom. She was running through ways in which she could get Carina off balance and not get shot in the process. *She seems reasonably professional. I will have to go hard and fast.*

'Hurry up, bitch,' Carina called as Melanie stood to do up her jeans.

'Almost finished, but I think I am getting my period. Can ... can you get me some hand towel please? I need to clean myself up,' she asked in her most pleading and appealing voice.

'Ahh, for God's sake,' Carina snarled and moved to the hand basins to pull a hand towel out of the dispenser. As she bent to pull the towel out, she placed her handgun on the bench. As she started to extract the paper towel, she felt a sharp pain as her left knee caved in when Melanie delivered a swift hard blow hoping to break her leg. Carina collapsed downwards hitting her jaw hard on the cement benchtop that dazed her momentarily. Melanie grabbed the handgun and stuffed it in her jeans. Carina had swung around and was trying to regain her feet as Melanie once again delivered a full-blooded kick, but this time she used a roundhouse delivery to the side of Carina's head. The woman instantly collapsed in a crumpled heap. Melanie dragged her into the cubicle, closed the door and locked it. She clambered up over the side of the cubicle and carefully headed out of the toilet block. *I need time and space between these bastards,* she thought as she quickly headed off into the bush.

No sooner had she gone 15 metres into the bush that she heard 'Mel!' She spun around to see Bob kneeling by a large ficus tree. She headed for him and collapsed into his arms. The trauma and relief welled inside her and she hung onto her man as tightly as she could. Bob held her for a moment feeling her shake and sob once or twice.

'It's okay Mel, I've got you,' he said, looking over her shoulder towards the toilet block and Benning's vehicle.

Melanie regained her composure and proceeded to tell Bob all that she knew and that Betty's airstrip was probably where the drugs were going to be flown out from tonight. Bob was on the two-way. 'Four this is One. I have Mel, I repeat, I have Mel. Change of plan. More to follow, over.'

'Copy, out.'

Bob and Melanie pulled back into the forest a little deeper so they could still watch Benning. Melanie explained how she had been tied, gagged and her recent escape from the clutches of Carina. 'Oh, and I got this as well' she added, pulling Carina's Glock from out of her jeans.

'Good girl,' Bob smiled, once again wondering who was the real hero in this saga, and once again was seriously impressed with her tenacity.

'Okay, Peter Bryant is on his way to the farmhouse … or what's left of it,' he said, nodding towards the plume of grey and brown smoke cutting through the azure blue sky in the distance. 'Greg is down the road apiece, hoping to nail Benning or any of the goons that might be trying to get back to town. However, now I am thinking we can kill two birds with one stone here.' He paused as Melanie cut in with 'I get it. Nail 'em at the airstrip.' She smiled as she looked at Bob's nodding in agreement.

'Exactly. But first ….'

Just as Bob was going to explain how to take out Benning and remove the threat of Carina who would be now regaining her senses, Kudlov's vehicle drove into the car park somewhat faster than the local speed limit. He was a man on a mission.

* * *

Carina started to come to and felt her battered jaw. First the benchtop, then a well delivered side kick had knocked her silly. *I underestimated that blonde bitch. I will kill her when I get the chance.* She looked around the vacant toilet block and realised her Glock was gone. *I really am gonna kill that bitch.* She walked gingerly out of the toilet block into the afternoon light that was fast fading. She saw Kudlov's shot-up vehicle pull up next to Benning who was now out of the Land Cruiser waiting for Kudlov to alight.

Benning could tell by the body language on Kudlov that things were about to get ugly.

'Vell, Frank, it has really fucked up this time,' he growled in a low menacing voice.

Benning was about to explain that the AFP had somehow intercepted their transmissions and give a plausible reason why things had gone so badly. But Kudlov was looking over his shoulder toward Carina who was now walking slowly toward the two men.

'Vot in the blue fuck is goin' on here, Frank?' Kudlov asked trying to piece together the unfolding drama.

'I ... I don't know. Carina, where's the woman?' he asked, hoping to take the heat off himself from the angry Russian. He turned to look at Carina who had a large red welt starting to appear on the side of her face.

'She got away. She jumped me and she's gone,' Carina offered, trying to clear her head that was throbbing from being well and truly smacked.

Benning turned back to Kudlov who now had his pistol pointed straight at Frank Benning's face.

'Giff me one good reason vy I shouldn't fucken' kill you, Frank. You are gonna cost me millions.'

'For fuck's sake, Marcos. Why are you blaming me? I've been the one making all this possible for the last coupla years,' he pleaded.

'That's true, Frank, that's true,' he said as he lowered the handgun. 'But now it is all over.' And he quickly raised the pistol and shot Frank between the eyes, killing him instantly. Blood spattered over the front of Kudlov's denim shirt. He looked down at the crumpled Benning and his shirt and methodically wiped spots of blood off his own face. 'Fuck you, Frank. Fuck you.'

Carina stood, waiting for the worst. She wondered if this mad Russian would waste her now as well. He looked at her and said quietly, 'Give me a hand to throw this piece of shit into that car and let's get outta here.' Carina gave an inward sigh of relief. Just when she needed a gun, she didn't have one. She grabbed her bag and Benning's gun from the car and removed any other material evidence that might link her or Kudlov to the shooting. She ran around to get into Kudlov's car when he looked at her with a concerned look on his ugly face.

'Vot do ya tink you are doin? Get in dat udder car and follow me!' he spat at her.

As Carina climbed into the Land Cruiser, she noticed people emerging from tents and vans heading towards her and Kudlov after the sound of the shooting. They immediately floored their vehicles and took off accelerating hard and spitting gravel from their rear wheels. They exited the car park and started heading south towards the turnoff back to Cooktown. The campers stopped and looked on, wondering what they had just heard, but there was nothing to see but a cloud of dust.

*   *   *

All Bob and Melanie had seen and heard was a pistol shot, saw a crumpled body hit the dirt and watched as they loaded Benning's body into the Land Cruiser. They looked at each other but said nothing. Bob was thinking of closing in and trying to stop Kudlov, but Melanie grabbed his arm as they watched the pair jump into their vehicles and exit at great speed. Melanie looked at Bob, 'That bastard takes no prisoners, does he?'

'Not a lot,' Bob grimaced, reaching for the two-way to call Greg.

'Four this One, get back to the caravan park asap,' he said curtly.

'Roger out.'

Bob was on the mobile phone calling Peter Bryant.

'Hey, Bob, what's going on?' he asked as if this sort of thing happened every day.

Bob couldn't help smiling to himself and played the cool hand response.

'Not much. Got Melanie back. That Russian just killed Benning, and he and the Asian chick have legged it.'

'Jesus! Okay, okay. Glad Melanie is safe. I'm at what is left of your safe house. We found a few bodies here, looks like the O.K. Corral.'

'Yeah, it was a bit like that, but they started it,' Bob said.

Melanie was tugging on his sleeve wanting to speak.

'Hang on a minute, Pete.' Melanie quickly ran through the conversations she had overheard while in the back of Benning's Land Cruiser.

Bob was back on the phone. 'Melanie reckons they are going to head towards an airstrip outside town about 25 clicks south on the Oakey Creek Road. The place is owned by a lady called Betty and she has reported aircraft movements there before.'

'Hang on, mate,' Bryant said quickly as he started spreading a map over the bonnet of his car. 'Right, got it. I'll get the local coppers to secure Betty and start assembling our guys from Townsville who are due here at any moment. We'll try and stop this lot before they have chance to get out of town.'

'Righto, we will head back to the farmhouse and recover what we can and see you at Betty's.'

'Nah, you stay at the safe house, you've had enough excitement for one day,' Peter Bryant said trying to sort out a plan in his head while on the move.

'You're kidding, aren't you?,' Bob snapped. 'We set these pricks up and we sure as hell wanna see them go down.'

'Okay, okay. But I am the incident commander and you do as you're told,' Peter Bryant said in his best authoritarian tone. 'I'll be up near the airstrip trying to sort out a plan to stop this bastard getting away.'

'Yes, sir,' Bob retorted with a grin on his face. "I reckon Kudlov will be there in 15 to 20 minutes.'

The battered red truck entered the car park slowly as Greg scanned the area for Bob and Melanie.

'C'mon, Mel, here comes Greg. Let's go and get some more ammo and water from the safe house and see if we can make ourselves useful.'

'Yes, Skipper,' she smiled up at him, the bruise on her face really starting to darken now.

Greg pulled up as the pair were walking across the caravan park with some of the caravaners still standing and watching as they climbed into the cabin of the truck and headed north back to the safe house. Bob quickly related what had happened to Melanie and Benning as Greg just listened on in amazement. 'Starting to get a bit serious now, eh?' he asked in a question not aimed at anybody. No one responded.

They drove down the farmhouse driveway to be greeted by firies from in town and the local police sergeant who was busy coordinating a young skinny bloke around getting him to take photographs of the bodies that Bob and Greg had been responsible for. They alighted and headed back to the shed looking for Barry. They came across one of the firefighters who had covered Barry's body with a small tarpaulin. Bob knelt down beside the inert form and lifted the canvas. He re-covered the blackened face and stood to face Melanie and Greg. 'I'm sorry guys, it's Barry.'

Melanie grabbed Bob's shirt and stood close to him and cried softly. Greg turned and quietly walked away, looking at the remains of the smouldering farmhouse. They were joined by Tim Brophy the local police sergeant. He looked at the silent trio and then down at the body of Barry. He softly cleared his throat. 'Can you ID this bloke for me, please?' he swung his gaze around the group and could see the impact of the killing on their sad faces.

Melanie quickly wiped her face and said, 'Yes, he is Barry Costello. He is an AFP undercover operative working for me. He was killed in the line of duty by a man I believe is named Marcos Kudlov, who is currently at large, armed and extremely dangerous.'

Tim Brophy entered the names in his pocketbook and looked up and asked, 'And you are Miss ...?'

'I am Melanie Ballantyne,' she said matter-of-factly without looking at Bob, who was hearing Melanie's real surname for the first time. 'I am an AFP special agent assigned to an operation that is classified at this time, but Agent Peter Bryant and I will brief you separately on that.'

Sergeant Brophy put his notebook back in his pocket and looked around at the carnage. 'Okey doke. I can't wait to hear the rest of this fairy tale,' as he headed off to greet an ambulance that had been ordered to remove the bodies from the crime scene.

Bob had not moved since Melanie had spoken. His brow was knitted, and his mouth was slightly agape. Finally, he said quietly, 'Ballantyne? I thought your name was Adams?'

'Yeah, sorry about that Bob, but Daddy gets upset if we throw the family name around too much when I'm working.'

'Daddy?' Bob asked as Melanie started pulling ammunition boxes out of the arms locker under the floor of the shed. Bob looked at Greg with a quizzical look on his face.

'Daddy?' he said again. Greg just looked at Bob and shrugged. He was going to stay right out of this one.

'We'll talk about it later,' Melanie said as she pulled another rifle out of a bag wrapped in oilskin cloth.

'You betcha we will,' Bob replied tersely, while taking the weapon and handing it to Greg.

'Mate, you better get that other four-wheel drive ready. We might need to reduce our profile a tad when we close on Betty's place. That red truck will stick out like dogs' nuts.'

'On it,' Greg said as he left to sort out another Land Cruiser and Bob and Melanie started reloading magazines and checking their armoury. Melanie averted Bob's gaze continuously as they worked feverishly to make themselves ready.

*   *   *

Peter Bryant was standing with several heavily armed tactical response group and Armed Offenders squad members about a kilometre down the road from the entrance to Betty's farm driveway. There was a second track that led towards the airstrip 500 metres further north of their location, but it had a deep creek to ford, making the last 300 metres only accessible on foot. Bryant produced a black and white sketch map of the property showing the ingress to the airstrip and the farmhouse.

'Right, we have got the property owner secured. She is currently being protected by our local police and will be kept out of harm's way … although she did volunteer to, quote "shoot them bastards".' He smiled as he recalled Betty's indignation that her airstrip was once again being used without her permission. He continued pointing at the sketch map. 'The airstrip is here, and it runs more or less north-south and is a good click from the homestead … here. We should be able to close on the airstrip from three sides if we ingress here and here. And you guys,' he said, nodding at the Armed Offenders team, 'will have to leg it around to the north to cut off any attempt to decamp north.' He went on to detail how they would close the area off with small arms fire if necessary.

'The tactical response leader asked, 'Where are the crooks right now?'

'They have put their Lear jet at the southern end of the strip, and my observation team reports that so far, two more vehicles have driven in and they are in the process of loading more stuff into the aircraft. From what our telephone intercept is telling us, they are about to fly out once the next vehicle arrives. I'm betting that will be Kudlov.'

'How many people are we looking at and are they all armed?' asked the Armed Offenders squad leader who was now mentally allocating troops to task.

'Our best guess is six. There is the leader, whom we believe is Marcos Kudlov. He is extremely dangerous and always armed with at least two weapons. He has a woman of Asian appearance we believe is Carina Thuong as his 2IC, and she is dangerous and will most probably be armed as well … with at least a handgun. She is not to be trifled with, gents, looks can be deceiving.' He looked around the dozen specialists who were all camouflaged, grim faced and nodding.

'Finally, there are a bunch of men who are part of Kudlov's gang, and they will also be most probably armed with a variety of long and side arms, so expect a deadly response when we move on them. Guys, we really want to stop this bloke from getting away. He has killed at least two operatives – albeit one we have since discovered was working against us.' He paused, adding soberly, 'But I hold him responsible for the death of Ian Taylor who he had murdered earlier this year.' Peter Bryant paused as he started to fold the sketch map. 'The last thing is that on that plane are hundreds of millions of dollars' worth of illegal drugs, and we need to stop it getting onto the streets. It is imperative we disable the aircraft. I'll leave you to brief your men, we move out in 10 minutes. If you hear that Lear jet start up, just get to the airstrip asap and disable it.'

Nailed

Kudlov was pushing his car as hard as possible along the bitumen road toward Betty's farmhouse and airstrip. He was pleased with his decision to pre-position the Lear jet at the airstrip away from Cooktown. He had a gut feeling that things were about to turn pear-shaped and needed to distance himself from observation and the authorities. Once on board his jet, he would head for a small airstrip on Balalae Island in Western Province in the Solomon Islands. From there, he would transfer his precious cargo to his boat that was already en route. The local coppers were easily bought off and he was confident that he could transfer his illicit cargo for entry back into Australia when things had settled down. Even when fully loaded, his plane had the legs to reach New Zealand, but he needed to go low-key and avoid any serious police surveillance. It was a circuitous route, but one that would avoid easy and unwanted detection.

Carina was working hard to keep the Land Cruiser on the track behind Kudlov as they headed toward the airstrip. She was amazed at how fast he was able to travel, given the poor condition of the road.

The failing afternoon light made avoiding potholes and washouts on the track difficult. The last thing she needed was to be stranded out here with little chance of avoiding the local coppers. Then, almost without warning, they suddenly burst out onto the side of the airstrip. She followed Kudlov right up to the Lear jet that was being loaded with the last of the gang's drugs and stash.

The pilot was standing near the access door and stairway waiting for his passengers. He had spent most of the day removing all of the seating in the passenger cabin to make way for the packaged drugs. The fuel and cargo load was at the maximum and he was hoping that there were no more than two more passengers. He would need all the grunt he could muster to get this aircraft safely airborne and headed for Western Province. It was going to be a long night.

*   *   *

Greg was driving like a man possessed as they hurtled down the track towards Betty's farmhouse. Bryant had refused them permission to enter the perimeter and to stay back from the airstrip. Greg looked at Bob, 'I've got an idea,' and they turned hard off the track and sped west towards a small hillock not far from the homestead and overlooking the end of the airstrip.

Bob looked at Melanie. 'Stay here, Mel, watch our backs and look after the car.'

She smiled wanly, 'Can't even see out of this bloody eye anymore, so I wouldn't be much good up there.' Her right eye was closing from where Carina had struck her with the pistol. 'You guys get up there smartly; I think I heard the plane start up.'

'Been here before mate?' asked Bob as they scrambled up the rocky rise.

'Yeah, we had to do some surveillance a while back, but the crooks were a no show.' They both settled down into firing positions leaning on some large basalt rocks and looking down onto the airstrip.

'Waddya reckon Bob, about 500?' asked Greg.

'Yep, that's what I'm working on,' he said as they both set their sights. 'Okay, I've got the nose wheel nice and clear. Can you take the pilot's window and scare him a bit?'

'Might kill him.'

'That's the price he just might have to pay,' a grim-faced Bob replied. 'Wait until we see what the Special Ops team are gonna do'.

Peter Bryant was monitoring his radio and had now been told that everyone was in position and awaiting the order to move in. The observation post had reported that there were now four vehicles near the Lear jet, and it appeared that Kudlov was about to depart.

* * *

Kudlov scrambled from his vehicle and headed toward the stairway. He spun and turned to the leader of the gang who were standing and awaiting instructions. They had surmised they wouldn't be flying anywhere and wanted to be paid and wanted to know where they should go next.

'Are ve loaded already?' barked Kudlov.

'Yes, sir,' replied a thick set man in his late 40s. 'What do you want us to do now, Boss?'

Kudlov threw a valise full of money at the thug and said, 'If I vos youse lot, I would get the fark outta here as quickly as possible.' He turned towards Carina who was hoping for a ride to freedom. 'All of you should head to somewhere outside Queensland and stay low for a month. Keep an eye out for an ad in the papers looking for workers for a honey farm.' He smiled to himself thinking he would never see this lot again.

'And Carina, you … you have let me down. You are fucken lucky I don't kill you. Piss off and do not try to contact me again.'

Carina's mouth suddenly went dry. She had witnessed Kudlov execute Frank Benning and knew of his savagery. She started to feel for her handgun in the back of her jeans but Kudlov was up the stairs and the pilot was behind him closing the hydraulic stairs and access door behind him. She had missed her chance.

'Right,' said the thug in charge of the money. He had quickly peered into the valise that was crammed full of bank notes, mostly 50 and 100 dollar bills. His eyes lit up. 'We'll meet in Trinity Beach at the BP roadhouse. If you are not there in 24 hours you will miss out on your payday. I reckon you should go back down through the Daintree as the coppers will be watching the Mulligan Highway.' With that, he and another hoodlum climbed into his four-wheel drive and started heading back down the track towards the main road. The rest of the gang all followed suit by climbing into their cars and heading down the dirt road. The three-vehicle convoy was moving at pace. Carina was left standing by herself. She climbed into the Land Cruiser with Benning's body still in the rear compartment. She decided she would dump him at the next opportunity.

* * *

The Special Operation teams and Armed Offenders squads were in position and had set up a blocking position on the track out to the main road. All had orders to shoot if they or a third party were threatened. The gloves had come off after the shootout up at the safe house. The observation team was finally seeing some movement by the convoy of vehicles.

'Zero Alpha, this is Nine Bravo, they are on the move, looks like an egress back to the main road at pace.'

'Roger. All call signs on the track stop those vehicles and hold all pax.' Peter Bryant was hoping that his cordon around the airstrip was tight and he had no holes in his perimeter.

The lead vehicle was suddenly hit with two shots into the radiator and another into the front tyre. The vehicle lurched to a stop as a third shot shattered the windscreen spraying the occupants with shards of glass. Two armed police on the side of the track were kneeling with their rifles pointed at the men as they scrambled out of their four-wheel drive. Comically, the second and third vehicles in the exiting convoy crashed into the rear of the disabled four-wheel drive. Carina heard gunshots ahead of her. She slammed on her brakes and slowed her vehicle and deftly pulled off into a thick copse of bush. She now decided she would leave on foot through the thick scrub. As she alighted, she grabbed her backpack but felt a searing pain as a bullet from one of the ambusher's M16 rifles hit her in the right leg. The high velocity round passed through the meat of her thigh, but she was still able to walk albeit with a limp and in agony. She dived for cover into the long grass and started crawling away from the Land Cruiser.

* * *

Bob and Greg heard the Lear jet start to warm up and saw the pilot moving his ailerons and flaps in his pre-flight checks. What they couldn't hear was Kudlov screaming at his pilot to get moving as fast as possible or he would shoot him in the leg.

'Okay, Greg, let's stop these turkeys,' Bob said quietly while centring his aim on the front tyre of the Lear jet.

'Copy,' Greg replied as he squeezed off a shot that smashed into the right-side window of the aircraft. The hardened laminated window stayed intact, but crazed and small flakes of glass fell into the cabin. Greg looked through his scope and saw the window was still intact. He started to readjust his aim to put another round through the cracked cockpit window.

Kudlov reeled back as minute pieces of glass were blown into his face. The window had actually saved his life, but now he was starting to panic.

'Get this fucken plane moving! Now, now, now!' he screamed at the top of his lungs.

'I'm trying but I can't roll until I have full power. This old airstrip was made for Second World War fighters and bombers, not a modern jet that's fully loaded,' he said, trying to stay calm, a feat not easy when seated next to a homicidal maniac with more guns than he wanted to remember.

The pilot now released the brakes and the Lear jet started to roll forward.

Bob's first shot aimed at the nose wheel missed. Through his six-power scope he saw the tell-tale plume of dirt and grass just beyond where he should have hit. *Steady Robert. Sniping 101. Lead a moving target.* He adjusted his aim and led the nose wheel by almost six inches. His next round blew out the front tyre of the plane which immediately dropped the nose of the aircraft dangerously close to the ground. The pilot felt a severe jerk of the steering column as the aircraft slewed violently to the left. Bob's following shot destroyed the nose wheel hydraulics and the aircraft nose thudded into the ground.

Greg now had to readjust his total shot. The window glass was now on an angle and he lost his best shot. Greg's second round tore into the starboard jet engine which immediately slowed and lost power.

Warning lights suddenly lit up and a loud warning alarm started telling the pilot of a possible fire in the starboard engine. The pilot immediately shut down both engines. He turned to Kudlov, 'The front wheel has been taken out. I can't steer. We've only got one engine. We're not going anywhere, sir.'

'Maybe not you, but I am outta here,' Kudlov said as he unbuckled his harness and headed for the exit door. He stopped, grabbed a small bag that held several hundred-thousand dollars in large notes and slung an AK-47 assault rifle across his back. He had his handgun, several spare magazines, and he would now have to fight his way out.

The pilot released the lock on the door to allow Kudlov to exit the aircraft. Red laser beams were now illuminating the cockpit as the surrounding police officers aimed at his head. He stayed in his seat, wishing he was somewhere else.

The access door opened and Kudlov peered out into the dim light as the sun finally settled behind the jungle canopy. He started to climb down the steps. He had a Glock in one hand, his briefcase in the other and suddenly realised that he had two red dots on his shirt aimed centre of mass into his barrel chest.

'Fuck youse!' he yelled as he brought his weapon up to shoot into the darkness. Before he could get a shot away two rounds slammed into his chest and exited through his back. He was killed instantly and fell forward, toppled down the stairs and smashed headfirst onto the grass runway.

Bob and Greg watched as the Special Ops team moved in to secure the body of Kudlov and two more police officers stormed the aircraft and secured the pilot still sitting nervously in his seat.

'Looks like they got 'em,' Greg said as he applied the safety on his rifle.

'Yeah, but did they get all of that mob in the cars?' he asked standing and started moving back down to the track to collect Melanie and check in with Peter Bryant.

Down on the road, the Armed Offenders squad had rounded up the fleeing criminals who were now sitting in the middle of the track with their hands behind their backs. All had been handcuffed and remarkably, none had been wounded or injured in the capture.

Peter Bryant closed on the scene as Bob, Greg and Melanie drove up in their vehicle.

'Nice work on stopping the plane, guys,' Bryant said, smiling at the trio. Bob looked at the surly group sitting in the dirt and suddenly turned to Peter Bryant. 'Where's the woman?' he asked, checking that he hadn't missed seeing her in the gloom of the headlights.

'She's not here,' Melanie said, looking back up the track. 'She was in the car that Benning had been driving. Has anyone checked back down the track?'

Bryant turned to the sergeant in charge of the Special Ops team. 'Sergeant Collins, take some men and sweep back up to the airstrip and clear both sides of the track. She may be wounded and lying doggo.'

'Sah'. He pointed at his squad and without a word, the team shook out into an assault line and started heading back up to the airfield.

*   *   *

Carina had now moved quietly away from the track and was heading towards Betty's homestead to get her bearings. Her immediate aim was to try to find something to dress her wound that was now bleeding freely. She came up to a small barbed-wire fence that surrounded the house. She could hear Betty talking to a male on the front veranda of the house. She gingerly climbed over the fence and saw bedsheets hanging off the clothesline. She quickly grabbed a sheet and headed back into the tree line. For the next five minutes, she slowly peeled off her blood-soaked denim trousers and quietly tore the bedsheet into a bandage. She made a packing for the entry and exit wounds and then applied a tight bandage around her thigh. She stood and tested her leg that was painful but manageable, given her need to exit the area – and quickly.

*   *   *

Senior Sergeant Peter Bryant called the Queensland Police team and Bob, Greg, and Melanie onto the track. 'Okay, once the Ops guys get back, we will head off into town. There's not much more we can do out here in the dark tonight.' He looked at the leader of the Armed Offenders team and said, 'I'll need your guys to picket the plane as a major crime scene tonight and we'll have a relief team here at first light, plus a shed full of forensics guys as well.'

The team leader nodded, saying 'Any chance of a feed for the guys, sir? We haven't had anything since we were scrambled this morning.'

'It's on its way. Use underneath Betty's house as your HQ. I am sure she will look out for you as well.'

'Sir.'

Bryant turned to Bob, 'Mate, take your group into Cooktown and meet us at the RSL hall in town. Sergeant Brophy is setting up a feed and place where we can have a quick debrief. We'll put you up in the motel next door for the night.'

'Roger,' Bob said. 'Has the safe house been cleared?'

'Yep. All done, but it's also being picketed tonight until forensics go through that as well.' He paused and smiled slightly, 'You've been a busy lot, haven't you?'

'They started it,' Bob said, and Greg just guffawed.

'Righto, get going. I'll see you around 8 or 8.30 tonight.'

The trio climbed into their vehicle with Greg behind the wheel. He turned and looked at Bob and Melanie in the back seat. 'Just wanna say that it was great working with you two.'

'Ditto,' said Bob who was quite exhausted from what had been a long day. 'Let's get into town and get cleaned up.'

'Amen,' replied Melanie whose right eye had now fully closed and was turning a pale shade of purple.

The trip back into Cooktown was quiet. Bob thought about quizzing Melanie on who she really was, but he could sense that both Greg and Melanie were really feeling the loss of their mate Barry in the shooting at the safe house. *Better to leave sleeping dogs lie, Bob, old son.*

Greg broke the silence. 'Will we head straight for the rissole?' Bob smiled at Greg's nickname for the Returned and Services League; he hadn't heard that term for a while.

'Yeah, mate. Let's see what has come out in the wash.'

They pulled up in front of what was once a small cottage that the local RSL members had turned into a clubhouse and meeting rooms.

This small low-level house was set up on stumps and was a stone's throw from the Endeavour River. The river was known to be infested with saltwater crocodiles who would take anything that entered their domain. In the gravel car park, there were now dozens of four-wheel drive vehicles with government plates and several that had none at all.

'Looks like we have quite a crowd,' said Greg nonchalantly.

They entered the clubhouse and saw Sergeant Brophy standing behind the BBQ on the side veranda of the building. He now had an apron over his uniform and was seemingly in his element as he flipped burgers and rolled sausages over the grill.

'Ah, gidday, you lot,' he said beaming. 'Grab a stubbie and tell me what you want to eat,' as he pointed to a vast collection of sausages and rissoles on the plates. 'There are bread rolls over there – already buttered – and a plate if you want to be genteel about it,' he said, smiling broadly at Melanie.

'Thanks, Sarge,' said Greg, holding out a roll, 'Hit me with a burger, thanks.'

Greg was grabbed by a local he knew as Bob and Melanie took their meal out onto the grass verge next to the clubhouse.

'I've got someone to tell Barry's brother about his death,' she said in a small voice.

'Any other family?' asked Bob.

'No, his Mum and Dad were killed in a bus accident about five years ago while on a holiday in Europe somewhere, and he only had his younger brother.'

'Ah,' Bob offered, not knowing what else to say.

Silence.

'Mel, I'm really sorry about Barry,' he started.

'Thanks, Bob. It's really hurting. I've never lost a close mate like Barry before.' She looked down at the ground. 'You know, I got him into all of this when I ran into him about four years ago. It's my bloody fault he's dead now.'

'No it isn't, Mel. Jesus, shit happens anywhere and anytime.' Bob tried to look into her one good eye. 'Barry knew the risks we were taking. He had been a soldier. We all put ourselves out there today. No one, I repeat no one — apart from those crooks – is to blame.' Bob finished his beer, looked at Melanie who nodded for a refill and went to grab another beer from the super-sized Esky on the veranda. He turned to go back to Melanie, and he saw Superintendent Ballantyne standing, talking to her. He was looking closely at her bruised and battered face. *Okay, well, this will be interesting, Robert. Now maybe we can get to the truth of all this.*

Bob sidled up to the superintendent who turned to face Bob.

'Ah, Bob McTaggart. Just the bloke I was looking for,' he started.

'Evening, sir,' Bob replied and then, looking at Melanie, said slowly, 'I believe you might be related to Agent Adams here,' he said trying to keep his poker face together.

The superintendent took his forearm and they moved a small distance away from a group of policemen who had just come onto the grass. 'Bob, I'm sorry about the subterfuge, but we really needed to find out – without a shadow of a doubt – that you were clean. Your link to Luigi Zappia in Townsville seemed very strong, and we had to make sure. With everything that was going on — as it turned out — with Frank Benning and company, I had little option. Benning took us by surprise. That bastard sold us all out after his marriage went belly up, and he was on six figures a year. Some people are just too greedy,' he sighed.

Ballantyne paused as Bob took in the situation and thinking *he was probably right, but did he have to send such a good looking, attractive, sexy woman to do it?*

The superintendent continued. 'Melanie has been an agent with the AFP for almost eight years, and this was her first undercover assignment with deadly risks.' He looked Bob directly in the eye. 'When Peter Bryant rang me from Canberra about his dilemma with a possible leak, we had to eliminate all possibilities.'

'Sure,' Bob said quickly, and before he could add anything else, Melanie was beside him, adding 'And me being your deckie allowed me to not only check you out but your boat as well,' she finished, looking Bob in the face with a slight smile.

'Okay, okay. And I guess you couldn't let me in on that because I am not a trained secret squirrel,' he offered.

'Something like that,' the superintendent said quietly. He offered his hand. 'No hard feelings, I hope, Bob?'

'No, sir,' Bob replied, 'Just took me by surprise, that's all.' They shook hands warmly.

'She always takes me by surprise,' her father stated. 'And call me Jim when we're not in front of the underlings,' he smiled. 'Gotta get ready for the debrief, I'll catch you later.'

Bob turned to face Melanie who was looking up at him. 'Am I forgiven too?' she asked in her very best husky voice.

'Maybe,' Bob said, trying his best not to look vulnerable. 'Just don't know what to call you, that's all.'

Melanie turned and headed for the Esky to get some more beers. 'Anytime is a good start,' as she walked across to the temporary bar.

Bob smiled to himself. *Just might do that young lady. I just might do that.*

* * *

At about 9.00 p.m., Peter Bryant called the assembled police and other agents who had been working the operation in together.

'Well, good job, everyone. This has been a climactic day for our operation. It has taken us over a year to bring this op to a head and, I am glad to say, almost to a close.' He paused, 'But it has not been without cost. As you know we lost Ian Taylor earlier in the year through foul play, and today we lost another good operator in Barry Costello. They, gentlemen, sorry — ladies and gentlemen,' he corrected, looking straight at Melanie, 'They paid the ultimate price that any police officer – regardless of service – has to pay in our fight against organised crime.' The assembled group just looked at each other and nodded.

'I just want to say thank you one and all for your efforts. Have a beer or three, go and get a good night's sleep because we still have a lot of work to do out at the airfield and the safe house.' He stepped down off the milk crate he had used for a dais and walked across to where Bob and Melanie were standing.

Peter Bryant shook Bob's hand. 'Well done, mate. The superintendent tells me he has explained how Melanie came to be your offsider. I won't apologise because I know that you don't need that. When I lost Ian Taylor, I was determined not to lose another operator.'

'I got it, mate, we're sweet,' Bob replied.

'Good. I gotta tell you but, you really had us worried when you went off air last week. But I saw how it all came together for you. Nice work … for an Army hack,' he grinned.

'Yeah, thanks. What happens to me now?' Bob asked.

'Well, I reckon after you debrief us out at the safe house tomorrow on how that all went down, you should get yourself back to Townsville on that boat. You still have a boat, don't you?' he asked.

'I hope so. It's tied up in Annan Creek; well it was two days ago. But I need help getting back to Townsville.'

'Ah yes,' Bryant smiled, 'Greg has volunteered to be your deckie. Melanie has got too much work to do and is not in the best of shape to be acting as a lookout at the moment.' Melanie punched his arm and said, 'Thanks a lot, Peter, but you're right. I've a shed full of reports to dictate and then sort out Barry's effects and so on.' She looked at Bob, 'Sorry, Skipper, you will have to get someone else to cook breakfast for you.'

'No sweat. At least now I'll have free run of the bathroom,' as he dodged a punch from Melanie.

'Oh, and Bob,' Bryant said as he was about to leave, 'I'll be in touch when you get back to Townsville. We need to sort out your boat and a few other things.'

'You're not going to take it off me, are you?' McTaggart asked, thinking that Zappia's boat might be confiscated.

'Nope, that is not on the cards. Don't worry about that,' he said as he walked off to talk to the Special Ops commander.

The evening drew to a close. Bob and Greg headed for the motel. Bob noticed that Melanie was talking long and hard with her father, the superintendent. *I wonder what scheme she is cooking up now?* Bob had wondered if the *Delfina/Office* would be surrendered to the Crown as ill-gotten gains. At least now he could still earn a buck.

*   *   *

'The following day passed quickly out at the "battleground," as Bob described it to Peter Bryant. The house was now just a smouldering ruin. Bob then took Bryant down to the Lion's Den and indicated where Kudlov had shot Benning. His final briefing to the police senior constable taking a record of all actions was at the small hill overlooking the airfield where the Lear jet was being unloaded and forensics personnel were gathering evidence and cataloguing material. Melanie was at the house, writing up her after action report and collecting Barry's belongings. Her face was quite swollen, and her eye was now a lustrous dark purple.

Peter Bryant sent a text message to Bob when he saw them arrive at the hill overlooking the airstrip. *Come over to the plane and check this out.*

Greg and Bob drove their vehicle up onto the airstrip and parked just outside the police tape surrounding the aircraft. A large white van was parked nearby that the forensics and drug squad people were using. Spread out on a large blue tarpaulin were dozens of packages wrapped in a variety of plastic waterproofing. The drug squad had assembled the drugs into cocaine, heroin, methamphetamine and, surprisingly, ecstasy tablets. The bulk of the haul however was cocaine and heroin.

Bob whistled softly. 'Jesus, how much of that shit is there?'

Peter Bryant glanced at a senior constable with a clue board in his hands.

'We have weighed it in as 3.68 tonnes.'

'Good grief! What the hell would all this be worth?' asked Bob, trying to take in the massive amount of illicit material spread out before them.

Peter Bryant cleared his throat and referred to his notebook. 'That's a street value somewhere around 100 million dollars – give or take a million.'

'My God,' exhaled Greg. 'No wonder Kudlov and his mob were prepared to fight so hard for it.'

'And kill for it,' added Melanie who had just been delivered to the airstrip by a fellow agent.

'Exactly,' Peter Bryant put in, 'Not to mention the enormous knock-on effect with kids addicted to this stuff and the damage it does to families and the community as a whole. In fact, the "worth" in crime, costs to the economy and so on is probably four times what is sitting here in front of you now.'

'Where the hell were they going to take it?', Bob asked.

'The pilot is still spilling his guts, but he said he intended to land in the Western Province in the Solomons. Kudlov was then going to transfer all this onto his boat which we will most likely apprehend tomorrow morning when it arrives at Balalae Island.'

They stood in silence as the drug crew started cataloguing and loading the packages into the van.

Bob turned to Peter Bryant and said, 'Well, Greg and I have finished here now. We are going to get back into town, organise a local copper to drive us out to the *Delfina* – or *The Office* — if she's still there, fuel her up in town and head back to Cairns.'

'Why Cairns?' Bryant asked.

'Well, Townsville doesn't have the trade that Cairns does for what I want to do, and that is get on my boat, cruise the seas and catch fish and make money.'

'Okay, let me know when you get there.'

'It'll be at the marina because the boat is gonna need some work, apart from being an unregistered vessel at present.'

'Right,' said Bryant who hadn't even thought that would be a priority for most people.

The two men shook hands with Peter Bryant. Bob kissed Melanie awkwardly on the cheek. He didn't know what to say or even if whatever relationship they had still existed. He was in No Man's Land. She smiled thinly but still warmly at him. Melanie still showed signs of grief and exhaustion. Greg gave her a hug as they said their goodbyes. Bob and Greg headed into Cooktown, and then picked up a local policeman who escorted them out to Annan Creek where *The Office* was still tied to the jetty.

'Better check it over in case someone decided to booby trap it,' Greg offered.

'Good idea. I'll go on board, you do an external.'

After 15 minutes of detailed checking, they waved the constable goodbye and cast off from Annan Creek jetty and headed into Cooktown. By midday, they were at the wharf at Cooks Landing marina and refuelling *The Office*. Bob had already decided that once he was back in Cairns, the boat would be slipped, repaired, and renamed. He had always wanted to move further north where the money was better, and the marina had very good slipway for work on the boat.

He was signing off the refuelling invoice when Peter Bryant walked into the marina office.

'Glad I caught you before you head off, mate,' he said warmly.

'Something wrong?'

"Nah nah, just wanted to update you that's all. You would have heard the Polair chopper flying around this morning. We've been trying to track Carina Thuong since she fled the airstrip. We found signs that she was probably wounded – no idea how bad but she was losing blood. She stole a bedsheet from Betty's clothesline, and from what we can piece together, she might also have stolen a trail bike and is now somewhere between here and Cape York or here and Cairns.'

'It's a big country. I don't like your chances of grabbing her. She seemed pretty tough to me and gave the impression she knew how to look after herself.'

'Yeah, I think you're right on all counts,' Bryant responded. 'Our bet is she will head for Brisbane or Sydney and try to hook up with Vietnamese bad hats until she is back on her feet.' Bryant then produced his mobile phone and brought up a few photos of two men who had been headshot.

'Recognise these guys?' he asked.

'Yeah, I do. This bloke was in the pub in town when we were here weeks ago with this other dude. I think his nickname was "Boots". They gave me some information but also triggered a warning that someone — and I guess it was Kudlov — was looking for the *Delfina*.' Bob looked at the photographs and realised that both men were dead. 'Was he wearing army boots?'

'Yeah, he was as a matter of fact. Geez, good recall, Bob. Anyway, they had a photo of your boat on their fridge in the place they were staying at and a whole pile of drugs that were being wrapped up for shipment.'

'What happened to them?' Bob asked, still trying to recall exactly what they had said in the pub.

'The neighbour complained of a smell and when the coppers checked it out, they found a real mess. Given that there were no signs of a struggle, it looks like a professional hit by people who knew them.' Peter Bryant finished by putting the phone back in his shirt. 'Someone has been cleaning house, I would guess. They've been dead for at least two days.'

'Christ, that mob didn't muck around. Not much loyalty between thieves, is there?'

'Not a lot. Oh yes, nearly forgot. The Border Protection mob grabbed Luigi Zappia at Brisbane International.'

'Oh yeah?'

'And he was carrying a shed full of cash in several suitcases. Quite a lot more than he declared, actually,' Bryant smiled. 'His warehouse in Townsville is being done over as we speak.'

'Good. Anything else?' Bob asked, wanting to get underway before the tide changed too much.

'Yeah, there is actually. Superintendent Ballantyne wants to make you a permanent offer for you to work for us.' He searched Bob's face for his reaction. 'Would you be interested?'

Bob paused, 'Let me think about that, Pete.'

Bryant said, 'The sweetener in the deal would be us paying for you to have the boat restored to what it was and a monthly retainer that is not too shabby. Plus, you get a deckie who is paid for by us.' Bryant was smiling at the lucrative deal being offered.

'Gee, you make it hard for a bloke to say no, mate. I'll let you know when I get to Cairns,' Bob said as he headed out of the office.

'Great, we'll talk then.' Bryant turned and walked off down the boardwalk.

Bob was back at the boat and Greg looked up and asked, 'What did Bryant want?'

'Made me an offer that I think I am going to find hard to refuse,' he grinned back.

They cast off and headed out into the channel of the Endeavour River as Bob drew up their nav plan for the trip back to Cairns. They would be cruising all night, but the seas were calm, and the evening sky was brilliantly lit with a squillion stars.

Epilogue

It had been almost a month since they had left Cooktown, and the boat was now high up out of the water in the Cairns slip yard. Two men were busy welding at the bow and foredeck of the boat, and Bob and Greg were working on cleaning and working on fittings that needed replacing or refurbishment. Once they had returned to the marina in Cairns, Bob had sorted out accommodation, marina berth leasing and was looking for office space on the wharf. Once Bob had accepted the offer to be a permanent part-timer with the AFP, it was as if somebody waved a magic wand. He was given a budget to restore and repair the *Delfina* to her former glory. He was paid for the last month with a retainer for the next quarter and things were looking good. It took him almost half a day to decipher the contract that Bryant insisted he read, sign, and return before anything could move forward. Greg said, 'It is just normal government bullshit but sign it anyway and take the money.' So he did.

The slipyard workers were busy studying a set of plans on how to rebuild the fly bridge. Bob asked if they could do it and they just shrugged and said 'of course'. They were used to working with heavier jobs like trawlers and coastal traders so this would be "fun". They asked about the fake portholes and Bob expressed ignorance, saying it was the previous owner's wife's idea. The rebuild was going to take two to three weeks, and then it had to be inspected and re-registered. He and Greg had sandblasted the entire hull and removed the name of the boat. They had sat around afterwards in the shade of the boat on very large paint tins, wondering what Bob was going to rename the vessel.

'I was thinking *Miss Demeanour*,' Bob said lightly. 'In view of all that we have been through these last few months.'

'I like it, Skipper,' Greg said, raising his stubbie to clink bottles. 'Here's to the *Miss Demeanour*.' They both smiled and then Greg looked over Bob's shoulder and said, 'Looks like we have company.'

Bob turned on his paint tin and saw a woman walking slowly towards them though the slipyard. She was wearing khaki cargo pants, khaki hiking boots and a khaki shirt. She reminded him of the photographers one sees in *National Geographic* television shows. On top of her dark red hair she was wearing an Akubra felt hat with a leopard print headband. He couldn't recognise her as she was sporting large dark sunglasses that hid a large proportion of her face.

As she closed on the duo, who were filthy dirty and clad only in shorts, work boots and even filthier short-sleeved shirts, they stood.

'Can I help you, ma'am?' Bob asked, hoping he was looking at a potential client.

'I hope so,' the woman responded as she removed her sunglasses.

'Melanie!' Bob exclaimed. 'I … I didn't recognise you with that red hair.'

'Yeah, well a girl has gotta keep things moving,' she said with a cheeky grin.

'Great to see you,' Greg chimed in as he stepped forward and gave her a quick hug. 'I've gotta go the marina office. I'll catch you later,' as he walked quickly off to the marina office. Bob just watched him, thinking there was nothing to do in the office. He turned to face Melanie.

'Sorry I can't offer better seating,' he said as he waved his arm in the direction of the paint tins.

'No need, Skipper. I won't be staying long. I'm back in town because the cottage up at Kuranda is up for sale and I was thinking of buying it.'

Bob's mind instantly rushed back to the incredible time they had spent "getting to know each other better", as Melanie had put it.

'Oh, really?' he said, looking for any other sign on her face that had now healed from the pistol whipping Carina Thuong had given her.

'Yes.' She paused and looked intently into his eyes. 'And I was wondering if you could come up with me and give me your opinion. You know all that bloke stuff about buildings and so on.' She smiled warmly at him, hoping he would say yes.

'I can do that,' he said nonchalantly, 'Greg can oversee the painting for the next couple of days … if you think it will take that long?' he asked, hoping she would say yes.

'At least two days,' she nodded, putting her sunglasses back on. 'Text me your address to this number and I'll pick you up tomorrow morning at 8 o'clock.' She handed him a business card that read *Melanie Cartwright, Eco photography.* He looked at the card and then into her green eyes. His mouth was slightly agape. 'Cartwright?'

'Uh huh,' she smiled and turned toward the slipyard gates. 'See you tomorrow. Don't be late.' He watched and admired the shape of her backside as she made her way across the yard. The PO Box address was Cairns. *Things are looking up again, Robert, old son.*

Greg returned from the marina office and looked at Bob looking at Melanie as she was walking out of the boat yard. 'Any problems, Skipper?'

'No mate, but it sort of reminds me of the ending to that Humphrey Bogart movie *Casablanca.*'

'Oh yeah, how's that?'

'Right at the very end as the aircraft is leaving, Humphrey Bogart's character Rick turns to this French copper and says something like "Louie, I think this is the beginning of a beautiful relationship".'

www.ingramcontent.com/pod-product-compliance
Lightning Source LLC
Chambersburg PA
CBHW070431170726
48291CB00002B/444